THE PINOCHET PLOT

THE PINOCHET PLOT
A novel by
DAVID MYLES ROBINSON

Terra Nova Books
Santa Fe, New Mexico

Library of Congress Control Number 2017961401

Distributed by SCB Distributors, (800) 729-6423

Published by Terra Nova Books, Santa Fe, New Mexico.
www.TerraNovaBooks.com

ISBN 978-1-938288-20-3

Author's Note

Although this is a work of fiction, I have incorporated real persons and events into the story. For example, everything pertaining to Augusto Pinochet and the politics and brutality of his regime is true, or allegedly true, other than any and all references to the fictional storyline and characters. He didn't have Ricardo Muñoz assassinated, because Ricardo Muñoz didn't exist. The CIA's MKULTRA program was real, as were the famous people alleged to have participated in it. The findings of the Church committee are represented accurately. The Indian groups I mention actually existed and actually met the various fates described. The statistics on poverty and food stamps are as factual as the official reports from which I took them.

My state of mind had been less morose than usual since I'd left the courthouse, but the rare smile I was sporting faded the moment I entered our reception area. Something was terribly wrong.

Tina, our young and usually exuberant receptionist, had obviously been crying, and when she saw me walk through the door, her tears let loose with a vengeance.

"What's wrong?" I asked.

She grabbed a Kleenex from the stack on her desk, patted at her swollen red eyes, and motioned for me to go back to the offices.

I'd never heard our law office so silent. The place was like a morgue. I didn't bother asking any of the secretaries what was going on and walked straight into my partner's office.

Cheryl was sitting at her desk, staring down at some file. But she didn't look as if she was really reading it. She, too, had been crying.

"What's going on?" I asked.

Cheryl hadn't heard me enter and jerked her head up in surprise. Her face softened when she saw it was me.

She stood and rushed to me.

"Oh, Will," she said as she threw her arms around me, "I'm so sorry." Two-second pause. "It's your mother . . . ."

My stomach instantly tightened, and I could feel my throat constrict. Does it say something about me that I knew in that moment that my mother was dead?

"What about her?" I said, barely able to choke out a response. But I knew. I knew with absolute certainty. Yet the words hadn't been spoken. It wouldn't be real until the words were uttered. I didn't want Cheryl to answer my question—to say aloud the words that would confirm the horrible truth I already knew.

But she did.

Cheryl was still hugging me, and when she spoke, it was into my neck. Her words were warm against my skin. I could smell the subtle vanilla fragrance she favored.

"She's dead, Will."

Cheryl paused but still held me tightly. I could tell there was more to come.

"The police say she committed suicide."

Despite the warmth of her breath and the closeness of her body, I felt a chill run through me. *Suicide?*

I must have shivered, because Cheryl loosened her hug and rubbed her hands up and down my arms. Then she walked me over to her couch and sat me down.

Suicide? Seriously?

My brain felt frozen: numb and stupid. I couldn't even cry. I felt totally and unambiguously vacant. All the processors had shut down.

Did you know that suicide is the tenth leading cause of death in the United States?

—2—

I had bounded into my office in a better-than-usual state of mind because I had just come from what I hoped would be my last court case for a very long time—if not forever. I was about to start a sabbatical from my law firm.

I had first asked myself the potentially epiphanic question, which in turn had led to my decision to step away from my law firm, when I had been sitting in an ultra-plush conference room on the thirty-fifth floor of the Bank of America Tower, staring out at a postcard view of San Francisco Bay. The question had hit me with surprising force: *When did I become such a dick?*

My client was being deposed by one of the name partners in one of the biggest and most expensive law firms in the city. My educated guess was that this particular partner, doing the job of a second-year associate, was charging his client about one thousand dollars an hour. The two lesser partners sitting to his side and doodling on their yellow legal pads were probably billing out at five hundred each. I, on the other hand, was only charging my client eight hundred an hour, which was four hundred more than I usually billed him. That was because it was a stupid case that I didn't want to handle and had tried my best to talk him out of pursuing.

But my client, a slick-looking fifty-year-old CEO of a large car-wash chain, had more money than he knew what to do with. So rather than use it for some good cause, he had decided to fight this slam-dunk lawsuit brought against him by another way-too-rich CEO, who was my client's partner in a private jet, a Learjet 95. My client owed his jet partner just shy of a million dollars, which he refused to pay because his partner had used the jet more than he had and, according to my asshole of a client, had thereby nullified their fifty-fifty agreement.

The real reason my client refused to pay was that he was pissed off that his partner, who owned a huge chain of quick-lube service stations, had decided to put automated car washes at many of his facilities, often within a block of my client's business locations.

"Just pay what you owe," I sagely told my client when he was first served with the lawsuit. "You have no viable defense and could end up getting hit with interest and their attorneys' fees." Which, of course, was exactly what my adversaries had presumed would happen—and was the reason why they had a senior partner billing out at a grand an hour on a basic assumpsit, or collection, case.

"I don't give a shit," my client said. "The fuckhead betrayed me. We bought that jet together because we weren't competitors and would have no business conflicts."

As he sat with one leg thrown over the left arm of my client chair, he tapped nonstop with his right hand, gouging away at the chair's beautiful rosewood arm with his heavy diamond-and-gold ring. I inwardly cringed with the certain knowledge of what that arm would look like when this client conference came to a merciful end.

"So his deciding to compete against you is a defense for not paying what you owe on the jet how, exactly?" I asked in the most sarcastic tone I could muster.

My client waved his left hand disamissively. "Come up with some good defense. Or countersue the cocksucker. Claim we had a noncompete agreement or something."

I sighed theatrically. "But you didn't. Look, you have no defense. You . . . are . . . going . . . to . . . lose. Can I be any more precise?"

"So what? I'll make him sweat while his high-priced shysters run up their fees, and then I'll settle for the amount due, with each side to bear their own fees and costs."

I shook my head in exasperation. "He's not sweating. He's not even thinking about this case. You're the one who will have to give a deposition. You're the one who will have to admit on the witness stand that you owe the money. You're the one—"

"Let's make a wager," he said, interrupting me. "I'll bet you ten grand that I don't pay any more than the amount owed. No interest. No fees."

I stood. "Jesus, now you sound like Mitt Romney trying to bet Rick Perry. If you want me to go forward with this case, I'm going to bump my hourly rate to eight hundred."

My client shrugged. "Whatever." He stood and turned to leave.

"Why don't we do this instead?" I said to his back. "I'll negotiate a deal right now where you pay the amount due. Then you give me the quarter million you would spend on fees and costs by fighting this case, and I'll donate it to a wonderful charity in your name."

My client turned and faced me. I could see that for the first time in our conversation he was truly pissed.

"Look, Will," he said through clenched teeth, his jaw pulsing with anger, "don't start up with any of your liberal bullshit. I earned my money, and I'll do whatever the fuck I want with it— and that doesn't include giving it away to worthless slugs waiting for a handout. I put up with you because you're the best mouthpiece I've ever had, but there are limits to my largesse. Just do your fucking job. Charge whatever you like."

And with that, my client walked out, and a few months later I found myself half listening at his deposition as the overpaid senior partner reamed my client a new asshole. I gazed down at the bay and watched a small regatta of midsized sailboats head toward the Golden Gate Bridge. I hate sailing, but at that moment I wished I was on one of those boats. Ironically, I wasn't particularly liberal. I wouldn't have been representing all these assholes if I'd really been political, as my father had been. I had what I referred to as "logical sensibilities," which I suppose put me just enough on the edge of liberalism to see how fucked up my clients were but not liberal enough to stop taking their money.

When did I sell my soul and become a complete dick? I asked myself again.

*　　*　　*

I have some psychological issues. I don't deny it. You probably would too if you had come home and found your father shot in the head when you were eleven years old. Or if you'd been forced to deal with your mother's depression and heartache following his murder. It's not as if I'm totally nuts or anything. It's just that I have some suppressed anger issues. I tend to suffer from what I refer to as "melancholia," which is a really cool word and which I don't equate with "depression." One of the dictionaries defines it as a "gentle sadness." That's perfect.

I suffer from more psychological ailments, but you don't really need a complete list now. Some will probably become self-evident as I relate my story to you. Some are completely irrelevant—none of your fucking business, if you must know.

The anger issues are mostly under control. I think my chosen profession has helped with that. Instead of directing my anger at the world in general, I've learned to harness it and turn it into passionate advocacy for my clients. Many, if not all, of those who have served as my opposing counsel over the years have decided that I'm a complete asshole. I know that because they've told me. Only some, not all, of my former girlfriends over the years consider me a complete asshole. To be fair to me, the former girlfriends who consider me an asshole do not do so because of my anger issues. They do so because I have problems getting close to people. I think I'm afraid that they will someday go away and leave me lonely and hurt—as if they'll get murdered or something.

So a year after my epiphany at the deposition of my client (who ended up paying close to 2 million dollars for his 1-million-dollar debt), when my adversary from that day's court appearance and I walked out of the San Francisco Superior Court building, I wasn't surprised when he didn't even acknowledge my cheery (for me) adieu and turned to walk in the opposite direction (despite the fact I knew very well that his office was on the same route I take to my office). I allowed myself an internal "I-don't-give-a-shit" shrug and began the trek back to my South of Market office. The August fog was thick, wet, and cold, and, as usual, I loved it. The fog was almost always a perfect complement to my generally morose state of mind, as if it added a sensory component to my melancholy. I loved knowing that if I were to head to the East Bay or down the peninsula south of the city, in no time I would be in eighty-degree weather under blue skies. I'm not sure exactly why I loved knowing that. Maybe because it made me feel sheltered and cloistered from the rest of the world. Sometimes we San Franciscans feel as if we live in a bubble. Or maybe that's just me.

Anyway, despite the cold shoulder from opposing counsel, my step was positively jaunty as I headed back to the office. "Jaunty" is not a word I've ever used to describe anything about myself before, so do not underestimate its use. I'd just come from what I planned to be my last court appearance. Tomorrow I would start what I'd been telling clients would be a "sabbatical" but which I hoped and presumed would be a complete retirement. After fifteen years of practicing law, the last eight of which I had become a real dick, I was fully and completely sick of it. Sick of my rich, arrogant, manipulative clients, and sick of the law that was stacked in their favor. I was sick of myself, doing their bidding, getting them out of trouble whenever they got caught crossing the line in the name of greed. I was sick of the political hack judges who sold their souls to get elected and somehow felt that putting on a black robe allowed them to be supercilious and demeaning to all who entered their domains.

Cheryl Granite, my law partner, one of my two best friends, and occasional lover, would take over the practice, although the name on the letterhead would still read Muñoz and Granite, Attorneys at Law. I'm Muñoz.

Travis Wheeler, my other best friend but not occasional lover, would stay on with Cheryl as paralegal and private investigator, as needed. Cheryl would move into my large corner office, and Travis would probably move into Cheryl's office. The new associate Cheryl had hired, Jimmy Martinez, would end up in Travis's broom closet of an office. Jimmy would one day become the first openly gay, same-sex-married Hispanic justice on the United States Supreme Court.

Cheryl used to refer to us as "fuck buddies," but I put a stop to that, which is kind of funny, considering how much I drop the proverbial "F-bomb" in normal conversations. "What the fuck? Where the fuck's my briefcase? What fucking law school did you say you went to?"

But there must be some weird puritan streak in me, since I never use the F word when it pertains to sex. I haven't figured out how that fits in my psychological profile. Cheryl thinks it's hilarious.

Our office—my former office, that is—is an old converted single-room occupancy hotel, or SRO. SROs were also called "residential hotels" and were prevalent in San Francisco back in the day. This is where poor people used to live. The rooms were usually small, about eight by ten feet, with a toilet and shower down the hall. Tens of thousands of poor working people in San Francisco used to live in SROs. Many still do. Here is what Justin Herman, executive director of the San Francisco Redevelopment Agency from 1960 to 1971, said about the downtown SRO neighborhoods of the South of Market: "This land is too valuable to permit poor people to park on it."

I doubt that the homeless people who are forced to sleep on the streets so that important attorneys like me can have high-rent loft offices are as enamored of the cold, wet bubble of fog as I am.

So I jauntily bounded up to our second-floor office space in my less-morose-than-usual state of mind and promptly found out my mother had committed suicide.

It was not until later that night, after Cheryl and Travis got me to my Pacific Heights home and fed me something and then finally left me alone, that I broke down and cried. After roaming the house and staring at my mother's beautiful paintings, I stopped at a self-portrait she'd done while my father had still been alive and cried. I cried and cried and cried, and then, exhausted by grief, I went to bed and listened to the foghorns in the bay. Then, at last, I slept.

—3—

I made my way to the office on automatic pilot the next morning. I needed to clean out my office, and now I needed to make arrangements for my mother's funeral. She lived in Los Angeles, but she'd taken her life at a small *posada*, or inn, in Santa Fe, New Mexico. Pills. That's the way I would have done it too. Admittedly, there'd been a few times in my life when I'd thought it all out. But, of course, I knew I was psychologically fucked up. I hadn't realized Mother was as well, at least to the point where she would take her own life.

I arranged to have her cremated there in Santa Fe. I decided I would throw some of her ashes into the wind in Tesuque, where I'd been born and where I had lived until my father's murder.

Tesuque, just outside of Santa Fe and part of Santa Fe County, is a Spanish variation of the Tewa name *Te Tesugeh Oweengeh*, meaning the "village of the narrow place of the cottonwood trees." There was a small creek lined with cottonwood trees behind our old hacienda. I'd bet my life that Mother had visited that spot before she did herself in. She loved that place. She must have painted that scene a dozen different times. In hot weather the three of us would often picnic there, under the shade of the billowy cottonwood trees. That was the first place I would spread some of her ashes.

The second place would be in Taos, about an hour up the road. That's where Mother had been living and working as a painter before she met my father. It's where we tried to live after he was murdered.

Around noon, Cheryl and Travis tried to talk me into going out to lunch. I demurred, telling them I wanted to finish packing.

I needed to catch a plane to Santa Fe the next day. I asked them to bring a sandwich back for me. I must have looked my normal melancholy self because, after studying my face for a few seconds, they looked at each other, shrugged, and left me alone. They were still gone when the mail came.

Tina knocked tentatively on my door and entered. She was young and embarrassed and unsure of how to deal with death. She held out an unopened envelope. I took it and studied the front of it as she silently withdrew. My heart began pounding, and I could feel the blood rush to my face. I sat down in the old leather desk chair I'd bought when I first opened the office. It creaked. The letter was from my mother.

It took me a while to get up the courage to open it. It was a long, handwritten letter. Mother's writing was as flowing and beautiful as ever. There was no obvious indication of stress. I wondered about when she would have written it in relation to taking her life. Had she posted it at the front desk of the inn and then calmly retreated to her room to die?

Here is what part of the letter said:

> *My dearest Will,*
>
> *First of all, my darling, you need to forgive me. I know suicide is a totally selfish act and that it is mean and cruel to those left living. But you and I have been through so much together that I know with absolute certainty that you love me just as I love you, with unqualified totality, so you will force yourself to understand and accept what I have done. You took care of me and protected me in some of the darkest days imaginable. So I know that you don't want me to live in the kind of pain—no, the word* pain *doesn't describe what I feel. It is anguish at the very core of my being. It is tortuous being alive. I know you have your own demons, Will. Who wouldn't after being through what*

*you have been through? I won't try to compare. I just
want you to understand and appreciate and accept that
what I am about to do is what I want. There is no
doubt. There is no hesitation. Even as I write this,
knowing how devastated you will be by what I have
done, I have no second thoughts. So I want you to
applaud my decision to take my life into my own hands
for the first time in so very long. I want you to be happy
that I am finally out of pain.*

 *Okay, so I have said all that. Probably more than I
needed to say. You can do with me as you wish.
Cremation would be my desire. Spread my ashes here in
New Mexico at a place or places you know I loved.
Please apologize to the owners of this inn where I am
staying. I'm sure they don't appreciate having to call the
coroner to cart away a dead body.*

I put the letter down on my desk and got up to close the door
Tina had left open. That was so like Mother to think about the
impact of her decision on those who would have to deal with it.
I had thought I was all cried out from last night, but to read her
words—I started crying again and made no attempt to stifle the
tears. I walked back to the desk, picked up the letter, and read on.

 *Now for the important stuff, my sweet Will. I don't
know if you accepted the police version of events
surrounding your father's death or not. We never really
talked about it. But I think you know that I didn't buy
the burglary-gone-wrong scenario. I believe your father
was assassinated.*

As I read on, I wiped at my eyes and tried to process what I
was reading. What Mother had written in her perfect penman-
ship on the way to her deathbed would change my life.

—4—

My father was a famous Chilean novelist. His name was Ricardo Muñoz, and he wrote beautiful love stories, creating magnificent concoctions of coincidence that could be interpreted as fate. I knew Father was famous—there were always big shots coming by our house in Tesuque to pay homage to the great writer. But I don't think even my mother, who was an American, realized how beloved he was throughout Latin America until he was murdered. Apparently Americans weren't as into complicated, mystical love stories as Latin Americans were. Mother and I sat in numb amazement as we watched videos of the Chilean news broadcasts showing thousands of people throughout Latin America taking to the streets in mourning for Father.

His death made the news in the United States, but by and large, he was just another Latino who'd been murdered.

Mother's suicide letter made it clear she suspected that Father's opposition to Chilean President Augusto Pinochet was the cause of his "assassination."

*   *   *

In 1973, Augusto Pinochet led a right-wing military coup to overthrow the democratically elected socialist government of Salvador Allende. Allende had been elected in 1970 and was able to take office despite the fact that, according to the Church committee report, U.S. President Richard Nixon and his national security adviser, Henry Kissinger, had ordered the CIA, under the direction of Richard Helms, to prevent Allende from taking power.

Three years into Allende's term, on September 10, 1973, a Chilean military officer reported to a CIA officer that a coup to overthrow the Allende government was being planned. The U.S. government refused to take any action to stop the coup, which succeeded and put Pinochet in power. Pinochet hated socialists, communists, and left-wingers in general. So he had that in common with the CIA and the administration of President Nixon. Father was a left-winger and, worse in the eyes of Pinochet and his cronies, an intellectual.

Father began writing vitriolic articles opposing Pinochet. He attended rallies. He wrote a column for a Santiago newspaper until Pinochet shut the newspaper down. Dictators got away with doing that kind of thing.

The first time Father was arrested, they only kept him for two days. Father thought they just wanted to scare him into shutting up. He saw many of his old friends in prison. It was like a reunion of sorts. He didn't shut up when he got out.

The second time Father was arrested, Manuel Contreras himself came to visit him in prison. Contreras was head of the infamous DINA, the Chilean intelligence service. It was later learned the DINA had assassinated many left-wing politicians and activists throughout Latin America. Contreras apparently wasn't content just to purge Chile of the dangerous lefties. Like a rat terrier, he went after the vermin everywhere he could find them. Would it surprise you to know that Contreras was on the payroll of the CIA?

Father had been a member of PEN International, a worldwide organization of writers dedicated to freedom of expression. When a writer somewhere in the world was oppressed, suppressed, and often jailed by a regime that didn't want people to hear what the writer had to say, PEN International would step in and try to help the writer. Sometimes it worked and sometimes it didn't.

Father's second arrest made him a cause célèbre among writers and intellectuals throughout the world. PEN held rallies for him in London, Paris, and New York. There was a star-studded benefit for him in Hollywood, which must have been nice, but I doubt many of those in attendance had read any of Father's books.

Contreras was supposedly very polite to Father when they met—polite in that menacing way that really dangerous people affect. In no uncertain terms, Contreras told Father that his ass was grass if he didn't shut the fuck up and get with the program. Father was released two weeks later. He wrote in his unpublished memoir, which I now have, that he lost seventeen pounds in those two weeks. He was beaten many times after that really polite meeting with Manuel Contreras. He pissed blood for a month after he got out.

Father had hoped his exposure through PEN International would shield him from anything worse than some prison time, but when they tried to assassinate him three months later, he decided enough was enough and applied for and was granted asylum in the United States. Do you think the American authorities found it ironic that this Chilean author had to flee Chile because the new American-backed dictator was trying to kill him? Probably not. But Father did.

*   *   *

I hadn't known much about Pinochet before Mother's suicide. Of course, I knew that he'd been a brutal dictator in Chile, and I do remember hearing Father and his friends talk about him. But I knew few details and almost nothing of the CIA involvement.

Below is a passage from the congressional Church committee report:

```
Covert United States involvement in
Chile in the decade between 1963 and
1973 was extensive and continuous.
```

```
The Central Intelligence Agency spent
three million dollars in an effort to
influence the outcome of the 1964
Chilean presidential elections. Eight
million dollars was spent, covertly,
in the three years between 1970 and
the military coup in September 1973,
with over three million dollars expended
in fiscal year 1972 alone.
```

I guess $8 million wasn't chump change in those days. Nowadays the CIA drops off bags of money to a puppet du jour in the Middle East, and nobody seems to care.

*   *   *

Father fled to the United States in 1975. His last novel before the move, *Arabella,* had become an international best seller. Maybe its success was due in part to the limelight from the PEN rallies. Most likely it was because the novel was less mystical, more forthright. It was a love story, set in Cuba during the height of the Cold War. Arabella was a Cuban-American spy who had fallen in love with a Cuban doctor. Both were intensely patriotic, and both wanted the same things in life—love, family, safety, social justice, and peace—so in the end, neither could truly understand why they were enemies.

Father met my mother, Susan Montrose, about six months after arriving in the United States. She was a famous artist in her own right. She had made her name painting, but by the time she met my father she'd become quite famous for her pottery. They met at an art gallery reception in Santa Fe. Father wasn't as famous in the United States as he was down south, but Mother knew who he was. She'd read all his books in their original Spanish, and she would later claim that she was wildly in love with him before she even met him. I doubt that, but it made for a good story over cocktails.

In any event, the two fell in love, married, and built a large adobe-style hacienda in Tesuque, near the foothills of the Sangre de Cristo Mountains, just outside of Santa Fe. They were a big-time power couple in the art world. Even some heads of state came to the house to pay their respects when they were in the neighborhood. Juan Carlos I of Spain was a big fan of Father's and came all the way to Santa Fe to meet him between visits with Gerald Ford of the United States and José López Portillo of Mexico. Pinochet never came, of course, but the widows of two great Chilean artists Pinochet and Contreras had assassinated came.

Cheryl insisted on sleeping with me that last night in San Francisco, and I didn't argue. We made love slowly, languorously —almost sentimentally. I don't know why I'd never married Cheryl. She was certainly the most sexually intoxicating woman I could ever want. She was part Cherokee Indian, and you could see it in her high cheekbones, which were rounded and elegant, and in her smooth, tawny skin. The rest of her was what we collectively refer to as "white." Her eyes were large and dark brown, and they could sparkle with delight one moment and flash with anger the next. They gave her away when she was trying to negotiate—not a good trait for a lawyer. She was about five feet nine inches, just four inches or so shorter than I am. She was on the thin side, although her breasts were a good handful, which is generally how I liked to measure breasts. We were a good team, both as law partners and as lovers.

Most women I had dated over the years had given up on me as any kind of love interest, but Cheryl understood me. She knew I was too afraid of losing her friendship to formalize our love interest. She knew I was too much of a pussy to commit to something as scary as an actual relationship.

Travis thought I was a complete idiot for not marrying Cheryl. He warned me over and over that someday she was going to fall in love with someone who would want to marry her. If that ever happened, I usually replied, I would be happy for her and would still have my two best friends. Giving up an occasional lover would be a small price to pay. I would say that to Travis, but I would feel a pain in my heart and an emptiness in my gut as I spoke.

Travis would shake his head in mock disgust.

"You're just like fucking Fox News," he would say. "Repeat a bullshit lie enough times, and eventually it becomes some kind of truth."

I think Travis would have married Cheryl if he weren't gay.

*　　*　　*

"So," Cheryl said as she lay beside me, "how long do you think you'll be gone?"

Her voice was husky from our lovemaking. She was lying on her side, caressing my bare chest.

"I'm not sure." I answered with my eyes still closed. "I've got to go to Santa Fe to take care of stuff there, and then I've got to go to the Malibu house and clean it out and shut it down."

I opened my eyes and turned my head to look at her.

She stared back at me with those huge eyes, and I felt something lurch deep inside me.

"I think I want to follow up a little on some of what Mother said in her letter." I turned my head and stared up at the ceiling, kind of shrugging as I did so, making it seem like no big deal. "You know, just check some things out."

Cheryl's answer was to continue to caress my chest and then, finally, she gave me her patented feminine grunt, which I knew meant "fuck you." But not in a bad way.

Father was murdered in his study at the Santa Fe house in 1988. I was eleven years old at the time, so I knew what death was. But I never expected that death would come and visit our house as if it were some uninvited dignitary.

Mother had taken me out of school for the day so we could drive up to Taos to meet with a gallery owner who was going to do a retrospective of the great Susan Montrose's work. It was a wonderfully fun day. There was not a cloud in the sky, and the flesh-colored cliffs bordering the highway to Taos were mesmerizing. Along the Rio Grande, off to the left, the leaves on some of the trees had turned bright colors of yellow, orange, and red. The majestic waterway now ran shallow with the lassitude of a river waiting for the winter storms to give it new life.

After her meeting, Mother took me to lunch on the Plaza, where a mariachi band played, and then we drove out to the Rio Grande Gorge. I walked along the sprawling bridge, which shook whenever a car or truck rumbled by, and I remember looking straight down from the steel deck to the Rio Grande, six hundred fifty feet below. I wondered what it would feel like to fall all that way.

*   *   *

Mother and I entered our house feeling lightheaded with happiness. We'd talked about convincing Father to take us to Santa Fe for dinner. I liked the patio of La Casa Sena. The September evening would be warm, and the lights in the trees dotting the patio would be twinkling, offering a cheerful welcome. The water fountain in the center of the courtyard would babble softly beneath the pleasant chatter of the guests. It always felt to me as if everyone there was happy, at least for that moment in their lives.

All the house servants had been given the day off. Father had been looking forward to the peace and quiet. He had intended to do some serious writing. So when he didn't answer our calls as we entered the kitchen via the attached garage, we both headed straight for his study, where we knew we would find him hunched over his old Corona typewriter.

He was hunched over it, all right. But there was blood all over his desk. The blood had come from a hole in his head. The hole had been made by a .38 revolver of some sort. That image is frozen into my brain, and I will never, ever be able to forget it. It's not the last memory of my father that I would like to have, but that's what I got.

I stood by Father's lifeless body and stared at the mess.

Mother was screaming, but I didn't hear her at first. When she finally came to her senses, she realized she had to get me out of that room. She was still sobbing, though—and uttering all these horrible sounds that didn't even sound human—as she yanked me by the arm and led me out of the study. I won't forget those sounds, either.

It was, all in all, an utterly unforgettable day.

The police were convinced Father had been murdered by burglars. Mother was convinced he had been assassinated by Pinochet. The police gave no credence to the assassination theory.

By the time Cheryl and Travis returned to the office with my sandwich, I had cried myself out—again—and had resumed sorting through the fifteen years of crap I had gathered. Some of the items were mementos from cases I'd won that had seemed so important to keep at the time—a defective emergency radio beacon for boats from my first multimillion-dollar verdict, for instance. But I tossed most everything into a trash bag. That's kind of what happens with our lives, isn't it? We collect and hoard and memorialize, and someday someone has to come along and clean up all the crap we leave behind. I wasn't even forty years old yet and I was cleaning up my own crap, so I figured I was doing someone a favor.

Travis read Mother's letter while I pulled down all the framed degrees and certificates from the wall. Cheryl had gone back to her office.

When he was done, Travis set the letter on the couch next to him and sat there in silence for a few minutes. "You okay, man?" he finally asked.

I nodded, climbed off the stool, and put the frame holding my United States Supreme Court bar admission into a box. Then I walked over to my desk chair and sat down.

Travis was a lean black man with a shaved head and piercing black eyes. He was a little older than me and in his early forties. But unlike me, he looked more like he was in his early thirties. We'd met in college, at Cal Berkeley. He and Cheryl were the only two friends I'd let into my life. I mean *for real* into my life. For real and forever. Like my mother had been.

I locked my hands on the top of my head and leaned back. "Yeah, I guess so." I nodded to the letter lying beside him. "It's a lot to digest. First the suicide, and then the part about Father being assassinated."

"What about the part about your stepfather—Chuck? That's some heavy shit."

I knew Travis wasn't finished, and I watched him run his left hand over his clean-shaven head, an affectation I knew meant he was mulling over what to say next and how to say it.

Finally, as was usually the case, he didn't try to sugarcoat anything and just came out with it.

"Do you think maybe she'd gone off the edge and had become delusional? Paranoid? No offense, but she obviously wasn't well wrapped."

I brought my hands down and leaned forward, elbows on the desk.

"I don't think so," I said. "The letter sounds pretty rational—at least the sentence structures are. The conclusions may be wrong, but I don't get the feeling they were induced by delusions of any kind. I mean, Dad may not have been assassinated by Pinochet's people, but I believe Mother believed he was, and I believe she'd believed it from day one." I paused, took a deep breath, and then exhaled. "As for the part about Chuck being involved with the CIA . . . shit, I don't know what to think about that."

Travis nodded fully this time. "I agree. Just playing devil's advocate. So what're you going to do about it?"

I shrugged heavily. "Damned if I know."

*   *   *

Cheryl and Travis took me out to a small trattoria near my house that night. Cheryl had read the letter by then, so all three of us were still in the process of digesting its contents. We ate in silence for the most part, although occasionally one of us made a comment or asked a question that provoked further discussion.

It was a strange dinner that would have probably made me uncomfortable had we not been as close as we were.

"Look, Will," Cheryl said after the dinner plates had been cleared and we'd settled back in our seats to enjoy what was left of the wine, "it's not like there's much you can or even *should* do at this point. I mean, Pinochet's long gone. The CIA isn't going to tell you squat." She ran the slender fingers of her right hand through her closely cropped dark hair. "Which leaves what's-his-name, your stepfather. And what're you going to do about him? Track him down and kill him?"

Travis started to laugh but stifled it when he saw the look on my face.

"That's one of the options," I said and sipped the last of my Barolo.

—8—

Mother was never the same after Father was murdered. She maintained some semblance of direction for a while by hounding the police day after day. Back then I thought she was just pissed because the police didn't seem to be making any progress finding Dad's killer. But now I understood that it was obviously more than that. When the police no longer took her calls or let her in to see the chief, she began hounding politicians. That didn't last too long. Suddenly the woman who had hosted heads of state could no longer get even her local representatives on the phone.

When she finally gave up trying to convince the authorities that my father had been assassinated, she decided we needed to leave Santa Fe. That was fine with me. Our house was no longer the magical and joyous place it had been when Father was alive. Now it was empty, silent, and sad—and it was good to leave.

Mother sold the house almost the moment she put it on the market. A wealthy Iowan bought the place. He had made a fortune from inventing and then manufacturing hot chocolate machines that were used in almost every coffee shop in America. Unfortunately, he and almost his entire family were massacred two years later by a serial killer who was on the run from police in five states. It was the Iowan family's bad luck that the authorities chased the fugitive right into our old house, where he decided to make his last stand by first killing everyone who was home at the time. He also took out six New Mexico state troopers before he was finally shot once in the head and once right through his penis.

Everyone said the penis wound was just a lucky shot.

Speaking of luck, it was pretty damned lucky for the Iowan's oldest son—and for all of us—that the son was not home at the time. Why was it lucky for all of us? Because that son went on to work for a man named Steve Jobs, and the son was said to have been instrumental in the development of the iPad.

After Father's death and then the massacre of the Iowans, no one wanted to buy our old house for years. By then, we were living in Los Angeles.

—9—

After Santa Fe, we tried living in Taos for a year, but that didn't work out. Mother thought that by being close to her old friends she could get on with her life and get over the loss of her precious Chilean writer. But her depression and irritability and general downer attitude about everything made it a chore for anyone to be around her. Gradually even her oldest and best friends faded away, so it was finally just the two of us. And that was no fun for me.

I'd become desultory and moody, and the last thing I needed was to be stuck trying to cheer up my mother when all she wanted to do was mope around and play with clay. I wanted to mope around and play video games and forget about how depressing our lives had become. We were a fine pair of mopers.

One day Mother announced, as she always did, that she was going to go out to the mailbox to get the mail. She still had on her torn and worn baby-blue daytime robe, which she claimed was her pottery frock. It was really just a skanky old robe. She ambled out in her robe and slippers, not bothering to pat down her disheveled hair that was electrified by the dry air. She came back a different woman.

When she walked into the house holding a letter and an envelope, she looked wild and scared. She wasn't ambling anymore. She was moving fast.

And she was *talking* fast. "Pack your things. We're getting out of here."

I didn't react right away, choosing instead to stare in confusion at her.

"Did you hear what I said?" she snapped at me. "Pack up! We're leaving!"

Mother never yelled at me, so that got my attention. I decided it would be best to do as she said and ask questions later.

* * *

There is a species of monkey called moustached tamarin that lives in the Amazonian lowlands of Peru. Researchers have discovered that when a female tamarin gives birth, usually to twins, if there are not enough male tamarins around to help with the chores of raising the babies, the mother will sometimes kill her own young. According to scientists, the explanation for such pitiless behavior is cold and calculated. Tamarin mothers are simply very good at evaluating their familial resources. If their babies have a poor chance of survival because there isn't enough help available to raise them, why make a pointless investment of time and resources trying to keep them alive? Better to cut their losses, bag the babies, and wait for a better season to breed.

Luckily for us, most human mothers aren't so cold and ruthless. Otherwise, Mother might have cut her losses and had me put down after Father died. She was obviously inept at raising me alone.

But when she got an anonymous letter that warm summer day in Taos, all of her maternal instincts kicked in and she went into protect-her-baby mode.

Here is what the anonymous letter said:

> *Bitch whore wife of the traitorous lunatic Ricardo Muñoz:*
> *We have killed your man, and now we will kill you and your weak and retarded bastard son, Will, unless you behave yourself. You know what we mean. Pay attention, or you and the kid will be butchered.*

Of course Mother didn't show me the letter at that time. Actually, she never showed it to me. I only saw it when I was going through her effects after her suicide. They had spelled my name correctly, but I don't think they'd had any evidence to support the claim that I was retarded.

In any event, when Mother got that letter in the mail, her maternal instincts kicked in faster than a snoot full of cocaine, and she got us the hell out of Dodge.

* * *

We drove to Los Angeles in Mother's Ford Taurus station wagon, which was packed full of our belongings. She'd arranged for a friend to hire professionals to pack up the furniture and artwork and ship them to us once we got settled somewhere.

The drive to Los Angeles from Taos was actually kind of fun. It was like being with my mother again. She wasn't mopey, and we pointed out the sights of interest and sang songs. We pulled off I-40 to go look at Meteor Crater, which is said to have been made fifty thousand years ago when a meteor crashed into earth. The crater is four thousand feet in diameter and five hundred seventy feet deep. It's not as deep as the Rio Grande Gorge in Taos, but it's still pretty impressive. I highly recommend spending the time to visit if you're ever in the neighborhood. You can imagine what the meteor would've done had it hit Los Angeles. Of course, now someone would capture video of it with their phone so you wouldn't have to imagine it—as they did in Siberia when the meteor hit in 2012. I wonder what will kill this planet first: a huge meteor that renders Earth uninhabitable or our own insatiable need to suck the planet dry. Wouldn't you love to be a fly on the wall of the world to see what ultimately happens?

Obviously we were in no hurry to get to Los Angeles. We were just in a hurry to get out of Taos.

—10—

I disembarked from the small commuter plane and squinted up at the hot August afternoon sun. Did you know that Santa Fe is the oldest and highest state capital in the United States? I figured it was probably ten degrees cooler here than it had been in Albuquerque to the south, but it was still a scorcher. The short walk across the tarmac to the small adobe-style terminal was sufficient for me to appreciate the air-conditioned interior. I checked in at the Hertz desk while the luggage was being unloaded and, less than ten minutes later, was heading toward town in a big-ass black Cadillac Escalade. It was more car than I'd asked for, but it was all they'd had available.

I drove straight to the mortuary, where I paid the bill and retrieved Mother in her temporary housing, an ugly fake bronze urn. Then I drove up toward the Plaza and parked on Washington Avenue, near the Inn of the Anasazi.

Anasazi is a Navajo word that is generally accepted to mean "ancient people," although it might also have meant "ancestors of our enemies," which I guess means that they forgot to kill off all their enemies. So they had that in common with Pinochet. They were Pueblo Indians who migrated from their ancestral homelands of northern New Mexico and Arizona in the twelfth and thirteenth centuries, possibly because of climate change or possibly because, like elephants and pretty much all humans, they had exhausted and destroyed their own environment. Probably the more conservative Anasazi people kept denying that the environment was affected by humans—right up until it was a wasteland. I'm sure the "ancient people" would be proud to have a five-hundred-dollar-a-night Rosewood Hotel named after them.

I chuckled to myself as I climbed out of the car and, before closing the door, said to the urn, "See, Mom? Fifteen minutes together again and you've already driven me to drink." I locked the car door and walked to the inn's bar for a midmorning margarita. I wondered if everyone who carried around the ashes of their loved ones spoke to them as if they were still alive.

I debated checking into the Anasazi for the night, but all the tourists apparently enjoying themselves seemed to depress me, so I didn't linger. Instead, I downed my drink and walked the two blocks to the *posada* where Mother had killed herself. It was a small place with red bougainvillea growing over the rust-colored adobe walls. The office was cozy and plush, decorated with Indian carpets and paintings. *At least she didn't die in a hovel*, I thought.

"Is the owner in?" I asked the twenty-something Latina woman at the counter.

"May I tell her who's asking and what your business is?"

I'd always hated those questions, and the asshole in me was tempted to say, "Yes, you may, and no, you may not." But she was so pretty and her smile was so overwhelmingly pleasant that I simply said, "Will Muñoz. My mother died here a few days ago."

The charming smile was immediately replaced by a genuine look of sadness and sympathy. *This chica never had to speak*, I thought. Her open face said everything.

"I'm so sorry," she said needlessly. "I'll go get my mother. She's the owner."

Moments later an older version of the beautiful young woman walked through the door separating the check-in desk from what I presumed was the back office. Her face was solemn and kind, and I accepted her condolences with as much grace as I could muster, given my deepening melancholy, which was tinged with impatience—impatience with what, precisely, I couldn't say.

I held out an envelope for the woman to take. "Please take this and consider it from my mother. I know she was sorry to have put you through this."

The woman frowned, clearly perplexed, and took and opened the envelope.

I had placed inside it a check for one thousand dollars made out to the name of the *posada*.

She breathed in sharply and looked at me. "What's this? You don't need to do this. You don't need to apologize for anything." Her voice was soft but firm. "Your mother seemed a lovely woman. She was very kind to us. It broke our hearts to find out how sad she must have been."

I shook my right hand, refusing to take the check she tried to hand back. "No, please. It had to be distressing for you. Maybe for your other guests, as well. Please take it. She would have wanted you to have it."

I hesitated and, probably sensing that I wanted to say something more, the woman withdrew her outstretched hand. Like her daughter, she didn't need to say anything more. I could see from her expression that she was urging me to continue.

I started to speak, but my voice cracked on the first word and I had to start again. "Can you tell me what she was like before she died?" I hesitated again, unsure what exactly I was asking. "I mean, did she seem depressed, or was she acting strange in any way?"

The woman put down the envelope and check and reached out across the counter for my hand. I let her take it. Her fingers were warm and slightly calloused.

"Yes, she did seem sad. But not depressed in any way people would notice. She was so dignified and, like I said, kind. I thought I recognized her name when she checked in, so I googled her and found she was the famous artist. My daughter has an old print of one of your mother's early paintings, and she asked your mother if she would autograph it. It was the only time I remember seeing her smile."

The woman stopped talking for a moment and let go of my hand. Her voice sounded heavy with sorrow when she added, "I thought nothing of it when she asked for some writing paper and envelopes. It was the last time any of us saw her."

*   *   *

I left the two women and drove to our old home in Tesuque. The house looked empty and the yard was overgrown, so I parked in the driveway. I stared at the front of my old house for several seconds before shaking off the temptation to try to look inside. This one house had seen so much love and misery. But I guess that's the job of a home, isn't it, to host all the stages of our fleeting lives?

"Let's go," I said to Mother.

I carried the urn under my left arm and walked around the house to the stream in the back. It was little more than a trickle— typical for August. The cottonwood trees were still green. Soon enough they would begin to turn yellow. Their rounded leaves were like large aspen leaves and quaked and shimmered in the breeze. I sat down in the shade and put Mother down beside me on the bank. I leaned back onto my elbows, closed my eyes, and let the soft sounds of the trickling stream and the rustling leaves wash over me.

How could the will to live be so strong in some people and so weak in others? Why did convicted murderers fight so hard to spend the rest of their lives in horrible prisons instead of asking to be put to death? How could people in horrible pain, on the verge of death, fight to live with every breath? And yet there were people like Mother—with health and every kind of creature comfort imaginable—who found dying so much more preferable to living. Of course, I understood that depression was a mental illness. I, of all people, understood how overwhelming sadness could be, how it could take over one's life. It just hurt me to know Mother had felt so much pain that her instinct for survival had been shunned and bullied and ultimately trampled by the will to die. It hurt me that Mother had hurt so much. And it angered me that someone had caused her so much hurt.

I looked at the urn sitting on the moist dirt beside me. "Why didn't you tell me you were in so much pain, Mom? Why didn't you call me or come up and stay with me? We could have gotten you through it."

I let the empty words drift away on the breeze, and I was suddenly struck by an enormous sense of exhaustion. I lowered myself until I was lying flat on the slope of the bank. I could feel the wet earth and rotting leaves beneath me. I stopped thinking and again let the sounds of the stream and the wind through the trees envelop me.

"*Envelopes*—plural!" I said to myself as I jerked awake, flinging my left arm out and inadvertently knocking over Mom's urn in the process. Still foggy and disoriented from sleep, I stupidly watched as the top fell off and the urn rolled lazily down the slope toward the creek, spilling pieces of Mom as it went. By the time I scrambled to my feet, the urn was sitting in the middle of the creek. I picked it up and looked inside. Mom was gone.

My back and butt were wet from the bank, and I felt a chill run through my body as the afternoon wind picked up. I don't know if I intended to say anything as I released Mother's ashes, but now, as most of her drifted downstream toward the Tesuque Pueblo, all I said was, "Bye, Mom. I love you."

I brushed myself off as best I could and picked up the lid to the urn, and as I trudged back to the car, I remembered my thought upon waking: the woman at the *posada* had said that Mom had asked for writing paper and some envelopes. Had she written more than the one letter? If so, to whom? Or had she just asked for extra in case she messed up her first attempt?

I drove back to Santa Fe—there was no longer any point in going to Taos—and got a room at the Inn of the Anasazi. It was late afternoon, so I cleaned up and went down to the bar for a margarita. This time, I didn't rush it. I sat at the banquette against the wall across from the bar and half listened to the conversations around me. This time it felt comforting to be surrounded by people, and I let the ambiance and the tequila mellow the hard edges of the surreal day. I decided that tomorrow I would check in with the police.

Did I mention we were wealthy? That's probably why I'd never been particularly political—I didn't need to be. I was free to live my life as selfishly as I wanted. Father and Mother had each made millions from their work. When we got to Los Angeles, Mother rented and ultimately bought a house on the beach in Malibu, which was where a lot of movie stars lived. We didn't meet any.

The Chumash Native Americans, the first people to settle Malibu, called the area *Humaliwo*. They didn't pronounce the first two letters of the word, saying instead "maliwo," which is how Malibu got its name. In the Chumash language, Humaliwo means "the surf sounds loudly," which is true.

The Spanish settlers, guys like Juan Cabrillo, landed there to get fresh water, and then the missionaries began to settle there. I suspect they forgot to pay the Chumash for the land. The Chumash were mostly wiped out by the missionaries, who brought influenza and smallpox with their good work.

Some of the billionaire celebrities who live in Malibu now would probably feel guilty about all this if they knew whose land they were living on. But the good news is that the surviving Chumash have a casino in Santa Ynez.

Mother hired a housekeeper by the name of Josephine, who was a large, buxom black woman with straightened hair and soft, chubby features. Josephine lived with us five days a week and then went to her home in Watts for the weekend, presumably to wash clothes and clean up after her family there.

Josephine had two daughters and four granddaughters living with her, which probably made her happy to come live in a large house in Malibu during the week. Dessa, her oldest daughter, had moved back into the house in Watts two years prior when her husband had up and left her after hearing she was pregnant again. It's a good thing Dessa was not a mustached tamarin. Otherwise, she might have calculated that it would be too hard to raise her new baby. One of the ways mustached tamarins commit infanticide is to crack the baby's skull and eat the brains. Anyway, Dessa's child, Deshawna, would eventually have a child who would become the first African American woman to lead the LPGA money list and to win a gold medal in golf at the Tehran Olympics.

I was twelve when we moved to Malibu, and it was a perfect place to get me out of my doldrums. I learned to surf and bought binoculars so I could watch all the girls in their bikinis from my back porch. I even made some pretty good friends in school.

Josephine called me "hotshot," probably because I was something of a smartass. She wouldn't take any shit from me, though. She'd call me in from the beach while standing on our back porch, and when I'd ignored her twice, she'd holler so loud the entire neighborhood could hear her. "Hotshot, you get your ass on in here now! Don't make me come and get you!"

*   *   *

Years later, while I was going through some of Mother's things, I found an article that had been cut out of a 1968 edition of *Ebony* magazine. The article featured a thirteen-year-old girl named Josephine Washington who had stood with a garden hose in front of her parents' little house in Watts during the 1965 riots. She'd gone door to door organizing a neighborhood watch group to keep demonstrators and looters away from their homes. If any of the bad boys came near their homes, Josephine and her neighborhood army would start yelling at them and shoot hoses at them until they went away to burn something else.

At first, after I read the article, I was sad that I hadn't known Josephine was a hero in Watts, but then I realized it hadn't really mattered at all. I couldn't have loved her or admired her any more than I had. So I just loved her memory all the more. She too was dead by the time I read the article.

*   *   *

Mom calmed down a bit after we moved into the house in Malibu. It was such a fairy-tale kind of place that it was hard to imagine anything bad happening there. Except fires. It seemed as if fires and mudslides were a constant threat in Malibu. Maybe it was the Chumash gods' way of saying "fuck you" to the billionaires.

Mom had begun working again, and although there was still an air of sadness around her, the fear and paranoia that had grabbed hold of her that day in Taos was slowly loosening its grip. Of course, I didn't know then what the cause of her fear was. She really had no one to share that awful letter with. She'd given up on the police by then. All she could think about was how to protect me. I don't think she cared the slightest about herself.

But, as they say, time heals all wounds, and I guess fear is a wound. As I grew out of my wimpy persona, I think Mother began to feel that the bad times were behind us. When an art gallery friend of hers pestered her into going out to some openings and parties, Mother finally relented.

*   *   *

After Mother had been going out fairly regularly for several months, she announced one day that she'd been invited to go to Mexico for the weekend with some of her friends, but she seemed reluctant to say yes. Josephine and I worked on her for days, telling her how good it would be for her. When Mom finally relented, Josephine and I high-fived each other, thinking we had pushed Mom into taking another step toward normalcy, and at first it appeared to have worked.

Mother came back from her weekend in Mexico looking relaxed and happy, and things were good for three days. But I came home from school on Thursday and learned Mother had locked herself in her bedroom. Josephine told me Mother had gotten a letter and had almost fainted when she read it. She said Mother's eyes had gone wide, her face had turned pale, and then her lips had begun to quiver. When Josephine had gone to her, Mother had waved her away and mumbled something about being okay and then had gone to her room and locked the door.

Josephine and I sat in the kitchen and speculated on what could have set Mother off this time.

"I just don't know," mused Josephine. "She's been so happy. She confided in me that she met a man she liked. I thought maybe your poor mama had finally turned the corner and was going to start living again."

But that's when things really started to go bad. Mother had received another threatening letter. Since I didn't know about the first one yet, I had no idea what was going on. What I know now is that the new letter was even worse than the first. It talked about killing us both, and it talked about things Mother and Josephine and I had done, which meant someone had been watching us. I never did see the letter. Josephine told me Mother said she'd given it to Chuck Evans, the man Mother had met, the man who would become my stepfather.

—12—

I knew the Santa Fe police had handled Mother's suicide, since it was a detective from that office who'd called me to give me the news. After a leisurely breakfast of huevos rancheros at the Anasazi, I called Detective Rolando Martinez.

"Sure, Mr. Muñoz, I remember you. What can I do for you?"

"I'm wondering if you, or anyone else in the department, received a letter from my mother."

After a slight pause, he said, "You mean a suicide note of some kind? Besides the one in the room we already told you about?"

"Yeah, I guess that's what I mean," I replied, realizing how stupid I must have sounded. "The owner of the inn where she died said she asked for some writing paper and envelopes. I got a letter from her that was delivered after her death, so I was wondering if anyone else received anything since she'd asked for more than one envelope."

"Nope," Martinez said. "Just the one short note to make sure we knew she was taking her own life. That's it. Anything else I can help you with?"

"No, I guess . . . wait," I said. "Can you tell me who handled the investigation into my father's death?"

Again he paused before answering. "He died in Tesuque, right?"

"Yeah."

"The Tesuque police wouldn't have handled it. It would've been the homicide division at the Santa Fe County Sheriff's Office. I wouldn't know which detective was assigned to the case— or even if he's still there."

I thanked Martinez and hung up. Then I looked up the address for the sheriff's office. I knew from experience that one could accomplish a lot more in person than from being handed off from one person to another on the phone.

Twenty minutes later I was sitting across from Captain Morrisey, who'd been a rookie in the CID when my father was murdered. Now he was well into his fifties and looked it. His face was craggy and tanned. His hair, what was left of it, was gray. Although he sat behind a desk, I could see he had a serious paunch. Despite the decades of police work, he had eyes that seemed to sparkle.

"Sure, I remember your father's case," he said in a deep and sonorous voice. "It was one of my first homicides. Bill Reyes was the lead detective on the case. He passed a few years ago."

The captain leaned back in his chair, bringing his large, round belly into full view.

"I heard about your mother. I'm very sorry."

"Thank you," I said automatically.

He sat silently a moment, looking uncomfortable, and then said, "So what can I help you with? I assume you know we didn't handle your mother's death."

I nodded. "Yes, I know that. I was wondering if your office might have received a letter from my mother. Something she would have mailed just before she died."

As I said this, it occurred to me how absurd it sounded. If they had received a letter from Mom, the captain would have brought it up and wouldn't have acted surprised to see me.

Now he frowned, shaking his head. "Not that I'm aware of. Why do you think we would've received such a letter? Your mother wasn't exactly a big fan of ours."

I offered a small smile and a shrug. "Just a long shot. She requested writing paper and envelopes from the hotel before she committed suicide. I know there was a short suicide note that the Santa Fe police have, but that wasn't in an envelope and there weren't any empty envelopes left in the room. She sent me a letter. So it makes sense that she sent another letter to someone."

The captain rocked back and forth in his chair, clearly mulling over the information. Then he picked up his phone and punched in some numbers. "Allison, did the department receive any kind of letter a few days ago from a woman by the name of Susan Muñoz?" He looked up at me. "Or Susan Montrose?"

I nodded to him, surprised that he remembered Mother had kept her maiden name.

Captain Morrisey listened for about half a minute and then rolled his eyes at me. Then he said into the phone, "Don't you think someone should've told me about it? Go downstairs and see if you can find it. Now, please."

He hung up and looked at me. "Sorry. Yeah, some letter came in addressed to Detective Reyes. The mail room has it. They were going to forward it on to Mrs. Reyes. Luckily, we still have it."

I didn't react. I couldn't imagine what such a letter could reveal that Mom hadn't already confided to me. It probably contained nothing more than some lonely and paranoid-sounding ramblings about how her former husband, Chuck Evans, had been involved in the death of my father.

The captain clearly wasn't into small talk, for which I was thankful, so he pretended to study some paperwork on his desk.

I leaned back in my chair and tried not to think of my mother, so sad, angry, and alone, writing her death letters, trying one last time to get justice. An old-fashioned overhead fan slowly rotated above us, performing no productive task that I could tell.

A few minutes later, someone knocked on the door as they pushed it open. A heavyset woman who looked Native American entered and handed the captain an envelope. She smiled and nodded at me on the way out.

Captain Morrisey studied the envelope for a moment before slitting it open. I watched him as he read the two-page letter, his lips moving almost imperceptibly. I couldn't read his expression. He would have made a good poker player. When he was done, he handed me the letter.

Once again, I noticed that Mother's handwriting was beautiful and easy to read. I'm certainly not an expert, but I could see no evidence of stress.

Here's what the letter from my dead mother to Detective Reyes said:

Dear Detective Reyes:

Please forgive me for imposing on you again after all these years. I'm hoping you are still with the sheriff's office. If you are not, will you please give this to whoever is in charge? I am about to take my own life, and I want this one final opportunity to convey information about my husband's death. Much of this we didn't know at the time, so I don't really blame you for not entertaining the idea that Ricardo Muñoz's murder was political. As you know, or at least as I told you, Pinochet tried to have Ricardo assassinated. This was while Ricardo was still living in Chile and was waging a war of words against the Pinochet regime. When Ricardo was murdered, I assumed it was Pinochet's people following up on their prior death threats. I can see why you would have a hard time buying that scenario.

What I didn't know at the time was that Pinochet and his people had obtained a draft copy of Ricardo's unpublished novel, The Daughters of Pinochet. *According to old acquaintances from Chile who were in a position to know what was going on, Pinochet was furious about the novel, which, as you might assume, portrayed him as a ruthless megalomaniac. What was worse, however, was that in the novel, the daughter of Pinochet was the daughter of one of his mistresses. When the child was thirteen, Pinochet decided that he wanted her, his own daughter, as his mistress. He threw his former mistress, the child's mother, into prison and raped the daughter into submission.*

There is a lot more to the story that would have enraged Pinochet, but you can imagine how abhorrent this kind of portrayal would be to the Latin mind-set. Being called a thug and a murderer is one thing, but incestuous pedophilia would have been too much. Remember that Pinochet had a wife and three daughters. So I think he would have done everything in his power to stop the publication of The Daughters of Pinochet.

I stopped reading and looked up at Captain Morrisey. He was watching me.

"Are you done?" he asked.

"No. Just read the part about Dad's novel. You got to admit it would have pissed off Pinochet and his supporters."

Morrisey nodded. "Did you know about the novel?"

I shook my head. "Not really. I mean, I knew there was an unpublished novel, but I had no idea what it was about. I remember asking Mother once if I could read it, and she refused, saying his publisher was holding the only copy and she'd been given strict instructions not to have it published and not to let it leave his office."

Morrisey grunted and nodded to the letter. "Go ahead and finish."

Please bear with me, Detective Reyes. I may be about to kill myself, but trust me that I am not insane. I understand that the novel itself is not a sufficient reason for the authorities to reopen the investigation into Ricardo's murder. There is more.

After Ricardo was murdered, I received two anonymous letters. Both letters threatened to kill me and my son, Will. The first letter ordered me to destroy the novel. The second letter didn't mention the novel, but they were horrible, scary letters, and I would be lying if I said I was not terrified for our lives. The first letter came not long after Ricardo's death and was the reason I packed us up and moved us from Taos to Los Angeles. The second letter came years later, just as I had begun to forget and start living my life again.

What happened next sounds ridiculous to me now as I write this, but at the time, when I feared for our safety, it made some weird kind of sense. A man by the name of Charles Evans came into my life. I won't bore you with the details, but suffice it to say I came to feel safe and protected when he was around. I told him about the letters, and he convinced me to marry him. For a while, I did feel safe. But then Will moved out to go to college in the Bay Area, and it was just Chuck and me and my maid, Josephine. Chuck became abusive toward both of us. He would go off on insane rants and would call Jo and me some of the worst names imaginable. Sometimes he would hit me—but never when Jo was around. He never hit Jo. I think he knew she would have killed him if he ever touched her.

Again, I won't bore you with all the gruesome details, but the psychotic rants of his became more and more common. During one of his last rants before I threw him out of the house for good, he said things that made no sense, referring to Ricardo's murder and to the novel The Daughters of Pinochet. He said things no one could have known about. He said he knew these things because he had worked for the CIA. Jo and I decided Chuck was completely mental and threw him out.

But Chuck kept calling the house, and when one of us would pick up, he'd start swearing and threatening *us. When I saw him sitting in his car on the street outside the house one afternoon, I called his friend Milton Fischer to ask for advice on what to do. Milton had been Chuck's best man at the wedding and always seemed to be around, never far from Chuck. It was a strange relationship that I didn't really think about until much later. I told Milton what was going on and how it was creeping me out, and I asked him if he could help or if I should just call the police.*

Milton was very deferential and even apologized for Chuck's actions. He said there were forces at work that I couldn't understand and that he could not explain. When I continued to press him, using the police as my leverage, Milton said something had happened to Chuck when he was young that had left him with brain damage. That was why Milton had to stick close to him. He said he couldn't tell me more and that he had already said too much. He promised to take care of Chuck and said I wouldn't be bothered again.

Milton was true to his word. I never heard from Chuck again, but I've been a mess ever since. I became reclusive again. I was scared of my own shadow. Jo tried to take care of me and get me to see a doctor, but I refused. Chuck had known too much about Ricardo. He knew about a completely secret novel that had been shelved. He kept asking me where I kept it.

I'm sorry to have been so long-winded, Detective Reyes. I realize you will probably think I'm as crazy as I think Chuck is. But if you think there may be some things worth looking into, I'd appreciate it. I will be gone, but my son should be given the opportunity to learn the truth about his father's death. I have sent him a letter as well. It is not as long as this, but I did share my concerns about Chuck and his knowledge about

things that were private. If I know my son, you will get
a call or visit from him before long. Help him if you can.

I handed the letter back to Morrisey, who took it and put it on his desk without saying anything. I'd been a trial attorney long enough to be able to read most people's body language, and I could tell what Morrisey was thinking by the way he leaned back in his chair, arms resting on the armrests, his head held at a slight angle.

"You think she was nuts, don't you?" I said.

He didn't move or say anything for a few seconds, but finally he leaned forward and put both forearms on his desk. "I think your mother was obsessed with tying Pinochet to your father's death, and I think it finally got to her." He paused, and I could see him work hard to soften his expression. "I feel for her. We never solved the murder, and it must've torn her up inside."

"Technically, the case is still open," I said. It wasn't a question. It was a statement.

Morrisey nodded.

"So don't you think you should at least do some preliminary checking based on her letter? Why not check out Chuck Evans and Milton Fischer at the very least?"

Morrisey stared at me for a long time. Was he trying to intimidate me? Read me?

I met and held his gaze until he finally broke eye contact and looked down at the letter. I waited.

"Okay," he finally said. "Here's what I'll do. I'll run Evans' and Fischer's names through all the databases we have access to, and we'll see what turns up. If there's nothing to pique our interest, I'll drop it and take no further action. If I see something worth pursuing further, I'll let you know." He looked back up at me. "Fair enough?"

I knew that was all I was going to get out of Morrisey, so I nodded and said, "Fair enough." Then I stood up and held out my hand. "Thanks for your time."

—13—

I could tell Chuck was a real prick from the first moment I met him, but I also knew the feeling was mutual. He couldn't stand to be around me any more than I could stand to be around him.

"Maybe you just need to give him more of a chance, hotshot," Josephine would say to me in the early days after he had entered our lives. But I knew she didn't like him anymore than I did.

Chuck was a big, tall, manly looking man. He was an intimidating presence. His face was angular and rugged-looking in that old cowboy movie star sort of way—James Arness and those guys. His blond hair was cut short, something just shy of a military-style buzz cut. To me, it was his eyes that gave him away. They were the one flaw in his features. They were too small and were kind of a nebulous gray color. They didn't appear to have any depth to them and were always moving, as if he was constantly unsure of his surroundings. How Mother failed to pick up on the eye thing is beyond me. As an artist, she was sensitive to what the eyes could tell about someone. I can only guess she was blinded by fear.

Chuck was supposedly a consultant—whatever that meant. It's amazing to me how selfishly uninterested in Chuck I was. I don't remember asking any questions about him. If Mother told me he was a consultant, I never asked what he consulted about or for whom. This older guy named Milton was always hanging around, but I never asked what his last name was or even who the hell he was. Despite never warming up to Chuck, I was happy that Mother had someone to take care of her so I could leave for college without feeling guilty.

One day during the summer before I would leave for Berkeley, and not long after Mother and Chuck had married, Jo took me aside and suggested I come and spend the weekend with her family in Watts. "Let's give them some time alone together in the house," she said.

I readily agreed. I'd grown to love Josephine and welcomed the opportunity to see where she lived and to meet her family. It would also be good to get away from Chuck for a few days, I thought.

The year was 1993, one year after the Rodney King riots. You remember Rodney King, don't you? He's the black man the Los Angeles police beat the shit out of after King led them on a high-speed chase. King was on parole at the time and had been drinking, so he decided to make a run for it rather than pull over when the first cop car turned its flashing lights on. Bad move, dude. When King finally stopped and got out of his car, he resisted arrest, and what occurred thereafter was all caught on videotape by a private citizen by the name of George Holliday, who lived in a nearby apartment. That was a big "uh-oh" moment for the cops. That was also one of the first big lessons that people still don't seem to have learned: always assume whatever you do is being filmed by someone.

Josephine's daughter Dessa had just moved back home, and Josephine's other daughter Serena had never left. So when I came to stay for the weekend, I was the only male in a household of seven females, ages ranging from two to forty-six. I was in heaven. The young kids crawled all over me and begged me to swing them upside down. They were thrilled to have a man to play with. The older ones waited on me hand and foot.

The three-bedroom house was a small, neatly kept stucco bungalow that had been built in the '50s. It was the same house that Josephine had guarded when she was thirteen years old. The front stoop was spacious and was where we'd all gather as dusk settled in.

Neighbors strolling by smiled and waved, and more than a few hollered up to Josephine, "Hey, Jo, who's the white boy?"

Josephine would laugh and answer, "He's my hotshot."

Being half-Latino, I wasn't used to being referred to as a "white boy," but in the eyes of the good people of Watts, I was just another gringo.

We all went to church on Sunday at the Watts First Baptist. I wasn't religious and would never be religious, but this church was actually fun. There was singing and praise-the-lord-ing and amen-ing and all sorts of happy stuff going on.

At one point the minister, a large, rotund balding man with smiling eyes, announced, "Brothers and sisters, I want you all to welcome our sister Josephine's guest here today and treat him to our famous Watts hospitality."

That got a huge laugh, and people turned in their seats to stare openly at me. I smiled and gave a little wave like a celebrity.

That evening, as Jo and I sat on her front stoop and the rest of the household busied themselves with preparing dinner, Jo put her hand on mine and gave it a light squeeze. We sat like that for a few quiet minutes.

The girls in the house chattered nonstop such that their conversation became a kind of background music. The noises of the neighborhood drifted in and out of my consciousness. A Marvin Gaye song playing in a house across the street. The occasional passing car. A far-off siren.

"Do you think your mama's gonna be okay?" Jo finally asked.

"You mean with Chuck, or just in general?"

Jo took a moment and then said, "Both, I guess."

I shrugged. The selfish side of me answered, "Sure. I think so."

"But you don't like Chuck. You think she gonna be okay with him?"

"Why not? Just 'cause I think he's a dick doesn't mean he doesn't love her and won't take care of her." I looked sideways at Jo. "Why? Do you think something's wrong?"

Josephine stared out at the street. The Marvin Gaye song had ended, and now Smokey Robinson was singing "Tears of a Clown." Before speaking again, Jo gently took her hand off mine and put it in her lap. "I guess not. You know I don't like him none, either. I don't like the way I see him treat her."

I squirmed uncomfortably. I'd be leaving for college soon, and I didn't want anything to screw that up. I wanted to believe Mother would be all right—that Chuck would be good for her. But in my heart I knew exactly what Jo was saying. I'd never seen Chuck hit Mother, so there wasn't any kind of overt abuse that concerned me. The hitting would come later, after I was gone. Mostly it was little things. A request would come out as an order. He'd cut her off in the middle of a story and take over the dialogue. He was dismissive of her artist friends. But the one big fight I remember was when Chuck referred to my father as a "pretentious commie intellectual." Jo and I were in the kitchen at the time, and as the loud, loathsome pronouncement came out of Chuck's mouth, we looked at each other with what can only be described as a mixture of shock and dread. We both knew that no one could insult Dad and get away with it. Jo put her hand on my arm, an unspoken order to stay where I was. The vicious tirade that erupted from Mother was scary in its own right. It went on for the better part of a minute before she ordered Chuck out of the house. He said something in a low, menacing tone that we couldn't hear from the kitchen, and then the door slammed and he was gone.

Like most cowardly spouse abusers, Chuck eventually came crawling back and whined and whimpered and apologized his way back into the household. He didn't look much like a Hollywood star in that role.

These were all things I didn't want to see or hear or acknowledge. But I knew Jo was right.

"Well, even though I guess I agree with you, there's really nothing we can do about it. Is there?"

Josephine shook her head slightly. "No, hotshot. I reckon not." Her voice sounded sad and resigned.

On Monday morning it was time to head back to Malibu. I gave all the ladies hugs and kisses and promised I'd come again, and then Josephine and I climbed into her little Toyota Corolla and returned to where the rich people lived their quiet and not-so-sober lives.

I had reason to think about that conversation with Josephine many times in the years that followed.

—14—

After spilling my mother in the river and talking to the cops, there was nothing more to do in Santa Fe that afternoon, so I caught the 2 o'clock American flight to Los Angeles. The two-hour flight gave me time to think. What, exactly, did I plan to do? Was I really going to try to track down Chuck and confront him? Was I going to try to solve Dad's murder even though the Santa Fe cops couldn't? Realistically, did I think Mother was right to think Pinochet would have had anything to do with Dad's death?

In the end, of course, I had no answers and no clear plan. I simply didn't know what else to do other than plod along and see what developed. For now, I would go to the Malibu house and begin the sad and dreary task of sorting through Mother's things. I wished desperately that Josephine could be there with me. But she, too, was dead.

Two years before Mother killed herself, she called to tell me Jo was dying. I'd known Jo had cancer. Mother had kept her on, but as the disease and the treatment ate away at her, eventually it was Mother who took care of Jo. Like clockwork, on Monday morning one of the kids would drive Jo to the Malibu house, where she would stay until Friday afternoon. The fact that it had become impossible for her to do any semblance of actual work was never acknowledged. The roles Mother and Jo played simply reversed as an unspoken matter of course. Josephine would lie on the couch most of the day while the television played their favorite talk shows and soap operas. Mother would fuss over her, making sure she was comfortable, making sure she got food in her.

I watched this strange and poignant transformation of the employer/employee relationship whenever I was able to get away from my life in San Francisco. I brought it up to Mother one Saturday when Josephine was home in Watts and Mother was cleaning the house, which she refused to do in front of Jo.

But Mother cut me off, saying, "I need her every bit as much as she needs me. We don't talk about it. We just both know what we know."

And that was it. My mother, who, frankly, had not been the most maternal of moms, had become nurse, sister, and best friend to her dying maid.

When Mom called to tell me Josephine was dying, I asked Cheryl to handle the court appearances I had over the next few days and then caught the next available flight to Los Angeles. I wasn't sure who I should be more concerned about: Mom or Jo. I knew Jo had her faith. Mom had Jo and me.

I drove straight to Jo's house in Watts. The front yard was not as well kept as it had been when I'd visited those many years before. The lawn was sparse and brown. A few pieces of windblown trash littered the yard. The flower beds next to the porch where we'd sat and waved to neighbors were barren except for some sick-looking twigs that had once been bushes. Transparent blue shopping bags hung from the twigs like some futuristic plastic flowers.

"House needs painting," I muttered to myself as I walked up the wood stairs.

Considering the number of family members who had been drinking at Josephine's trough over the years, there was no excuse for things to have fallen in disrepair. *It must break her heart*, I thought.

Serena answered the door. She was younger than me, but she looked old, worn, and sad as she peered out to see who was on the stoop.

After a few beats, she realized it was me and broke into a huge grin and pulled me toward her for a hug. "Oh, Will, I'm so glad you came. Mama will be so happy to see you." She pushed me back to arm's length and added, "She's bad, Will. She don't have much time left."

The house was dark and quiet when we finally walked inside. The ever-present sound of happy children I remembered was gone. The wonderful aromas of cooking were gone. Instead, the house smelled like sickness. The stuffy air reeked of medicine, disinfectant, laundry, and conflicting perfumes. We turned left into the living room, which now served as a hospital room. Josephine was lying on the couch, propped up with several pillows. Oprah was on the television, but someone was turning the volume down even as we came into the room.

"Mama, look who's come to see you," Serena said.

I walked to the couch, and as I looked down at Jo, I had to catch myself to keep from crying out. The once robust woman I'd grown to love like a mother was rail thin. Her face was gaunt, with dark purplish bags under her eyes. She wore a bandanna on her head.

She peered up at me and then, like Serena, finally recognized me. "My hotshot," she said in a soft voice, clearly straining. I gently held the thin hand she stretched toward me.

Someone pulled a chair up beside the couch, and I looked back to see it was Deshawna. I nodded to her but immediately turned back to Jo and sat down.

"Y'all leave me and hotshot alone for a few minutes," Jo said. Then she pulled me close. Her grip was amazingly strong, considering how frail she looked. "Come close, Will. It hurts to talk."

I started to say something, intending to tell her she didn't have to talk, but she cut me off.

"I'm so glad you came, honey. I need to tell you some things—things I didn't even tell your mama. I was too worried about her." She coughed into her clenched fist, and I could hear the rattle in her lungs.

I spotted a glass of water sitting on a nearby side table and brought it to her. "Here," I said and let her sip from the straw.

She nodded to me appreciatively and then continued. "That Chuck was a bad man. Worse even than you and I thought. One day, not long before your mama finally threw him out of the house for good, I caught him upstairs in the storeroom. He had no business being up there. He was going through boxes of things that belonged to your father. I asked him what he thought he was doing, and he told me it was none of my business." Jo let out a kind of chuckle, which sounded more like a gurgle. "He said it was none of my *fucking* business, if you must know. Anyway, I told him he had no right to be going through Mr. Ricardo's things. But he ignored me and moved from one box to another. I asked him what he was looking for. I said I knew where everything was 'cause I'd helped Miss Susan pack everything up. When I said that, Chuck stopped what he was doing and looked at me. 'I'm looking for a book. An unfinished book,' he said." Jo stopped talking and pointed to the water glass.

I held it for her as she took some more sips. The house was so still I could hear the old antique clock ticking in the corner of the living room. The glare of the television images played across Jo's face.

"I told him that there weren't no unfinished books in any of the boxes. All of Mr. Muñoz's published books were downstairs on the bookshelf. There was one box of books that Mr. Muñoz had owned that were in Spanish, but other than that, there wasn't no books. Chuck stared at me like he was trying to decide whether to believe me. I watched him looking at me, and then I turned to leave. I told him I was going to get Miss Susan." Jo took a deep breath and wheezed.

I motioned to the water to see if she wanted some more, but she shook her head.

"That's when the bastard jumped up and grabbed me," she said. "He grabbed my arm, real hard-like, and he put his face up in mine. 'You don't get her,' he said, 'and you don't say a thing about me being up here. You understand?' His voice was rough and real threatening. His face was all scrunched up, mean looking. 'Or what?' I asked. 'You gonna beat me up like you beat on Miss Susan?' Chuck laughed when I said that. He let go of my arm but kind of pushed me as he did, and I fell back against some stacked boxes. 'Shit no,' he said. 'I'll beat the shit out of Susan if you tell her I was up here. So why don't you get your black ass back to work and leave me alone.' "

Jo yanked her hand away from mine. "Ouch!"

I looked down at my hand, confused, and then realized I'd been squeezing hers in anger. "Jeez, I'm sorry, Jo."

She choked out a laugh and put her hand back in mine. "That's okay, hon. Ain't nothing. So anyway, I didn't say anything to your mama. I was scared for her."

Jo started coughing again, and this time she accepted the water. I assumed she was through with whatever she had to tell me, but when she finished sipping on the straw and I'd put the glass down, she pulled me close again.

"A day or two after that confrontation in the attic, I saw Chuck's suitcase sitting on a stand in their bedroom. I got excited, thinking he was finally going to move out. There was no one home at the time, so I opened the suitcase to see whether or not Chuck had really been packing. There was nothing in the suitcase but a notebook—one of them spiral ones like schoolchildren use."

Jo closed her eyes and swallowed a few times, exhaustion creeping across her face.

Finally, she looked ready to continue. "I knew I shouldn't have done it, but I couldn't help myself. I looked in the notebook. At first I didn't know what it was. It was all newspaper clippings. Then I started to read them."

I could feel her grip tighten on my hand.

"They was all news stories about people that been murdered. I think the first one was from 1987 or so. I flipped through the notebook, skimming most of the articles. I was afraid Chuck would come home and catch me. But when I saw the news articles about your father, I know I let out a little cry. I still didn't know what I was looking at, a scrapbook of some kind, but there were many clippings after those about your father. They were all people that had been murdered. The last entry was only about a year before."

Jo stopped talking, and the room fell silent. I could hear low voices in the kitchen, and once in a while I could detect what sounded like a dish being put on top of other dishes. Someone was probably drying and stacking dishes.

After a while, Jo said, "Chuck is capable of anything. He's evil." She was struggling to talk now, her voice having deteriorated into a painful-sounding rasp. "After Chuck was finally gone for good, I should've told your mama. But I couldn't see what good would come of it. He was gone from our lives—and good riddance. Then the past year or so, your mama started talking about how she didn't think your father was killed in a burglary and about how she thought he was assassinated by that guy from Chile. She was obsessed with it. It was almost all she wanted to talk about. Maybe I should've told her about the notebook and about how Chuck had been looking for some unfinished book then." Josephine sighed heavily. "But then I got sick, and your mama started taking care of me and stopped talking about your father."

Jo gave me one of the saddest smiles I've ever seen. I waited for her to go on.

"I don't know, hotshot, maybe my getting sick was good for your mama. But you need to watch her. She ain't got nobody now that I'm about to pass. I'm scared for her." Jo started coughing and couldn't even take a sip of water. She'd probably said more in the past ten minutes than she had for weeks.

Serena and Deshawna came in when they heard the coughing.

Jo tried to wave them away, but she was too weak to protest.

I got up and bent over to kiss Jo, but she took my hand again and pulled me close. In a barely audible whisper, she said, "Look in your mama's frock drawer in her studio."

She didn't say anything more and let go of my hand, so I kissed her on her sunken cheek. If there is a smell of someone dying, that was what she smelled like: a vague, cloying smell of decay. It was the saddest, most unbearably memorable odor I ever hope to encounter.

Serena walked me out to the front stoop.

"Do you need anything? Any money for her medical bills or anything?" I asked.

Serena smiled and shook her head. "Your mother paid for all of Mama's bills. She's a fine lady."

I nodded. "They both are."

Josephine died the very next day. I was glad I was home with Mother when Jo passed. It was an awfully hard time. I tried to talk Mother into selling the house in Malibu and moving up to San Francisco, but she would hear none of it. She made all sorts of excuses, but in the end I suspect she didn't want to interfere with my life. Now, of course, I blame myself for not being insistent and forcing the issue. Would she still be alive if I hadn't left her alone in that big house? I never asked her about what Jo had said about Dad being assassinated or about the scrapbook Jo had found. Frankly, by the time we put Jo to rest, I'd forgotten all about that conversation. Mother never told me her suspicions about Pinochet.

Until she wrote her suicide note.

—15—

The trip from Santa Fe to Los Angeles seemed to take forever, and I was tired and more melancholy than usual by the time I finally got to the house in Malibu. It was one of the older houses on the beach: a wood-framed three-story affair. The front of the house had no real character, since it was too close to the highway to be anything more than a driveway and entry. But once you walked into the house, the views of the Pacific Ocean were stunning. I know Mother spent a small fortune on the weekly window cleaners for the floor-to-ceiling windows, but it was worth every penny. The day was clear and cool, and the sky was as blue as Los Angelenos could ever hope to see. The blue-green ocean frothed from a pretty decent swell, and for half a second I actually considered digging out my wetsuit and surf-board. But I was just too tired and confused. I felt as if I had no direction.

I decided I needed to talk to someone. After I tossed my bag onto my old bed, I plopped down on the living room couch and, staring out at the ocean, called Cheryl at the office.

"So how are you, pards?" she asked.

We had been calling each other "partner" or "pards" ever since becoming law partners.

"Confused," I said. "And sad."

"To be expected. Don't worry about it now. Did you take care of your mother's ashes?"

I chuckled and told her the story about knocking over the urn in the creek in Tesuque. "So I didn't need to go to Taos," I said.

"Obviously you harbored a subconscious desire to avoid Taos, so you *accidentally* spilled your mother."

Her sarcastic wit made me smile. It also made me miss her—and Travis. I said as much.

There was a slight pause on her end. "Gosh, Will, you must be more fucked up than I thought."

"I must be. Did I actually say something nice?"

"Why don't you come on home? Take a few days around here to gather your thoughts. When we get a break, the three of us can go back down to Malibu and help you clean out the house."

I thought about what Cheryl was offering. A part of me had wanted her to make that offer from the moment I called. It was tempting to agree, and I almost did so. But then I thought of Mother and the pain she'd been in and the letters she had written before killing herself. I'd run away from her troubles all those years ago when I left for school, and one of the things that was making me so sad now was realizing how selfish I had been over the past fifteen years while I had been building my law practice. Yeah, I called her twice a week like clockwork. And I visited her whenever I felt I could get away. But it had become a rote and superficial relationship. Shit, I hadn't even known she was so bad off that she was contemplating suicide.

"I think I need to see this through sooner rather than later," I told Cheryl.

I heard her sigh. "See what through, exactly? What are we talking about here, Will? Cleaning out your mother's house or chasing after her ghosts?"

"They're my ghosts too," I said, a little more aggressively than warranted. I decided to change the subject. "How's the business?"

Again I could hear Cheryl breathe deeply. Not exactly a sigh. More like a deep breath to help her let it go. Finally she replied in a light tone, "God, you've got some assholes for clients."

I laughed. "Duh. Who in particular are we talking about?"

"George Halpern, for one. Mr. Carlo."

George Halpern was the owner of a huge franchise pizza operation called Mr. Carlo's Pizza. His net worth was somewhere north of one hundred million dollars.

"No shit," I said. "But what's going on with him? I thought we were about to get a settlement with the plaintiffs' attorneys."

"I think we'll get it," Cheryl said. "But Travis and I decided it would be good to take George out to dinner to wine and dine him and make sure he was on board with everything, especially since he hadn't had many dealings with me before you left. So we took him to Boulevard, and he started getting liquored up and went into this long rant about lazy workers and government entitlement programs and how our welfare system is creating a class of people who want something for nothing and blah, blah, blah." Recalling the incident was enough to raise Cheryl's voice a notch or two in timbre. She was obviously angry. "I mean, there he is—a prick who's getting sued by his own employees for screwing them out of $20 million worth of overtime and benefits— and he's bitching about people on food stamps getting a hundred bucks a month. What the fuck, Will? Why are we representing people like this?"

I closed my eyes to the multimillion-dollar view. "What'd you say back to him?"

"What'd you think I said? I asked him how many of his employees were on food stamps because he refused to pay a livable wage. I asked him how many poor schmucks on welfare would have to rip off the system to get anywhere close to the twenty million bucks he screwed his people out of. I—"

"What'd you really say?"

"Nothing, of course. We let him get soused on martinis. We rolled our eyes at each other, and I cussed you out under my breath, and finally we got him to agree to the settlement."

"Sorry about him, pards. There's only a couple more complete assholes on my client list. The rest are only marginal assholes."

I heard Cheryl's humorless harrumph, and I missed her all the more. I don't know how my practice had evolved from representing individuals who'd been screwed over by large corporations to representing the large corporations, but somewhere along the line, I'd sold out. Cheryl, in the meantime, had stayed the course of slaying dragons. I admired and envied her for it. Just as I had turned my back on my mother, I had turned my back on the principles of law I most believed in.

What does it say about the survivability of a nation in which, according to various economic studies, 95 percent of income gains from 2009 to the present have accrued to the top 1 percent? George Halpern and many of my other clients are one-percenters. Hell, I guess I'm a one-percenter based on my inherited wealth. When had I become so selfish? When had I stopped representing the people who needed someone to help them stand up to the bullies who thought their wealth somehow made them better, smarter, harder working, and above the law?

"You still there, Will?"

I gazed out at the water, willing my mind to clear. "Yeah, I'm here. I really do miss you guys. I'm going to take some time here to clean out the place and decide if I want to put it up for sale. In the meantime, I might look into some of the things Mother wanted me to check out."

I told her about the second letter Mother had sent to the Santa Fe Sheriff's Office.

There was silence on the line when I finished, but I let it play itself out.

"Okay," Cheryl finally said in a resigned voice. "Let me know if you want to use Travis for anything. Maybe he can speed up your quest. Assuming we wrap up Mr. Fucking Carlo's settlement, I won't be needing him for a while."

"Thanks. And thanks for being so understanding."

Cheryl really did laugh then. "I'm not being understanding at all, you schmuck. I'm just hoping insanity doesn't run in your family."

"Ouch."

* * *

I don't know why I actually felt better after talking to Cheryl. It's not as if it had been that uplifting of a conversation. But I dragged my ass off the couch, changed into a sweat suit I kept at the house, and went out for a long walk on the beach. On the way back to the house, with my nose red and runny from the wind and the chill in the air, I remembered Josephine's last words to me:

"Check your mama's frock drawer in her studio."

16

Mother's studio was on the third floor. The wall facing the ocean was all glass. She had installed a huge skylight that comprised about half of the roof over that room. A potter's wheel sat on the opposite side of the room. A couple of easels graced the bright side of the studio. Obviously, Mother had been painting again. There were twenty or so canvases of finished paintings stacked along one wall. They would be worth a fortune.

I walked over to one of the easels, pulled off the sheet draped over the canvas, and stared at an unfinished painting of my father. It was scarily and uncannily realistic. Usually Mother painted in a more abstract style. The painting of my father was so pure and so perfect that, had it been finished, it could have been confused with a photograph. The eyes were the most amazing. How could she have painted eyes that conveyed everything she loved about Ricardo Muñoz? Humor, intelligence, curiosity, love—yet I also sensed an underlying sadness. I stared at the painting for several minutes. At first I simply marveled at the artistry. Then I really began to see my father. I felt my gut wrench. My eyes filled with tears as I realized how unreal he had become to me. Had it been torturous for my mother to paint this picture? Or had it been uplifting and wonderful for her to capture her long-lost love? Why had she not finished it? I wondered if it had simply become too much for her to look into those deep, penetrating eyes she had re-created.

I finally closed my eyes and turned away from the picture. "Oh, Mother," I said aloud.

I carefully covered the canvas again with the sheet and then looked around the room. An old, paint-stained wood chest stood against the wall where the finished canvases were stacked. I walked over and opened the top drawer. It was filled with folded frocks that Mother had worn while working. I reached inside the drawer and felt around beneath the clothing, eventually discovering a brown-paper package that had been tied with string. I set it on top of the dresser and continued to search the drawer. On the opposite side from where the package had been was a leather-bound book that I also placed on the dresser top. My search of the rest of the dresser revealed nothing of interest. I picked up the two discoveries and took them downstairs into the dining room, which was just off the living room and also faced the beach.

I took a seat at the dining table and opened the leather-bound volume first. On the first interior page, in beautiful script writing that I immediately recognized, were the words *Private Journal of Susan Montrose*. There were hundreds of pages filled with Mother's handwriting. I closed the book and pulled the paper package to me. I untied the string and removed the brown-paper cover. As expected, I uncovered a thick, typewritten manuscript. On the title page were the following words: *Las Hijas de Pinochet, una novela de Ricardo Muñoz*. This was it: *The Daughters of Pinochet*, my father's last work.

I'd been told there was only one copy of the book and that it was with my father's American publisher. Yet here was the original manuscript, rendered in the unmistakable typeface of Dad's old Corona typewriter. I stared at it for a moment and then gently touched the typewritten words, as if I would somehow be able to feel the soul of my father through this tactile connection. But when I tried to visualize him writing this book at his desk, all that came into my head was the vision of him hunched over, shot through the head. I pulled my hand from the page, as if my touch was the cause of the nightmarish vision. But, of course, I knew better. I'd been having that vision for almost thirty years.

The book was written in Spanish, and, although my Spanish was okay, it was not good enough to read and comprehend a long and probably complex novel. I wondered who I could hire to translate it. There were several interpreters I'd used over the years in court. I thought of one in particular, Manuel Carrera, who was originally from Chile and who, I reasoned, would be able to pick up on any specific Chilean idioms. I called the office and got his phone number.

Manuel seemed pleased to hear from me. "*Hola, compadre. Como estas?* Tell me it isn't true. You've retired?"

"Who knows? For now I'm calling it a sabbatical. So that's the company line if anyone asks."

"Sure thing. So . . . to what do I owe this pleasure if it's not business?"

"I have a potential job for you. Something different. Do you ever do any literary translations?"

"*Claro que sí.* Of course. I used to do a lot before things got busy with the legal interpreting business. What do you have?"

I hesitated for a second. I don't know why. "You know that my father was Ricardo Muñoz, yeah?"

Manuel chuckled on the other end of the line. "Sure." It was his turn to pause for a beat. "Don't tell me you have something of his to translate."

"I do. It's a full manuscript of a novel that's never been published."

He gasped. "*Mi Dío.* Are you serious, Will? You wouldn't mess around with me like that, would you? Of course I'd be interested. The great Ricardo Muñoz! My God!"

I'd never known the somber, middle-aged interpreter to get so excited. He sounded like a child being told he could go to Disneyland.

"There is a catch though, Manuel."

"*Ay.* There's always a catch. What is it?"

"Secrecy. You have to swear to secrecy. No one is to know what you're doing—or even that the book exists. Can you agree to that?"

There was silence on the other end of the line.

"May I ask why?" he finally asked. "The world should not be deprived of a long-lost novel by Ricardo Muñoz."

"I can't explain everything. At least not now. I have the feeling you'll start to understand as you go through the book. But I haven't read it, so I can't say for sure. I want to take this one step at a time. First thing is for me to be able to read it, and that's where you come in. My Spanish isn't good enough."

This time there was no hesitation. "Okay, sure. I'll be honored."

I interrupted him before he could continue, since I was pretty sure what his next question was going to be. "I'll pay whatever your going rate is. When can you start?"

"When can you get it to me?"

"I'll have it FedExed to you right away. You'll get it tomorrow."

After we ended the call, I took the manuscript to a copy service that had a FedEx outlet. I made two copies of the book and then shipped one off to Manuel Carrera in San Francisco. I sent the original and the other copy to my law office with instructions for Travis to put them in the firm's safe. I don't know why, but I felt as if some kind of burden had been lifted, at least temporarily, once the manuscript was out of my immediate possession.

It was late afternoon when I got home. Mother's journal sat where I'd left it on the dining table. One part of me wanted to start reading it now, but I knew myself well enough to know I was too mentally unsteady. I knew the words of my mother would be sure to have a profound impact on me and that the end result was sure to be more than mere melancholia.

I put the journal into the bottom drawer of the dining room credenza and then clicked on the television. Some background noise and diversion would be good. The lead story on the evening news was about a plan by the House Republicans to cut a large portion of the food stamp budget. Shit. My melancholia was being replaced by anger.

Did you know that about 75 percent of the people on food stamps are the elderly, children, veterans, and disabled? A large percentage of the remaining 25 percent are the working poor—hard workers whose wages are not enough to put food on the table for their families. I thought again about my rich clients like Mr. Carlo and their obnoxious sense of entitlement, which they displayed even while they were defrauding consumers or competitors or even their own government. My father would have been embarrassed for me, I thought. And rightly so.

I clicked off the television—that had been a bad plan—and poured myself a Tito's vodka on the rocks. Drink firmly in hand, I walked out onto the deck overlooking the ocean and watched as a few runners and walkers took advantage of the waning sun. The first signs of a colorful sunset were already visible, so I walked down the wooden stairs to the beach and sat on the sand to listen to the lapping of the mild surf. I tried to think of nothing but the beauty of the moment.

I was never really good at that.

17

I was up with the sun the next morning and, as is my practice, clicked on the television news. Why I wanted some talking heads yapping at me first thing about bad news—or, in the case of politics, *irritating* news—was something I'd often thought about. The best answer I could come up with was that I needed something new to clear my head of the nightly demons.

The "breaking news" was the murder of Willy Williams, a professor of economics at USC and longtime advocate of the working poor. He'd been found shot in the back of the head while sitting at his computer at home. One of his teaching assistants had gone to his apartment after he hadn't shown up for class and, finding the front door open, had entered and discovered the body. The apartment appeared to have been searched, but given that Professor Williams had lived alone, no one could say whether anything was missing. The police were calling it a murder in the course of a burglary.

Sound familiar? I relived all over again the moment when my mother and I had entered his study and found my father slumped over his typewriter. A burglary gone bad. But even as I tried to escape that image, something nagged at my sorrow. Something other than my father's murder. But I couldn't reel it in.

I would later read that the dead professor had been working on an article when he was shot. Police had found the following passage still on his computer screen:

> *Following the election of Barack Obama, wealthy*
> *Americans, led by a few mega-rich right-wingers such as*
> *the Koch and Carson brothers, capitalized on the anti-*

*Obama hysterics (Kenyan-born Muslim socialist) and
essentially bought themselves a radical right-wing party
that became known as the Tea Party. These wealthy
Americans believed this new radical right would work to
cut taxes and decimate regulations, two things they
needed in order to continue to accumulate and hoard
wealth in America. How these puppeteers were able to
manipulate voters who were not rich and who had very
little to gain from these policies is a topic that merits
substantial discussion on its own. Suffice it to say it is
my opinion that it would not have worked, at least not
as well, had they not had anti-Obama mania to rally
their troops. What these wealthy puppeteers did not
anticipate, however, was how absolutely crazy these
minions and those they elected actually were. It was one
thing to take food out of the mouths of people, but it was
quite another to be so radical and so crazy that they
would turn on their masters and actually work to
destroy the American economy.*

I wondered who Williams' target audience was. Did he harbor
some illusion that those manipulated voters would see the light?
I decided he was either writing a historical perspective or preach-
ing to the choir, which seemed to be the norm in today's American politics.

My mother never told me what Dad was writing when he was
shot in the head.

*   *   *

I shut off the television and went for a run on the beach. The
image of my father and the nagging thought of something or
someone else disappeared almost immediately, and I soon realized
I actually felt good. The endorphins made me almost giddy.

What struck me as I pounded the hard-packed sand near the shoreline was that I had no responsibility. No clients. No mother to feel guilty about ignoring. No money worries. I could quite literally do whatever I wanted. I told myself that if I didn't want to follow up on the details of Dad's death—murder—then I didn't have to.

It was a funny thing about me, I thought as I walked across the warm sand back to the house: I'd always been much more willing to do something once I had decided I didn't have to do it. I'd made my decision to go to law school only after I'd consciously decided that I didn't need to, that I wouldn't have to practice law just because I had a law degree. I'd opened my law firm after I'd decided I didn't need to work and that therefore it might be fun to open my own office with my two best friends from college. Maybe that was why I had eventually found myself representing reprehensible clients and not caring about politics. I hadn't needed to.

And so it was that, after running my way to an epiphany, I decided to investigate my stepfather to see if he was in any way involved in the death of my father. The fact that Josephine had caught him snooping in the upstairs storeroom, looking for a book nobody was supposed to know about, was enough to spark my interest. I couldn't reconcile in my mind why Chuck would have been secretly searching for a book about a deposed dictator written by a dead writer.

But the story about Jo finding a notebook full of news stories about murdered people, including my own father, had been the clincher. Was it possible that those were all people Chuck had murdered? If not, why would he have such a scrapbook? If so, why would he have murdered all those people? What, if anything, was the connection among the victims?

—18—

Here's a tip: If you ever find the journal of your mother who just committed suicide, don't read it.

Over the course of the next few days, as I pored over my mother's journal, I went from feeling "footloose and fancy-free" to heartbreakingly sad. She'd started writing the journal not long after meeting my father in Santa Fe. Mom wrote about her love and passion for Dad in such a simple and unaffected way that my own emotions became fragile and schizophrenic. One moment I'd smile at the joyousness of Mother's passion, and the next moment I would cry over the waste of an almost perfect love. What greater reason to live than to experience absolute love? What greater tragedy could there be than to have that love unceremoniously terminated by murder?

I could barely get through the passages written in the days and weeks following Dad's murder. I could physically feel Mother's torment and despair.

The tone of her writing changed when she received the first threatening note. This was the first time I became aware of why we had suddenly packed up and moved from Taos to Los Angeles. Her subsequent entries also gave me the first hint of why she thought Augusto Pinochet was behind Dad's murder.

Here is what Mother wrote the day after she received the note, which she'd stapled to a page in the journal:

> *This threat to kill us makes me more convinced than ever that P was behind Ricardo's death. Two months before the murder, Ricardo told me that Sam Chesne had sent* The Daughters of Pinochet *manuscript off to*

the interpreter who handled all of Ricardo's work. The
fellow is Chilean and lives in New York, although he's
originally from Santiago. When I asked Ricardo if there
was any risk that word of the book might leak to P's
people, he admitted that it was possible. But as was so
typical of Ricardo, he just put his arms around me and
told me not to worry, and, really, it was impossible for
me to worry about anything when that man wrapped
me in his arms and held me close. Then, just two weeks
before he was murdered, Ricardo told me Sam said the
publisher might not publish the book. Ricardo was
furious and called them cowards and many other
names. I was secretly glad. I had never asked Ricardo to
give up his political activities and essays, but in
Daughters, he was more politically and personally
abusive than I had ever seen.

I knew Sam Chesne had been Dad's U.S. editor. *Arabella* had
been published in the U.S. by Serapeum Press and Sam had been
assigned as his editor. When my father moved to the U.S., Serapeum became his primary publisher and Sam Chesne and Ricardo Muñoz became a team. I know Dad trusted him
completely. But the fact that the manuscript, which I'd not yet
read, had been sent off-site to a Chilean-born interpreter seemed
kind of risky to me. Obviously the manuscript must have made
its way to Santiago and gained the attention of Pinochet. But
then, I thought, who could have foreseen that Pinochet would
put a hit on someone over a novel?

One entry in Mother's journal broke my heart. It was written
one month after I had left Los Angeles to go to college at UC
Berkeley:

Will has been gone for about a month now, and it feels
like my life has been turned upside down. There is an

*emptiness inside me. As if I am no longer a whole
person. No longer a complete entity. Chuck has gotten
worse in the short time since Will left, almost like he'd
been waiting for Will to leave. I don't even know this
man. He has become even more overbearing and
abusive, and he scares the hell out of me. The other day
he hit me. It was only a slap, but it hurt. And it scared
me. I don't even remember what we were fighting about.
Or even if we were really fighting. It was like he came
into the studio and began yelling and swearing at me. I
just stood there, holding a paintbrush, while he went on
and on about what a "fucking cunt" I was. His eyes
were huge, and spit flew out of his mouth, and when I
finally told him to calm down, he really went off, telling
me not to tell him what the fuck to do. That's when he
hit me. Then he stormed out of the house, and I didn't
see him again until two days later. He came back like
some puppy with its tail between its legs. He apologized
over and over until I finally told him it was okay, that I
forgave him. I despise myself for being so weak. But I'm
also scared not to have him around.*

*Oh, Will, how I miss you! I didn't realize how
backward I had everything. It wasn't Chuck who was
there to protect me, to protect us. It was you. Now you're
gone, and I have only Jo. Thank God for Jo. I dread the
weekends when she goes home and leaves me with
Chuck. I wish I could be selfish and ask Will to come
back. I won't do it, of course.*

—19—

Travis and Cheryl came down to spend the following weekend with me at the Malibu house. They both had been to the house many times. The entry opened onto a large, open-plan living, dining, and kitchen area with hardwood floors and Oriental rugs in muted colors. The leather sectional couch was light gray, and the dining and side tables were all koa wood, imported from Hawaii. But like everyone else who walked into the house—no matter how many times they'd been there—they both walked straight to the floor-to-ceiling windows and stared out at the Pacific Ocean.

"Toss your bags by the stairs and kick off your shoes," I said. "I'll make us some cocktails, and we can sit outside for a while."

"I can't believe you took some of these guys on as clients," Cheryl said when we'd settled into comfortable deck chairs, cocktails in hand, watching the slow progression toward another beautiful sunset. They'd settled the pizza king's case and were slowly but surely clearing the decks of my caseload of asshole clients.

"I know, I know," I said. "Look at it as some perverse form of self-flagellation. I don't think I ever gave it much thought. I just started taking cases." I took a sip of my vodka. "You guys know I've never been very political, or much of a social activist." I smiled. "No matter how hard you tried to make me one. But then one day I realized who I was representing and what I'd become. Like I told you at the time, I had an epiphany."

Travis chuckled. "Don't worry about it, man. We'll clean up after you, and now you can move on to the next bizarre episode in your life, which is to solve a thirty-year-old murder."

"That *is* what you intend to do," Cheryl said, "isn't it, Will?"

I didn't answer right away, so for half a minute or so, the pounding of the surf was all we heard.

Finally, I nodded. "Yep. At least I'm going to see what I can find out."

I told them about the conversation I'd had with Josephine on her deathbed and about finding Dad's manuscript where she had said to look for it. I told them I'd sent it off to be translated. And I told them about finding Mother's journal.

"It's on the dining table if you feel like looking through it," I said. I turned to Travis. "If you can hang around for a while, maybe we can try to find out where Chuck is living. Even better, maybe we can find that Milton Fischer dude and see what he was talking about when he told Mother that Chuck had suffered some kind of brain damage."

Travis looked to Cheryl, who was, after all, his only boss now.

She gave a small nod. "If Will's going to go off on this wild-goose chase, I'd just as soon have you with him to make sure he doesn't get himself in deep shit."

"*Hellllooo*," I said, "I can hear you."

*   *   *

We kept the rest of the weekend light, rarely talking about work or about Chuck. Cheryl and I made exquisite love every chance we had. We all kicked in and made a feast on Saturday night: roasted chicken, chile rellenos stuffed with goat cheese, and a watermelon, feta, and basil salad. There were long stretches of time when I didn't think about the fact that my mother had committed suicide just a few days before.

We ate an early dinner Sunday night at an oceanfront bistro before driving Cheryl to the airport. She and I kissed long and hard, and I felt a kind of wrenching in my gut that I hadn't felt before during any of our previous good-byes.

I think Cheryl felt it as well, because when we finally pulled away from each other, she gently brushed my cheek with her right hand and looked me in the eyes. "Be careful," she said softly.

I started to reply, but she put a finger to my lips.

"I don't just mean in the physical sense," she said. "Be aware of what you're doing and how you're handling it."

I knew what she meant, of course, and I nodded and kissed her finger before she took it away.

Then she turned to Travis and kissed him good-bye. "Take care of our boy, T." And with that she was gone.

—20—

Travis and I started with the obvious: the internet. But there were so many hits for Charles Evans that it was immediately clear we wouldn't find him that way. There were a lot of hits for Milton Fischer as well, and other than discovering that they had each lived in Los Angeles, at least for a while, we didn't find enough background info on either man to narrow the search.

"Did you find any other personal papers of your mom's?" Travis asked.

I nodded. "All of her correspondence and bills and miscellaneous stuff are in the desk in her office. I haven't started to go through any of it yet."

Travis told me to carry on with cleaning out Mother's closets and dressers. "Let me know if you find anything tucked away somewhere. In the meantime, I'll go through her desk, if you don't mind."

I nodded my assent, and we went our separate ways.

I'd been too young to help clean out Dad's stuff after he'd been murdered. As I pulled dresses, blouses, and skirts out of Mother's closet and laid them in piles on the bed, I thought about how horrible it must have been for her to sort through Dad's things. Here was a dress I remembered Mother wearing at one of her art shows. Here was the blouse she'd always worn while attending functions at my school. I held it up. It was a turquoise silk blouse that was styled to resemble a Western cowboy shirt.

I stopped for a moment, holding the fabric to my face. I could smell the mild citrus perfume she'd worn. I closed my eyes and could see her in their bedroom at the Tesuque house. The room was large, with Spanish tile floors and long, rough viga beams running the length of the ceiling. A plaster kiva fireplace, painted a dark orange, sat in the corner. She would have kept the room dark as she went through Dad's closet, and I imagined her holding his favorite sports jacket up to her face to smell him one more time. She would have been crying, of course. For weeks after he was killed, I can only remember Mother crying, her beautiful face distorted into an ugly sadness.

I shook myself out of my depressing reverie and resumed the task at hand. One pile for the thrift shop. One pile, mostly coats, for the homeless shelter in Santa Monica I knew Mother had helped support.

I was practically done with her main closet when Travis entered. "How you doin', man?" he asked in a sympathetic voice. "It's gotta be a bitch to go through her stuff."

I folded the last of her blouses and put it on the pile for the thrift shop. "Yeah. But what's worse is that I keep picturing her doing this for Dad. Can you even imagine?"

"Hell no." He picked up one of the piles and held it awkwardly. "Where do you want these? Downstairs?"

I nodded and picked up another pile. "Yeah. You find anything in her desk?"

We began walking downstairs, each holding our bundle.

"I found the address where Chuck was living before he married your mother," Travis replied. "An apartment in Studio City."

I had five big boxes sitting in the living room, waiting for clothes, and we each dumped our load into a box.

"So where does that get us?" I asked. "I doubt he went back to live in the same place. Shit, that had to be, what, around twenty years ago?"

Travis turned and walked into the kitchen. "Want a beer?" he called over his shoulder.

I followed him. "Sure."

We popped the tops off a couple of bottles of Stella Artois and sat at the kitchen bar.

"Yeah," he said, answering my last question, "about that, according to the marriage certificate. So I called the apartment manager and asked who would have the records of old tenants. This guy sounded like an irascible old coot, but when I gave him a story about how I was helping a friend look for his former step-dad because his mother had recently passed away and had left something for her ex, he mellowed out and told me he'd been the manager back when Chuck Evans lived there. He remembered Chuck because he'd been such an asshole—his words." Travis paused and took a long pull on his beer. "So this guy tells me he might have the old records somewhere in the building's basement. Each tenant has to fill out some form. The manager keeps one copy, and the other copy goes to the management company—some real estate outfit in the Valley. He's supposed to call me back."

I didn't say anything. I was trying to think things through. I could see Travis seemed happy about the progress he'd made, but all I could think about was that we were going the wrong direction. Who cared about where Chuck had lived twenty years ago? We were trying to find him *now*.

I looked at Travis and could see he'd been watching me. A small, lopsided smiled played at his lips. He could read me like a book, and I suspected he knew exactly what I was pondering. He confirmed that a moment later.

"The more we find out about who Chuck Evans was," he explained, "the better chance we have of finding out where he went after your mom kicked his ass out. He had to work somewhere to make money. We don't even know what his profession was—or is. All we know is he told your mom that he and this Fischer guy were"—Travis made air quotes with his fingers—"consultants."

Travis had asked if the apartment manager remembered a friend of Chuck's by the name of Milton Fischer. "He didn't know him by name, but he described some guy he said was virtually inseparable from Chuck. It fits the description you gave me of Fischer. The manager even remembers accusing Chuck of illegally subletting part of the apartment to this guy. They were that close."

We were interrupted by operatic music coming from somewhere on Travis.

He retrieved a cell phone from his pants pocket. "Hello? Hey, that was quick. Find anything?"

I watched as Travis listened to someone I presumed was the apartment manager. Travis made a writing gesture to me, and I got up to fetch him a pen and paper. He began writing as soon as I gave them to him.

After another moment he said, "That's wonderful. I really appreciate the help. You take care of yourself now."

Travis looked at me after he stowed his cell phone. "Chuck put his occupation down as security consultant. The business name was Fischer Evans Security, with an address in North Hollywood. I have the address. I also have the address of Chuck's residence before he rented the place in Studio City." Travis broke into a big smile and rubbed his cleanly shaved head before spreading his hands wide. "Vegas, dude!"

I had to laugh. "Don't you think we should check out the security company here in L.A. before we go traipsing off to Vegas to check out what has to be a twenty-five-year-old address?"

"Shit, you're no fun."

But Travis was already typing "Fischer Evans Security" into his search engine. We got a hit, but it linked to an obsolete, blank site. Travis gave a small grunt.

"Must be out of business by now. Probably just let their domain lapse." He tried searching for variations on the name but came up empty. "Shit bricks," he said. "Looks like we're gonna have to do some old-fashioned investigating."

*　　*　　*

Two hours later, we were sitting in a seedy office in an old stucco building on Sepulveda Boulevard in Van Nuys. The walls were cracked and stained where water had leaked from the rusty rain gutters. There were bars over the two frontage windows. The sign on the outer door read *Valley Management Company*, and we were now sitting across from the owner, a corpulent, wispy-haired white man named Hugo Hyman. It had taken a few minutes for Travis and me to compose ourselves after giggling like a couple of teenagers before we were able to enter the office, which was sparsely furnished with a '50s-era reception desk, a yellow-and-brown-striped upholstered couch, and two hanging pictures, both of which were fading photos of Lake Tahoe, in black plastic frames.

After explaining to a tired-looking fake-blonde receptionist what we were looking for, we were granted access to Mr. Hyman himself. His office was more of the same—linoleum flooring, a wood veneer desk, two client chairs that had obviously come as a set with the desk, and three metal filing cabinets against one wall. There were no pictures or photos on the off-white walls.

He was holding a manila file folder up to his face. I could see an old coffee cup stain on the cover of the file. I could also read, in large caps, the name on the file:

FISCHER EVANS SECURITY—LANKERSHIM BLVD.

After a moment of seemingly intense study, Hyman put the file down and looked at us. His face was a pasty gray, and there were dark circles under his dull-looking eyes. "So," he said in a high-pitched, nasal whine, "whattaya wanna know?"

I had to force myself not to look at Travis, lest I lapse into uncontrollable laughter.

I was relieved when Travis answered in a composed voice. "We're trying to track down the two principals of the company: Mr. Fischer and Mr. Evans. So anything you can tell us would be most appreciated. When did they rent from you? Did they give a forwarding address? Did they give any references? That kind of thing."

Hugo Hyman looked from Travis to me. "And you're a lawyer?"

"Yes, sir, I am."

"So is it okay for me to give out this information?"

"Absolutely," I said, although frankly I had no idea what kind of expectation of privacy someone filling out a rental application would or would not have.

Hyman appeared to think for another few seconds before pushing the file across the desk to Travis. "Here's everything I got. Help yourself."

Travis began reading and jotting down notes while Hyman and I just sat there.

Finally I said, "Do you remember Mr. Fischer or Mr. Evans?"

Hyman looked surprised that he'd be asked such a question. "*Wellll*," he drawled, "I think I kind of remember them. Strange duo. The one guy—I think it was Fischer—was kind of short and skinny and had this big mop of curly black hair. I took him for a fellow Jew. The other guy was big. At first I thought he must be a movie star. Handsome fuck."

"Did they say what kind of security company they ran?"

Hyman shrugged, causing his whole body to jiggle like a huge bowl of Jell-O. "Something about providing bodyguard and personal security services. The small guy—Fischer, I guess—said he'd been in the security business with the government some years before. I don't remember if the big guy said anything about his background."

Travis had stopped taking notes and was listening now. "Did you ever become aware of any of their clients?" he asked.

Hyman shook his head even before the question was finished. "Nah. I never talked to them face-to-face after that first meeting. They paid on time and gave me the requisite termination notice when they left."

Travis and I looked at each other and stood. We shook hands with Hugo Hyman and thanked him for his time and turned to leave.

But Travis stopped and turned back. "Did you call any of the references they listed on their application?"

Hyman chortled and shook his head, the wattles under his chin flapping as he did so. "Nope. Hardly ever do—unless the applicants look real seedy."

We left Hyman and walked back through the outer office. The receptionist was playing a card game on her computer and never looked away from her screen as we thanked her on the way out.

—21—

"So," I said, "did we learn anything?"

We were sitting in a Denny's restaurant, not far from Hugo Hyman's office, with a cup of coffee in front of each of us. It smelled and tasted burnt. A boy of about age ten at the next booth was whining about not getting the dessert he wanted. I made brief eye contact with the father, who looked as if he wanted to smack the kid upside the head.

"A little," Travis answered. "Fischer's address was different from Chuck's Studio City address, so we have that as a possible lead. The company's business account was with Bank of America. The company's prior address was Las Vegas, so I think we can assume these guys have been together since before either of them moved to L.A.." Travis took a sip of coffee and grimaced. I knew him to be something of a coffee snob.

"You mean back to L.A.," I said.

Travis nodded. "Yeah. But the best potential new leads are the two references they put on the rental application. Names and phone numbers. I think I recognize one of the names from your mother's journal, but we'll have to check it out when we get back home."

"Who was it?" I asked. "Maybe I know the person."

Travis looked down at his notes. "Larry Miscovich."

I shrugged. "Never heard of him."

The young waitress came to the table and asked if we were ready to order.

Although we'd pulled into the Denny's because we were both hungry and eager to go over what we'd learned, we shook our heads.

"Can we get the check?" I asked.

I chuckled to myself at how alike Travis and I were—Cheryl too if she'd been there. We didn't even have to communicate what we were thinking, which was: *if the food is as bad as the coffee, there's no way we're staying here.* The kid in the next booth was in full scream mode now as his father dragged him away from the table toward the exit. The mother, a morbidly obese woman perhaps in her thirties, sat serenely eating.

Before we left the restaurant, Travis checked his iPad for the location of Fischer's last known address. It wasn't far. He entered the data in the map app, and we paid the bill and left.

*　　*　　*

Fischer's address turned out to be a plain brick two-story apartment building on East Verdugo Avenue in Burbank. A couple of scrawny date palms in front of the building bracketed an old, rusted metal sign that said *Tropical Palms Apartments*. Next to the permanent sign, a real estate sign stuck into the weed-riddled dirt said *One and Two Bedroom Apartments Available*.

Travis parked his rental car, and we walked through the open wrought-iron gates that led to an interior courtyard, haphazardly decorated with various potted plants. To the right was a door marked *Manager*.

Our knock was answered almost immediately by a middle-aged woman in a plain yellow dress covered by a stained blue apron. She had a pleasant smile.

We explained we were looking for a gentleman by the name of Milton Fischer, who we understood had lived in the building at some point.

"Sure," she said immediately. "I remember Milton. Nice man. Kind of quiet, but always polite. Paid his rent on time and never gave anyone trouble. What do you want with him?"

Travis gave her his best smile, which was almost always irresistible. "He and his partner did some work for a good friend not long ago, and we were hoping to hire him. But the business is shut down, and we can't seem to find him."

"Well," the woman said, "he only moved out a couple years ago. I think I still have the forwarding address he gave me." Without waiting for further prompting, she turned and disappeared into her apartment.

We were leaning against her doorframe when, five minutes later, she reappeared with a note card in hand. "Sorry it took so long, but once the last of the mail dried up, I guess I lost track of the damn thing." She held out the card. "Go ahead and take it. I ain't got no more use for it."

Travis took the card and thanked her.

"Did you ever see another man with Fischer?" I asked. "Big handsome guy?"

The woman tore her smile away from Travis and looked at me. Her smile disappeared and morphed into a small sneer. "Sure. He was handsome okay, but he was kind of scary. He never gave me the time of day. Just looked mean and angry pretty much every time I saw him—which was only a few times. I didn't know his name."

"Did you ever see anyone else with Fischer?"

"Nope. Just that one big lug."

We thanked her again and walked back to the car.

"Lug?" I said. "When was the last time you heard someone referred to as a big lug?"

"Musta been in the movies, 'cause I honestly can't remember ever hearing someone say that in person."

*   *   *

After we returned to the car, Travis again inputted Fischer's address into his iPad map. It directed us to an upscale-looking apartment building in Toluca Lake, but it turned out to be nothing more than a mail-forwarding drop. The tenant in the unit to which the mail was forwarded said he hardly knew Fischer at all. His name was Albert Weissman, and they'd been introduced at a movie industry party by Weissman's agent, who seemed to know Fischer well. Fischer and Weissman got to talking, and toward the end of the evening, after Fischer had learned that Weissman was having a dry spell in his acting career, Fischer offered to pay him a thousand dollars to receive and forward mail for a year. Weissman naturally jumped at the offer. By the end of the year, the flow of mail had stopped altogether. The new forwarding address was in Las Vegas.

Travis looked at me with one of his lopsided grins.

"Don't even," I said. But I couldn't help but smile.

—22—

Back home in Malibu, I put together a late lunch while Travis perused Mother's journal.

I was just putting our plates down on the dining table when Travis said, "Here it is. Larry Miscovich. I knew I recognized that name."

Travis showed me the journal entry:

> Got talked into going to a party yesterday with a lot of Hollywood types. It was at the home of Larry Miscovich, who is apparently a pretty big-time producer. I'd never heard of him. Bel Air. Valet parking. Quite a few actors I actually recognized. Larry introduced me to a guy I assumed was an actor. His name is Chuck Evans—even an actor-type name. He's super handsome but in a way very different from my darling Ricardo. I guess that's good, because I would never be able to have any kind of relationship with someone who reminded me of Ricardo. Is it weird that I'm even writing about having a relationship? Something about Chuck must have struck some kind of chord with me. Besides being so good-looking, he seemed super nice. Very attentive. We talked for quite a while. He introduced me to his business partner, Milton something, who was the opposite of Chuck: a small, wimpy-looking guy who didn't make much of an impression on me. They are security consultants. I asked what that meant, and Chuck said they did all sorts of things but the most fun was providing bodyguard

services to celebrities. At the end of the evening he asked
me out, and I surprised myself by saying yes. It will be
my first real date since Ricardo was murdered.

By the time I'd finished reading the entry, between bites of my sandwich, Travis had googled Larry Miscovich. I knew I must have read that entry when I'd gone through the journal, but I hadn't remembered reading that Chuck's "consultant" work was security.

"He has some pretty good movies in his credits," Travis said of Miscovich. "I don't see much of anything in the past couple of years. Must be retired now. Says here he's seventy-two."

"He still in Bel Air?" I asked.

"Don't talk with your mouth full, man. It's gross. Yeah, still in Bel Air."

Five minutes later, while I was washing the dishes, Travis entered the kitchen and announced we were having cocktails at Larry Miscovich's house that evening at six.

"How'd you manage that?"

"Oh, a little of this and that. He remembered your mother and that he was the one who introduced her to Evans. I explained that you're a big-time attorney now and that you're trying to find your former stepfather and Milton Fischer to discuss some unresolved issues. I kept it as vague and as mysterious as possible, and Miscovich invited us over. I get the feeling he isn't quite on the A-list anymore and welcomes some company."

*   *   *

Larry Miscovich's home was fairly modest by Bel Air standards. It was an older Spanish-style house with a red tile roof and an entry courtyard, complete with a fountain in the center. His front door was made of a heavy, dark wood. When we knocked, we immediately heard a dog's high-pitched barking, followed by a man's muffled voice.

I'm not sure what I was expecting Larry Miscovich to look like, but it was not the man who opened the door. He was holding a small, white-haired dog in his left hand. Thankfully, the dog's irritating barking had stopped. The man was wearing a full-length off-white caftan trimmed with what looked like gold silk piping. His face was tanned and taut, with very few lines—obviously the product of many Botox injections. His white hair was combed forward, à la Donald Trump, but wispier.

He looked at the two of us and then let his attention fall exclusively on Travis, who was dressed immaculately in a light-weight gray Armani suit with a baby-blue tie. He had his diamond stud earrings in both ears, and his brown head was freshly shaved and shined. When I had noticed his outfit before leaving, I had turned around and gone back to my room to change out of my jeans, sport shirt, and loafers, opting instead for navy pants, a white linen shirt, and a light gray linen sport coat. No tie.

"Oh, my God!" Miscovich exclaimed as he stared at Travis. "It's a dirty version of Mr. Clean. I love it!" His voice, as you might have guessed, was effeminate and gushing.

I glanced at Travis to see how he'd taken the greeting, but he was smiling and offering his hand, which Miscovich took with his first three fingers and thumb and held on to for what seemed an eternity.

"Mr. Miscovich, so nice of you to agree to meet with us," Travis said, cool as ever. He turned to me, although Miscovich was still holding his hand, and said, "This is Will Muñoz."

Miscovich finally dropped Travis's hand, tore his gaze away, and looked at me. After a couple of seconds, in a much more butch voice, he said, "A pleasure." He shook my hand with a firm grip. One pump, and then he pulled his hand away and invited us into the house.

I glanced at Travis as we followed Miscovich inside, and he gave me his mischievous grin and shrugged. I knew he knew that

I was wondering how someone's gaydar could be so fine-tuned he could tell us apart at first glance. I felt kind of hurt.

We followed our host through the entry, which was decorated with glazed Spanish tile that gave way to polished hardwood floors. Large rugs with what looked like Indian designs covered most of the floor of the great room, which was furnished with several big distressed leather couches and easy chairs. The tables and credenzas were all made of dark, heavy wood. Floor-to-ceiling windows along one wall looked out onto a sizable patio and pool.

I didn't make it all the way into the room before stopping to stare at a huge painting. It was one of Mother's: an impressionistic view of the cottonwood grove and stream that ran through the back of our property in Tesuque, where Mother's ashes now more or less resided. I vaguely recalled her painting this piece. She had finished it before Dad was murdered, and I remembered marveling at its size.

"I'm a devoted fan of your mother's work," Miscovich said as I stood before the painting. "I have several smaller pieces, and over there I have one of her pots." He pointed to a stand on which rested a large, intricately designed pot.

I eventually followed him to where Travis stood, looking out at the immaculately landscaped yard surrounding the pool. "Beautiful house," Travis said as we joined him.

Miscovich seated us in a cozy section of the room where we could talk.

As if on cue, a manservant entered and asked if we wanted anything to drink.

I asked for a Tito's vodka on the rocks, and Travis ordered a glass of chardonnay.

Miscovich was already drinking something out of a silver goblet. "So," he said after we had all settled in with our drinks, "you want to know about Chuck Evans and Milton Fischer. May I ask why?"

I'd been thinking about how to answer his question. I didn't want to lie if I could help it. "Does it matter? I mean, are you still friends with them?"

Miscovich laughed. "Oh, God, no. I wouldn't say I was ever friends with either of them, actually. They're both right-wing bigots and homophobes." He paused for a moment. "And Chuck is just plain scary."

"Yet you introduced Chuck to my mother, and they ended up getting married."

My voice must have had a little harder edge to it than I had intended, because Miscovich stopped smiling and straightened defensively. "And I'll be forever sorry about that. It was before I knew what a scary asshole he was—excuse my French. Frankly, I was totally surprised your mother didn't see through him right away, or at least soon enough not to marry him."

Travis joined the conversation for the first time, defusing the tension that had suddenly filled the room. "Let's go back a bit if you don't mind, Mr. Miscovich. We'll—"

"Oh, please. Call me Larry."

Travis nodded. "Thanks, Larry. We'll tell you why we're looking for Evans and Fischer, but I wonder if you can tell us a little about them first. For instance, how did you meet them?"

Miscovich took a sip of whatever he was drinking and maintained eye contact with Travis. "I'd heard of them through an old friend of mine in Las Vegas. They'd provided some bodyguard services for several big-name performers and had done a professional job. One of my actresses in *Blow Out*, the movie I was producing at the time, was being stalked, and I was looking for some security for her. My friend in Vegas set up a meeting here, and I was impressed enough to hire them. I discerned immediately that Milton Fischer was the brains of the outfit, and Chuck Evans was the brawn."

"Did you learn anything about their past?" I asked. "What credentials they had for that type of work?"

Miscovich looked at me as I spoke but then returned his gaze to Travis as he answered. "Milton was ex-CIA. Chuck had been working with him ever since Milton resigned from the CIA. He was much older than Chuck and, from what he told me, had met Chuck at UCLA during some sort of career fair where the CIA was recruiting." Miscovich shrugged and gave a small smile. "Other than that, I checked with a few of their past clients, all big-time celebrities, and they had nothing but rave reviews. So I hired them."

"Did the job go well?" Travis asked.

Miscovich looked serious all of a sudden. "Well, yes," he said after a noticeable pause. "Chuck attached himself to my starlet and had a couple of minor confrontations with the stalker, who was some middle-aged psycho from the Midwest. But then, after about a week, the stalker disappeared and Chuck told us we didn't need to worry about him anymore."

"Meaning what?" Travis asked.

Miscovich gestured with his left hand as if to say, who knows?

"At first, we simply assumed Chuck had talked to the guy and probably scared the shit out of him."

"But something caused you to change your mind about that," I suggested.

Miscovich's face darkened, and he nodded. "Yeah. But not for about a year. In the meantime, I continued to use them as needed and referred them to some agents and managers who needed similar services for their stars." He stopped and looked at me. "It was during that time frame I had them over to the party and introduced Chuck to your mother."

"So what changed?"

"Maybe nothing. But about a year after their first gig for me, I heard that the stalker's decomposed body had been found in a side drain in the Los Angeles River. It took the cops a long time to identify the body. Since my actress had filed several police reports against him and had even obtained a court injunction, once the cops ID'd the body, they came around to interview all of us."

"So what happened?" I asked. "Had the guy been murdered, and if so, were Chuck and Fischer implicated?"

Miscovich frowned and shook his head slightly. "Oh, he'd been murdered all right. One shot to the back of the head, execution-style. The cops interviewed everyone, including Chuck and Milton, but they were never able to pin the murder on anyone."

"But you had your doubts," Travis said.

"Sure, wouldn't you? One minute this bum is stalking my star, and within a week of hiring those guys, he disappears, only to later turn up dead. Wouldn't you wonder why Chuck had been so sure the guy wouldn't bother her anymore?" Miscovich looked down at his goblet. It must have been empty because he looked up and called out, "Enrique!"

A moment later, the valet entered the room and, without asking or being asked, took the goblet from Miscovich. Then he turned to us and asked with a slight hint of a Spanish accent, "Would anyone else like a refresher?"

We nodded in the affirmative, and he took our glasses as well.

Miscovich had what I can only describe as a contemplative look on his face while he waited for his drink.

No one spoke until we each had fresh cocktails.

Then Miscovich turned to me and said, "I understand things turned pretty sour between Chuck and your mother. I heard some rumors of physical abuse."

I nodded. "Yeah. I was only around for about a year or so when they first got together. You're right, though. He's a real asshole. According to our maid, things got really bad after I left for school."

Miscovich shook his head from side to side. "I'm so sorry I had any role in their coming together. I admired your mother so much. I also admired your father. At one point I'd even toyed with the idea of turning one of his early novels into a movie."

"Why didn't you?"

"I didn't think I could do it justice. His novels were so complex and had so many plots within plots that I finally decided I wouldn't fuck with it." He smiled at me. "So. You gonna tell me what this is all about? I can't imagine why in the world you would want to hook up with Chuck again."

I took a deep breath, glanced at Travis, and decided to tell Miscovich the truth. "As you probably know, my mother took her life recently. She—"

"Oh, my God! I didn't know. I'm so sorry."

"Thank you," I said. "She left a couple of letters, one for me and one for the police in New Mexico, where Dad was murdered. In those letters she explained that she suspected Dad was assassinated by someone hired by Augusto Pinochet, who was the president of Chile at the time. Dad had been a big opponent of Pinochet and was on the brink of publishing a pretty explosive novel based on his private life." I paused and took a sip of my drink. "Anyway, during their time together, Chuck apparently said and did some things that caused Mother to suspect he may have been involved in Dad's murder. Our maid, Josephine, also had her suspicions."

No one said anything for close to half a minute after I finished speaking. The house was deathly quiet.

Miscovich leaned forward in his chair as he studied me. "You mean to tell me your mother thinks Chuck Evans murdered her husband and then later married her?"

I hesitated for a second before answering and decided not to correct his use of the present tense. "I can't say for sure if she thought Chuck had murdered Dad, but I can say she obviously had some suspicions."

Miscovich sat back in his chair and took a sip from his goblet. He turned to Travis. "Wow. If that's true, Chuck is one sick motherfucker." He didn't ask us to pardon his French.

"So, Larry," Travis said, "are you still in contact with Chuck and Fischer?"

Miscovich shook his head. "Haven't heard hide nor hair of them for several years. Last friend I referred them to called me a month or so later and started yelling at me. He said Chuck was a maniac who'd almost killed some teen-ager who got too close to his rock star client, some chick. He was afraid the teen's parents were going to sue his star." Miscovich patted his comb-over. "That was the last time I had anything to do with those assholes."

"Did Fischer ever elaborate on what he did at the CIA?" Travis asked.

Miscovich was already shaking his head. "No."

"But he did say he was stationed here in L.A. and that Chuck had gone to UCLA?"

"Yeah. That's all I know. Sorry."

We sat in silence again for another minute. I didn't know what else to ask. I stood up. "Mind if I wander around a bit and check out the other pieces of my mother's work?"

Miscovich waved a hand in the air. "No, of course not. Make yourself at home."

I walked from the great room into a smaller room lined on three walls with books. A stack of what looked like scripts sat on a desk. One of Mother's paintings hung from the lone wall without bookshelves. I recognized it as an impressionistic scene of Taos Mountain—Pueblo Peak. I stared at the medium-sized painting. Mother had painted it in the house where my father had been murdered all those many years ago. Here I was in a producer's mansion in Bel Air, looking at a physical thing that had been created by my mother—created at a time when she still had her beloved Ricardo and when I was running around in ignorant childhood bliss.

It struck me that all the platitudes I'd heard over the years about how art lives on, even after the artist dies, contained some truth. As I stared at Mother's painting in this stranger's house, I felt a powerful connection to her that I'd never felt while looking at her work in our own home. I guess it was the separation, the discovery of her in a totally unexpected place, that made the feeling so strong and so emotional.

"You ready, Will?"

I jumped. I hadn't heard Travis come up behind me. I tore myself from the painting and nodded.

—23—

Travis and I sat on my redwood deck the next evening and got seriously drunk. It had been a beautiful Indian summer day, and the looming sunset, aided by the ever-present Los Angeles smog, figured to be spectacular. We'd started with a few bottles of Pacífico but then began to supplement the beer with shots of Don Julio Silver.

"Why do they call it an Indian summer?" Travis asked.

"Not sure. I've heard different explanations, including that it was traditional harvest time and that it was the time when the Indians finally ended their raids on the European settlers." I started to laugh but ended up snorting. "I'd wager it comes from whatever is the least complimentary to the Indians."

Travis grunted what I assumed was his agreement.

Did you know that many of the Indian tribes in California were very small? Some, like the Yahi, numbered only in the hundreds, which made it pretty easy for settlers to kill off entire tribes. The fact that there was gold in them thar hills made the genocide all the more acceptable. In 1854 alone, the federal government paid more than $1.4 million in bounties to kill Indians. The going rate was five bucks a head, 50 cents a scalp. I wondered how that compared per dead capita to the $8 million the CIA had paid to Pinochet and Contreras to kill leftists.

I thought about this and other horrific things humans have done and continue to do to each other as I watched one of the most majestic nightly events conjured up by nature. The contrast between the perfection of nature and the imperfection of man was striking. When I'd first begun wondering how I'd become such a dick, I'd pretty much limited it to what I was doing for a living. For a buck I didn't need, I was representing assholes with wealth beyond most people's comprehension—assholes who bitched and moaned about their employees, calling them whiney workers who didn't appreciate the fine minimum-wage jobs they were given.

As time passed, my comprehension of how big a dick I really was expanded. I wasn't just a selfish hypocrite; I was an enabler. Simply not agreeing to represent these people would have accomplished nothing beyond a significant reduction in my income, which I didn't need anyway. But by doing nothing to stop the assholes, I was enabling them. Dad had refused to be an enabler.

I said all this—in somewhat slurred and less-than-articulate English—to Travis as I downed yet another Don Julio.

"Eventually I realized it was people like my father," I said, "people who spoke out against tyranny, oppression, and poverty, who were . . . were . . . ." My alcohol-laden brain ground to a halt as I searched for the right words. "Not dicks," I finally said.

Travis nodded solemnly, but said nothing while we watched the final descent of the sun. Two beers later, he asked me how I intended to remake myself into a non-dick.

"I'd planned to volunteer at the Innocence Project for a while. Maybe I'll still do that once I get done with this quest."

"Whatever this quest is," he said.

I threw back a shot of tequila. "Yeah, whatever."

We'd spent much of the day processing what we had learned from Larry Miscovich, and while Travis had gone to UCLA to look through school records, I had stayed home to work the search engines. Afterward, we had compared notes and had been mutually shocked to find we had both zeroed in on the same incredible hypothesis—and it had nothing to do with a "career fair."

Our hypothesis was based on the fact that Milton Fischer had been in the CIA, stationed in Los Angeles, and had established some kind of contact with Chuck Evans. The contact had to have been prolonged enough for the two to get to know each other and agree to work together. The only prolonged contact involving students in the 1960s in which public records show CIA participation involved a highly illegal and supersecret project code-named MKULTRA. The goal of MKULTRA and its many subprojects had been to see if the human mind could be manipulated into doing, forgetting, or confessing, among other things. The CIA had worked closely with the military on these projects.

Students had been the prime subjects—lab rats. Most had been volunteers who had jumped at the chance to make some extra money, but many had been unsuspecting individuals who had not volunteered or consented to anything. UCLA was one of the few colleges on the West Coast that had participated in the program.

Here is part of an internal memo from former CIA Director Richard Helms:

> *We intend to investigate the development of a chemical material which causes a reversible, nontoxic aberrant mental state, the specific nature of which can be reasonably well predicted for each individual. This material could potentially aid in discrediting individuals, eliciting information, and implanting suggestions and other forms of mental control.*

In other words, the CIA and the United States military were experimenting with the use of various drugs to exert mind control. Some of the psychotropic substances used in the experiments were heroin, barbiturates, amphetamines, psilocybin, and others, including a super potent hallucinogen called quinuclidinyl benzilate, which was code-named BZ. Had Milton Fischer been a part of that CIA project? Had my stepfather been a lab rat?

"The only problem," Travis said after we settled down on the porch with our first Pacífico, "is that I could find no record of

Chuck Evans. Of course, I didn't expect to find anything about Milton Fischer."

"How'd you end up finding MKULTRA?" I asked. I'd found it fairly easily by searching the internet for references to the CIA and colleges.

"After I left records," Travis answered, "I went to the library and found the oldest staff person I could find and asked about any relationship between the university and the CIA back in the '60s. I got lucky. The woman wasn't old enough to have been working there then, but she said she'd been a student at that time and had heard about a drug experiment program the CIA was involved with through the psychology department. She said there'd been a big brouhaha once it'd been made public."

Travis had then gone to the psychology department and tracked down a couple of professors who'd been around back in the '60s. One was ancient and had refused to talk to Travis about any kind of experiments on students.

"He would probably have known the most, which I'm guessing is why he wouldn't talk," Travis said. "He was probably involved and would be humiliated to admit that he'd actually used live human beings as mind-control experiments. The only other prof who'd been around back then was a guy named Dr. Ansell White-man. He joined the faculty in 1966. Didn't even have his Ph.D. yet. He'd heard whispers about the project, but at the time it was so top secret he didn't really know what was going on. Years later, when things began to come to light, he found out that several professors he'd worked with and admired had been involved with the program. He thought it was disgusting and unethical, which is why he was so willing to talk about it. Dr. Whiteman acknowl-edged his older colleague had in fact been involved in the proj-ect." Travis took a long pull on his beer. "Supposedly the project was stopped by the end of the '60s."

"Maybe," I said, checking my notes, "but in 1977 a guy named Victor Marchetti, who'd been with the CIA for fourteen years, claimed the CIA had continued conducting experiments well into the '70s. He said the claim that the MKULTRA project had been abandoned was nothing more than a cover story."

"Incredible."

"Took the word right out of my mouth. Do you think it's possible Chuck was one of the lab rats?"

Travis shrugged. "Don't know. First we need to find some evidence of his having been at a school where they were doing the experiments. As I said, I couldn't find any Chuck or Charles Evans."

I'd finished my beer by this time and was contemplating the addition of tequila. "Or he could just have been a volunteer and not been a student."

We talked some more and drank some more, and then, as I said, we got seriously drunk.

24

Cheryl called the next morning to ask how things were going and to tell Travis she needed him back at the office. Apparently, she'd just taken a new case in which it looked as if a big pharmacy company had doctored the test results during the approval process to cover up certain pretty important side effects, such as death. There was going to be a ton of discovery to do, and Travis would be critical. We agreed Travis would head back the day after tomorrow. We had two days to find Chuck Evans and/or Milton Fischer before I'd be on my own.

The first day was pretty much a bust. Travis searched more records at UCLA and also at USC and Cal State L.A. I went in search of articles of incorporation or other business records of Fischer Evans Security or similar names. The California secretary of state's regional office, where articles of incorporation had to be filed, was on South Spring Street, in downtown L.A. I spent the morning fighting the freeways and breathing the smog. Once there, I went through the data banks and came up with nothing. I called Travis to see where he was and if he wanted to meet for lunch, but he was on his way out to Cal State L.A. and didn't want to stop and come back to town. So I had a deli sandwich before heading to the Los Angeles County Clerk's Office to see if any partnership agreements had been filed. Nothing.

The fact of the matter is that a partnership can be created simply by two or more people agreeing to go into business together and to share in profits and liabilities, although it would be pretty stupid not to memorialize whatever the agreement was. Partners are jointly and separately liable for the liabilities of the partnership. So if Chuck murdered a stalker, for example, and the stalker's family sued, both Chuck and Fischer would be liable for damages. Of course, under that scenario, monetary damages would be the least of their problems.

By the time I got back to Malibu, I was tired, frustrated, and cranky. It was as if the smog had tailed me home. I missed my S.F. fog.

Travis wasn't much better. We went to dinner at Guido's, had two bottles of wine and too much pasta, and talked little.

*　　*　　*

When Travis came down for breakfast the next morning, I was flipping pancakes and actually smiling, a sight that immediately caught his attention.

"I haven't seen you look so pleased with yourself since you banged Cheryl for the first time," he said.

"You are *sooo* crass. How'd you like it if I talked about one of your boyfriends like that?"

Travis laughed out loud. "Unlike you, I don't announce to the world that I just banged someone."

I flipped a pancake onto a plate and handed it to him. "Jeez, you've got a long memory."

Travis took the plate, picked up a couple strips of bacon that were sitting on a platter, and took a seat at the counter. "So what's got you in such a good mood?"

I turned off the burner and took my own plate of pancakes and bacon to the counter. "I called an old friend of mine from law school as soon as I got up this morning. He's now managing partner in a big-time firm in Reno, with a branch office in Vegas. It took less than an hour for his people to find a current business address for Fischer Evans Security. The home address for Fischer and Evans is one and the same. Must be living together now."

Travis finished chewing a bite. "Vegas?"

"Yeah. Shall we catch a flight this morning?"

Travis started to smile but then caught himself. "Shit. I gotta be back at work tomorrow."

"Not a problem. You can catch a flight to San Francisco tonight."

"How about first thing in the morning?"

It was my turn to laugh. "You're the one who has to deal with the wrath of Miss Cheryl."

*　　*　　*

The Las Vegas office of Fischer Evans Security was in a non-descript two-story concrete block of a building on South Decatur. The exterior of the building had been plastered with stucco in swirling patterns, but that was the extent of cosmetics. The stucco had been left its original gray color.

We entered a small vestibule with bare concrete floors and spotted a directory on one wall across from the stairs. There was no elevator—something that had probably been grandfathered in. The building was clean, and the directory showed a couple of accountants, three attorneys, and a mortgage broker. Reputable but low-end, I figured.

Fischer Evans was on the second floor. The sign on the frosted glass window in the top half of the door read *Fischer Evans Security*. The door was locked. Travis knocked, but there was no answer.

I reached for my cell and called the number I'd gotten from my law school friend. We heard the phone in the office ring three times, and then my call routed to voicemail: "You have reached Fischer Evans Security. There is no one in the office at the present time, so please leave a message," a male voice said. I hung up.

When we got back to the rental car, Travis punched in the home address that was listed on the business documents. It was in Summerlin, an upscale development in the foothills. Travis didn't seem too happy about getting so far from the Strip.

The house was a large, Mediterranean-style two-story home. The small front yard was well kept, but the house itself looked deserted. We walked to the front door and rang the bell a few times and then knocked. No answer.

Travis walked to a front window and peered inside. "Completely empty," he pronounced.

"Shit." I walked back to the sidewalk and looked at the neighboring houses. The one to the left, which boasted an almost identical design, sported a basketball net over the garage. I walked up to the front of that house and rang the bell.

A Latina maid answered. "*Sí?*"

"*Hola, Señora,*" I said and then asked to speak to her employer. "*Es tu empleador en casa?*"

"*Sí. Un momento.*"

She closed the door, and I heard a click.

I chose to assume she was just being cautious. I heard the click of the lock a few moments later, and the door was opened again, this time by a dark-haired woman dressed in golf clothes. She looked to be in her thirties.

"May I help you?" she asked, her tone polite but brusque.

I gave her my best courtroom smile. "I hope so. My associate and I are looking for the two men who lived next door to you, Milton Fischer and Chuck Evans. Would you happen to know where I can locate them?"

The woman shook her head. "As far as I know, there's never been two men living next door. We've lived here since the houses were built. No one's ever lived there. I'm not sure who owns it." She gave me a small, almost mischievous smile. "But they've been great neighbors."

"And you've never heard of Milton Fischer or Chuck Evans?"

She shook her head. "No. Sorry." She started to close the door but then opened it again. "You might try McCaskill Realty. They were the realtors and property managers for the subdivision. They might be able to help you. Their office is over on South Rampart, just off Summerlin Parkway." She closed the door before I could thank her.

"May as well give it a try," Travis said when I told him about the realtors.

*   *   *

Geri Kelly looked like a realtor: well dressed, with perfectly coiffed blonde hair and a forty-something face that had seen at least two series of Botox injections. She was wearing red linen slacks and a sheer gray silk blouse with a black bra underneath. The office was in a strip mall and was nicely appointed with half a dozen desks. Geri Kelly was the only one in the office. I got the feeling that whoever the principals in the real estate firm were had scored big while they had sat back and taken deposits for the new homes. They likely had sold out the subdivision just before the crash, which had hit Vegas hard. Now they were probably minimally staffed while waiting for a recovery.

Geri lost some of her welcoming charm once she learned we weren't interested in buying anything, but she did her best not to look too disappointed. We explained who we were looking for, and she excused herself and moved to a desk toward the rear of the long office, where she began typing on a computer. Three minutes later she was back, holding a card, which she handed to me.

"The house is owned by a holding company by the name of MF Properties. We dealt with a Mr. Milton Fischer. The house has never been occupied. All mail to the house is forwarded here, and we in turn forward it to Mr. Fischer. I'm afraid I can't give out his address without his permission."

"Can you at least tell us if it's here in Vegas?" Travis asked.

Geri nodded. "More or less. Henderson."

We sat for a moment more, wondering if there was anything further we could get out of Geri, but I couldn't think of anything.

Neither, apparently, could Travis. He stood and held out his hand to shake with Geri.

I followed suit.

"Do you get the impression these guys don't want to be easily found?" I asked in a facetious tone when we got back in the car.

Travis started the car. "I'm starting to get that impression. What now?"

I sighed heavily. "How do I know? You're the fucking investigator."

"Ouch. Testy, testy."

We headed back toward the Strip in silence.

25

One of the other West Coast colleges that participated in the MKULTRA program, or at least allowed its students to participate, was Stanford. That's where Ken Kesey, the author of the book *One Flew Over the Cuckoo's Nest*, volunteered. Kesey, of course, came away from the experiments a creative genius, totally enamored of LSD. I wasn't aware of any evidence that he'd been turned into some kind of killing machine.

On the other side of the country, however, a man named Theodore Kaczynski might have participated in the MKULTRA program while at Harvard. He didn't end up a creative genius. His only famous writing consisted of a long, rambling diatribe, which was called a manifesto. Has there ever been a "manifesto" written by a regular dude? Anyway, some people have tried to claim that Kaczynski should be considered the father of the Tea Party. He certainly hated lefties, technology, science, and big government. So he had that much in common with the Tea Party types. But I reckon he was too fucking crazy to pigeonhole into any one ideology or political group, even the Tea Party.

In case you don't remember Ted Kaczynski, he was also called the Unabomber, and he mailed letter bombs that killed three people and injured twenty-three others. He must have been given something stronger than LSD.

Then there was Sirhan Sirhan, who was alleged to have been under the influence of hypnosis at the time he shot Robert F. Kennedy. His attorney, Lawrence Teeter, pointed the finger at the mind-control techniques developed in the MKULTRA program.

Although I'd not yet proven that Chuck Evans had participated in the MKULTRA project at UCLA or anywhere else, I kept coming back to the fact that he and Milton Fischer, formerly of the CIA, had been together for decades. Had Chuck's former CIA handler become his business partner? Or, potentially more chilling, was it possible that Fischer was still Chuck's CIA handler?

I stared at my desktop computer in my room at the Palazzo Hotel. Travis had the room next to mine, but he had promptly cleaned up and gone out, presumably straight to the nearest blackjack table. He, Cheryl, and I had often taken weekends off from our studies at Berkeley and driven up to Lake Tahoe, where Travis would hunker down at the tables for hours at a time. Cheryl and I would hike, take boat rides, and make love, and then we would track down Travis and drag him away from the tables to go to dinner. If he was winning, we made him buy dinner. If he was losing, I bought dinner. Cheryl's family was poor as church mice, however poor that is, so Cheryl was never required to ante up.

I looked at my watch and realized I'd wasted three hours doing more MKULTRA research while making no progress at all on finding Chuck. But I'd learned that forty-four American colleges or universities; fifteen research foundations or pharmaceutical companies, such as Eli Lilly and Co.; twelve hospitals or clinics; and three prisons were known to have participated in MKULTRA.

And the craziness wasn't just limited to the United States. In Canada, a Scottish psychiatrist by the name of Donald Ewen Cameron had been involved in experiments designed to reprogram the human psyche. Some have claimed that his research was really all about effective torture techniques. Oddly, at least to my way of thinking, Cameron had been on the Nuremberg Medical Tribunal in 1946–47 and later became the first chairman of the World Psychiatric Association and served as president of the American and later the Canadian psychiatric associations. Would it surprise you to know that Dr. Cameron's research had been funded in part through a dummy corporation set up by the CIA?

In 1973, then-CIA director Richard Helms ordered all files relating to MKULTRA destroyed. But, in the immortal words of Texas governor Rick Perry, "Oops." In 1977, through a Freedom of Information Act request, twenty thousand pages of documents pertaining to MKULTRA, mostly pertaining to funding, were brought to light.

I decided enough was enough and finally shut down my computer for the night. I would try to find Travis to see if he wanted to go to the Mario Batali restaurant for dinner. I wondered if somewhere, not far away, my stepfather and his CIA handler were sitting down to their own dinner.

26

In the end I had dinner by myself. I'd spotted Travis at a black-jack table. There was a huge pile of chips in front of him, and standing behind him with a hand on his shoulder was a handsome black man about our same age. The hand-on-shoulder bit gave it somewhat of a proprietary air, so I decided not to intrude. Instead, I wandered around the Palazzo and the connected Venetian, occasionally getting jostled by tourists as they gawked at the fake everything. For fifty bucks or so you could buy a couple-hundred-yards ride in a gondola while an aspiring actor/singer gondolier tried to sing Italian opera. For free you could watch jugglers and mimes and more aspiring actors/singers do their bit in "Saint Mark's Square." As usual, the crowds increased my melancholia and crankiness.

I had a pizza and bottle of Chianti at Spago and then, on a whim, pulled out my cell phone and called the business number for Fischer Evans Security. At the voicemail prompt, I said, "Hello, this is Will Muñoz, the former stepson of Chuck Evans. I would like to talk and maybe meet with him if possible. I am in Las Vegas now and can extend my stay for a day if necessary." I gave my cell number and hung up.

Then I wandered around some more before heading to bed.

*　　*　　*

The call came at 7:46 the next morning.

"Mr. Muñoz?"

"Yes," I mumbled, sitting up and wiping sleep from my eyes.

"This is Milton Fischer. We got a voicemail from you last night."

If I hadn't been awake before, I was now. "Yes, yes, thanks for calling back. But I was calling for Chuck, not you."

"Well, I'm not so sure it would be a good idea for the two of you to talk. Why don't you tell me why you want to talk to him, and we can discuss it."

I grabbed the glass of water I'd had sitting on the nightstand and took a sip. "Why would I do that?"

There was a pause on the other end. I guessed Fischer was taken aback at the snub.

"Look, Will—may I call you Will?" He didn't wait for my assent. "I think maybe you and I should meet for a few minutes. We can talk about some things. There are forces at work here you don't know about and probably wouldn't believe even if you did. Chuck may look macho, but he's very fragile, and being confronted by his former stepson may not be in his best interest."

I didn't miss a beat. "Oh, you mean shit like you having experimented on him with dangerous drugs while he was a college student and you were in the CIA? Those kinds of forces?"

There was dead silence for a good fifteen seconds on the line. "We need to meet. I can come to wherever you are right now." His tone had turned hard.

I decided to quit messing around. "Okay. I'm at the Palazzo. Call this cell when you're here, and we can decide where to meet. Most everything is pretty quiet at this time of the morning."

"I'm on my way."

I climbed out of bed and saw a note under the door. It was from Travis. He'd left early to try to catch the 6 a.m. flight to SFO. *Shit.* I logged on to my computer and soon found what I was looking for. Then I picked up my cell and made a call.

Fifteen minutes later, I was sipping coffee and watching a couple of dead-eyed seniors play one mindless game of keno after another. Several men and one woman were working their laptops in the free Wi-Fi zone, saving the $25 a day for what they could get for free at any Hilton Garden Inn. When my phone buzzed, I answered and directed Fischer to where I was seated.

Despite the fact that he had to be in his seventies now, he looked much like I remembered him from our few meetings twenty-something years earlier. He was short and wiry. His full head of curly hair was gray, but he'd lost little of it. He had bushy eyebrows and overgrown nose hairs. His eyes were dark—maybe brown, maybe black—and they seemed to be constantly moving. His cheeks were sunken. His mouth was downturned, giving him a perpetual look of disdain. He looked like an angry old man. He was wearing pressed gray slacks and a yellow golf shirt with a logo on the left chest. He walked straight to me.

I stood and shook his proffered hand, which was thin and bony. His fingernails were cracked and yellowish.

"It's been a long time," he said without further preamble.

"Sure has."

"I hear you're a big-shot attorney now." As on the phone, he didn't wait for an answer. "So what d'you want to see Chuck about? I'd have thought you'd never want to see him again." His tone was harsh, but I noticed his body language was defensive and tentative.

"You know my mother died recently?"

"Yeah. We heard. Sorry for your loss." There was no sorrow in his voice.

"Hmm. Thanks. Anyway, she left a letter for me and also for the Santa Fe Sheriff's Office in which she said she believed Chuck might have had some kind of involvement in my father's death."

Fischer's half laugh, half snort was clearly meant to be derisive. "That's ridiculous."

He leaned in to me. I could smell stale coffee on his breath.

"Look, Chuck's had his problems. He never should have married your mother. I tried my best to stop him. But your mother had her share of problems, as well. She was delusional, and toward the end of their relationship, she was getting worse. Her craziness had a bad impact on Chuck, who had his own demons to deal with." He sat back again. "They were two screwed-up people who never should have been together."

I could feel the blood pounding in my temple. I wanted to stand up and coldcock the motherfucker, but I used all my anger management skills to remain seated and appear calm.

"Is it true Chuck participated in a CIA-sponsored mind-control program?" I asked.

Fischer gave me a look that I can only describe as a cross between a smile and a sneer.

He didn't look like he was going to answer me, so I kept talking.

"Were you in the CIA? Were you in charge of Chuck when he was in the program? Are you still in control of Chuck?"

Fischer shook his head. "Like mother, like son," he said. "You seem to have let your imagination run wild. What happened to Chuck was that he volunteered for a program run by the psych department at UCLA so he could earn some extra money. He was given some LSD and a couple of other drugs to see how he would react. I'm not sure how many times he did that, and I was not involved in any way. I didn't even know Chuck then. But I was a good friend of one of his father's friends, and since I was living in L.A. at the time, he asked me to keep an eye on the boy. I don't know if the drugs did something to Chuck or if he was messed up beforehand, but the boy I found was definitely damaged goods. I think he'd suffered some brain damage. Maybe it was from the drugs. Maybe it was from a baseball injury—he'd gotten into UCLA on a sport scholarship. He was a good kid most of the time. He could be absolutely charming. But there was a dark side he sometimes had difficulty controlling. I liked him. We hit it off. When he got out of college and I was starting up a security consulting firm, I asked him to come work for me."

Fischer got up and went to the counter and came back with a cup of coffee and sat down.

"What did Chuck do when he couldn't control his dark side?" I asked.

Fischer shrugged. He seemed more relaxed, as if he thought he'd sold the story.

"You saw some of it with your mother," he said. "He could turn mean and ugly, and sometimes it could get physical, although that was rare."

"Hmm. Rare. Did he ever kill anyone?"

"Not that I know of," Fischer answered quickly.

"My mother said Chuck knew things about my father's murder that he shouldn't have known. That no one other than the police would know."

Fischer shrugged it off. "By the time Chuck married your mother, he'd been working with me in the security business for years. He knew how to dig for information—even classified information. I guess he was interested in your mom and had dug around to find out as much as possible about her, including her prior marriage. That seems pretty normal to me."

"You guys still provide bodyguard services?"

Fischer looked mildly surprised. "You're aware of the nature of our services? May I ask how you know that?"

I ignored the question. "Did Chuck kill the stalker in L.A. he'd been assigned to watch?"

Fischer shook his head and pursed his dry, cracked lips. There was a big piece of dry skin barely hanging on to his upper lip. I felt like reaching over and ripping it off.

"I don't know what case you're talking about," he said, "but it really doesn't make any difference. Chuck didn't kill anyone. His anger has been well under control, and he's never done his job in any manner that was less than professional." He leaned in at me again. "Let's get down to it. You want to know if Chuck killed your father? The answer is no. We were in business together by then, and I knew pretty much everything Chuck did. He didn't know your father, he had no business with your father, and he had no reason to kill your father. As far as I know, Chuck hasn't even been to Santa Fe."

I remained seated when Fischer stood up.

"Now, as I think I've answered all your questions and I see no reason for me to arrange a meeting between you and Chuck, I will take my leave. You have a nice trip back," he said.

"Why was Chuck going through my father's things, looking for an unpublished manuscript about Augusto Pinochet?" I said to Fischer's back.

He stopped and turned to face me.

"Who says he was?" He held up a hand to stop me from answering. "It doesn't matter. I don't care to know. If what you say is true—which, considering the delusional bullshit you and your mother seem to have fallen prey to, is unlikely—I would venture to say that Chuck knew your dad's writings were worth a lot of money, so maybe if he found one that hadn't been published yet, he could sell it. Frankly, I don't care." He turned and walked away.

I quickly looked around and spotted a large, casually dressed man with short-cropped hair sitting at a slot machine not far away. He was looking at me and did not seem interested in the slots. I nodded to him, and he gave a slight nod in return. Then he stood and followed Fischer out of the casino.

27

"So I called my friend in Reno again, and he had one of their investigators here in Vegas meet me at the Palazzo before my meeting with Fischer," I said into the phone.

"And?" Travis asked.

"Hold on a minute." I pulled off my shoes and climbed onto the bed. "About a half hour later, he called with an address in Henderson. A townhouse. He saw Fischer go in. He hung around for another hour but didn't see anyone else go in or out."

"So what you gonna do now?"

"Don't know. Any ideas?"

The line was silent for a few seconds. "Nothing legal," he finally said.

"Yeah," I half laughed. "I had the same thought."

Travis went quiet again. When he spoke, I could hear the seriousness in his voice. "Where you going with this, man? I mean, what d'you expect to find? A smoking gun with your stepfather's picture on the stock? A written confession?"

It was my turn to take some time to think before answering. "I'm not sure. But there's something weird about Fischer and the way he answered my questions. He was lying—that much I can guarantee. But why? And about what?" I paused and took a deep breath. "I think this is about more than my father's death."

The words had come out of my mouth, but I couldn't say what precisely had inspired them.

As was so often the case, Travis knew how my mind worked. "You mean like Chuck was a serial killer? Some kind of killing machine created by that drug program?" Although his tone was sarcastic, I could tell it was forced, as if he could embarrass me out of pursuing whatever course of action I was pondering.

"You think that's farfetched?"

"Uh, yeah."

I let out a big breath. "Maybe so."

My phone beeped.

"I'll call you back," I said to Travis.

"Mr. Muñoz?" a man asked as soon as I'd hung up on Travis and answered the new call. "This is Captain Morrisey from the Santa Fe Sheriff's Office."

"Hello, Captain. I have to say I never expected to hear from you again. What's up?"

"I told you I'd run those names and see what we came up with," he said in a defensive tone. "I'm a man of my word."

"I'm sorry," I said. "I didn't mean to be rude. Did you find out anything?"

"A little. Kind of interesting. It appears that Chuck Evans, your stepfather, was not his real name. Have you ever heard him referred to as Charles Evanovich?"

"No, never. Why? Is that his name?"

"As best I can determine, yes, they're one and the same. Charles Evanovich was born in South Africa. His parents immigrated here in 1958, a decade after the first apartheid laws were passed. They'd been outspoken critics of the laws. The father was a college professor."

"Wow," I muttered.

"Wow what?"

"Well, it's just that the Chuck Evans I knew was a bigoted conservative, but you're telling me his parents were apparently the absolute opposite."

"Yeah. It's interesting. Evanovich had only two arrests that I could find. Both of them were when he was in school at UCLA. The first time was in his freshman year, when he was caught up in a sweep of SDS demonstrators." Morrisey paused. "In case you're too young, the SDS was the Students for a Democratic Society, a pretty radical leftist group."

"Yeah, I've heard of them. So you're telling me Chuck was a member of the SDS?"

"Can't say for sure, but he was arrested while demonstrating with the SDS."

I started to say something, but Morrisey cut me off.

"But here's the weird part. Two years later, when he was a junior, Evanovich was arrested again during a demonstration. Only this time he was with some far-right white supremacy group."

"So," I said, my mind reeling with the possible scenarios, "either he was faking at one of the demonstrations, or something happened in between to cause him to do a political and philosophical one-eighty."

"Seems like. But anyway, Evanovich, or Evans, didn't legally change his name until many years later. Just before he married your mother, in fact. Although from what I can tell, he'd been using the name Evans for a long time before that."

"What about Fischer? Were you able to find anything on him?"

"Not much. He was with the CIA, and he was stationed in Los Angeles during the same time frame Evanovich was at UCLA, but I couldn't find out what his job was or whether he had any connection to Evanovich during that time. All I know is that he left the CIA in 1973 and started up his security consultant company the next year."

I was processing the information as fast as possible. Fischer had pretty much admitted to me that Chuck had been involved in some kind of experimental project, but that was about as far as he had been willing to go. In fact, Fischer had claimed he had no involvement in the program. Yet now we knew for sure that he'd been in the CIA and in the same city as Chuck while those experiments had been conducted. And it was now a matter of public record that the CIA had been involved in experimental drug programs on college campuses in the '60s and into the '70s.

"You still there?" Morrisey asked.

"Yeah. Sorry. Just thinking. Were you able to tell if Chuck had been to Santa Fe at any time around the time of my father's death?"

Morrisey grunted a laugh. "Sorry. Not going to be that simple. He could've come and gone a million times without anyone knowing about it. So far, we have some interesting information, but other than his marriage to your mother, we have nothing connecting him to your family."

"So you gonna follow up on anything? You said it was interesting information."

"Yeah, I did. And it is. But there really isn't much more I can do as things stand. It's not like I don't have other cases to work on."

"Sure. I understand," I said. "I'll let you know if I learn anything more. I presume you'll do the same?"

"Of course, but I wouldn't hold my breath."

I could tell Morrisey was about to say more, so I kept quiet.

"I can't tell you what to do, Mr. Muñoz. And I certainly understand your interest. But maybe you should let sleeping dogs lie. I mean, if what you're thinking is even remotely true, then you're dealing with one seriously insidious bad guy. Really."

I thanked the captain for the information and warning, and when I'd hung up and tossed the cell phone to the side, I continued to sit on the bed, thinking. Was it possible that Chuck Evans had assassinated my father on behalf of a Chilean dictator who'd been put in power with the help of the CIA? Further, was it possible that, years later, for reasons I could not begin to fathom, he had married my mother? It was absurd. It was fantastically ridiculous. I had nothing whatsoever to link Chuck to my father's death other than my mother's suspicions. And yet . . . .

I reached for the phone and called Travis back.

—28—

Despite Travis's love affair with whatever Las Vegas has to offer him, and despite my culinary indulgences in the city, I've never really been able to ignore the stench of greed, corruption, and decadence upon which Vegas was built. From the ruthless mobsters to the hypocritical Mormon bankers who backed many of the first casino owners to the current crop of casino owners like Adelson, Wynn, and Trump, who funnel tens of millions of dollars to right-wing causes, Las Vegas is a distillation of the evilest elements of our American system of capitalism. But, as is the case with most everything, it's dangerous to think only in black or white. The temples to greed and lust also create tens of thousands of jobs and bring great entertainment to those lucky enough to afford it.

I thought about these things as I walked across the Strip to Caesars Palace, where I was scheduled to meet the private investigator who had helped me track Evans and Fischer. Travis was still tied up with the case Cheryl was working on and had suggested I keep working with this guy for now. I could hear a little wistfulness in his voice when he learned I was still in Vegas.

As I walked into the monolithic faux Roman entrance to Caesars, I wondered if Jay Sarno, the original designer and owner of the casino/hotel, having used money loaned to him by the Teamsters, had intentionally capitalized on the irony of building a pantheon of decadence based on one of the last great empires, which had collapsed and died under the weight of its own greed and corruption. I walked through the Forum shops, dodging the growing crowds, and made my way to Mesa Grill, Bobby Flay's restaurant. I hadn't met the investigator my law school friend had referred me to, but I'd seen him from a distance that morning when he'd shown up to tail Fischer. So I recognized him immediately. He was sitting against a banquette, facing the entrance.

He stood when he spotted me, and I noticed that he was about my height: a little over six feet. He had short graying hair, a prominent ruddy nose, and a thick neck on an equally thick frame. His name was Alvin Barker.

We shook hands and sat. I saw he already had a margarita in front of him, so I ordered the same.

"Thanks for your good work on such a short notice," I said.

Barker shrugged and smiled. "Just doing my job. Any friend of Jason's is a friend of mine. I hear you two went to law school together in Frisco."

I cringed. Nobody who knows anything about San Francisco calls it Frisco. To those of us who have lived and worked there, calling it that is like scraping fingernails across a blackboard.

"Yeah," I said. "I ended up staying in *San Francisco*, and Jason made a good move going to Reno."

A touch of the old asshole in me emerged as I emphasized the actual name of my city, but Barker didn't react.

"Anyway, if you're open, I could use you for some more work," I said. "My regular investigator is tied up on a case with my law partner." I figured Barker didn't need to know I wasn't in the game anymore.

Barker took a sip of his drink. He'd picked an end table, so there was no one on the one side of us. An elderly couple had just been seated on the other side. The restaurant had filled up with the lunch crowd.

"Sure," Barker said. "Same case?"

I nodded. "I want to find out as much as I can about the two guys you found for me. I've learned from a detective in Santa Fe that Chuck Evans changed his name from Charles Evanovich in the late '80s, so I'll want some background on him from his days as Evanovich."

I'd given a lot of thought to what and how much to tell this investigator. In the end, I had adopted my former perspective as an attorney. What would I want a prospective client to tell me about a case? Everything. So I told him everything. We were interrupted only by the waitress as she took our orders and then when she placed our meals in front of us. I told Barker about my dad's murder, about the awful notes my mother had received, about the unpublished novel, about my mother's suspicions, and finally about the possible drug experimentation at UCLA, including Fischer's possible role as a CIA agent based in Los Angeles at the time. It took all of lunch and two more margaritas to tell the whole story, and I have to admit I felt a little bit foolish as I told it.

Barker interrupted me only a couple of times, so I had no idea what he was thinking. He sat silently for several long minutes when I was done. He rubbed at the salt on the rim of his glass and spent more time staring down into his drink than he did looking up at me.

I just sat and watched him, giving him time. The constant cacophony of the slot machines surrounding us had long ago receded into the background and become white noise.

When he finally stopped fidgeting and looked me square in the face, he had a crooked smile on his lips and a sparkle in his light blue eyes. "I like it," he said. "It's so farfetched there just might be something to it." He held out his hand for me to shake—a signal I took to mean he was on board.

We talked about fees for a bit. His calendar was wide open, which meant he could devote himself full-time to the case for the foreseeable future. We settled on two thousand bucks a day, regardless of how many hours he spent in a given day. His son Billy worked with him, and Barker said he would use him as necessary and cover his fees from the two grand. He would also cover up to a hundred a day in expenses. I would cover everything else. I made it clear I might replace him with Travis once Travis was free.

Barker walked me back to the Palazzo. It was a balmy fall day, and it felt good to be outside of the unreal cocoon of the casinos. The sidewalks were crowded, and the ubiquitous porn hustlers obnoxiously flicked their cards advertising naked women. Most of the hustlers were Mexican. Some were women. I ignored how irritated they were making me feel and imagined what it was like to try to make a living standing on a sidewalk for hours at a time in all kinds of weather, trying to get rid of the stack of cards you were allotted on a given day. The street hustlers were one of the more visible of the many dark sides of Vegas.

Barker had some suggestions on where to start. I wanted to find out what, if anything, had happened to cause Chuck to change his politics while in college. How had he gone from demonstrating for one of the most radical leftist student organizations to demonstrating for right-wing white supremacists? Or, as I'd surmised earlier, was one a fraud? In which case, had he been a spy? Perhaps for the CIA?

I'd forgotten to tell Barker about the scrapbook Josephine had found in Chuck's room. As we walked, I filled him in on the notebook full of news stories about people who'd been murdered. Again I had more questions than answers. Who were those people? What were their political affiliations? And, most importantly, why had Chuck been so interested in those articles?

Barker and I parted at the entrance to the Palazzo, and as I wandered aimlessly around the casino and into the Venetian, I thought about the strange world we humans had created for ourselves.

29

I flew back to Los Angeles the next day. The house in Malibu was a bit of a mess, since I was still in the process of cleaning out Mother's things. I had to decide what to do with her paintings and pottery, of which there were plenty. She'd clearly spent most of her time in her studio in the past couple years. I called a gallery owner in Westwood I knew she'd worked with, and the woman agreed to come out and have a look sometime in the next few days. There was more than enough inventory to put a show together. In the meantime, I would go through everything and mark whatever I'd want to keep for myself.

I was just taking a box of shoes to the garage when a FedEx truck pulled up. Two minutes later, I was opening a box containing what I assumed was the English translation of *The Daughters of Pinochet*. I'd asked Manuel Carrera to send both the Spanish and English versions back when he was done. That wouldn't necessarily stop him from making a copy, but at least he'd have to think about it before violating my stern conditions. Both versions were there, as was a note from Manuel:

> *Will: this is brilliant! You've got to let it get published.*
> *It's a great read, although I can certainly see why*
> *Pinochet and his family would be pissed. But that*
> *makes it all the more delicious. If you decide to publish,*
> *please let me be the official translator. I would give*
> *anything to be associated with any work by the great*
> *Ricardo Muñoz. Thanks for trusting me to do this for*
> *you. My invoice is attached.*

I put the note aside and picked up the manuscript. Was this what had gotten my father killed? If so, there had to be a lot more to the story than a fictional account of Pinochet being an asshole. Now that I had the English version of the novel, I found myself oddly ambivalent about my motivation to read it. Once I started reading, I would be hearing my father's words. That was how he wrote. I could hear his voice in his writing as clearly as if he was speaking directly to me. I wasn't ready for that right now. I knew it would have the effect of pushing my ever-present melancholia toward that awful state of depression.

I put the book down and went back to the business of cleaning out the house—as if that wasn't depressing enough. After an hour of my thoughts continuously returning to the book, I finally gave up. I grabbed the manuscript off the dining table and settled into my favorite chair on the deck and started reading.

*   *   *

I didn't know what the libel law in Chile was, but in the United States, even with the public-figure exceptions, I was fairly certain substantial parts of *Daughters* would be problematic. Accusing even a brutal dictator of adultery, incest, and pedophilia had to cross some sort of legal line. But then, who needed the courts when you had assassination squads at your disposal?

The novel was, of course, beautifully written. Dad had somehow been able to blend and then contrast the physical beauty of Santiago de Chile, where the bulk of the story takes place, with the beauty and inherent goodness of the Chilean people, even while so many of them supported a man capable of unspeakable acts of inhumanity. As Pinochet is put into power with the help of the CIA, he becomes more and more of a Jekyll and Hyde character. He is a husband and father and at least feigns being a religious man. But as he and Manuel Contreras scheme to rid the country and region of left-wing troublemakers, his willingness to order torture and death seems to have a profound effect on him: a numbing, desensitizing effect that begins to pollute the core of his character. Father had craftily seduced the reader into the subtly evolving mind of a man as he turns into a demon. Even as Pinochet orders monstrous acts of cruelty, and even as he discards his longtime mistress for his own daughter from that mistress, the reader feels empathy toward the monster. The book had been so perfectly written that, by the time Pinochet has his mistress murdered for refusing to quietly hand over her daughter, the reader mentally nods to himself: *yes, this is exactly what that man would do.* And then, just as the reader—or at least I as the reader—begins to wonder if he too has fallen prey to the desensitization process, Dad has his Pinochet character dive even deeper into the pit of depravity and cruelty, and the reader is jolted back to his senses, ashamed for having allowed himself to feel any empathy toward that man.

I read all that afternoon, and when it got too chilly on the deck, I moved to the couch in the living room and read until dinnertime. I'd planned on going out to dinner, but instead I called for a pizza to be delivered. I finished the book late that night while lying in bed.

It took me a long time to go to sleep.

30

I called Sam Chesne, Dad's U.S. editor, the next day. He seemed genuinely pleased to hear from me. After giving me his condolences about Mother—and after the usual bullshit about how we were both doing—he asked if I was calling because I'd decided to publish *Daughters*.

"Why would I do that, Sam? You know Mother thought that manuscript is what got Dad killed."

I could hear Sam expel air, as if he was already frustrated with me. "It's a great book, Will. Ricardo's readers deserve to be allowed to experience his last work." He paused for a beat. "Besides, I know it'll do well and make us all a pot full of money."

"I don't need any more money, Sam. And I agree the book is beautifully crafted and written. But as a lawyer, I'm wondering how you think you could get away with avoiding the libel suit Pinochet's family would be sure to bring. I mean, even public figures have certain rights, and from what I can recall from law school, accusing someone of adultery and crimes is considered to be libel per se, meaning you don't even have to prove damages."

"I know all that," Sam replied in a tone that sounded and felt dismissive. "Our lawyers said there was no way we'd publish the book as is, so your father and I talked at length about that. We decided all we'd need to do in order to avoid the courts would be to change the Pinochet name. We'd go from a real person as the subject of the novel to a fictional character—a fictional character who happens to have many historical and personal similarities to Augusto Pinochet."

"Hmm. But you never got that far? Everything I've seen still refers to the man Pinochet."

"Nah. Ricardo was playing around with variations on the name and I had asked legal for an opinion on our exposure if we changed the Pinochet name. In the meantime, I gave a copy of the manuscript to the interpreter we'd used on all of—"

He stopped just short of finishing his sentence. I waited. I knew he wasn't finished.

"I never thought for a moment the fucker would send a copy off to Chile, but I'm convinced that's exactly what he did. He denied it, of course." I heard Sam exhale heavily. "In any event, Ricardo died before any final decisions on publishing had been made."

I grunted my acknowledgment, not trusting myself to respond politely.

"Sooo," Sam said slowly, "if we make the changes and run it by legal, you want to let me publish?"

I had always liked Sam, at least based on the limited contact I'd had with him over the years. But now there'd been a sea change in my view of him. I no longer thought of him as Dad's collaborator. If Dad's novel had played any role in his murder, then this man, who called himself Dad's friend, was partially culpable, or at least negligent.

"I'll think about it, Sam, but don't hold your breath. In any event, I'm still too involved in tying up the loose ends following Mother's death to give it serious thought. Having only now read the book, I was just wondering about the libel angle."

Sam started to say something potentially argumentative, but I cut him off and told him I'd be in touch.

I hung up and sat quietly for several minutes. The call had disturbed me on many levels. Because I had a history of anger issues, I'd learned to rely on self-taught techniques to sort through my thoughts and, in the process, separate my feelings. Which ones were based on anger? Which ones were based on rational thinking? It was hard to say after the conversation I'd just had with Sam Chesne.

In the end, I decided there probably wasn't much Sam could have done differently. He had to get the manuscript translated. It was, after all, my father who wrote it with the real Pinochet as the villain.

—31—

By mid-afternoon I gave up my halfhearted attempts to clean out the rest of Mother's closet and grabbed a Pacífico from the fridge and settled into my usual spot on the deck. The fall day was cool and pretty damn clear for Los Angeles. A few people strolled on the beach. A Portuguese water dog, the only one enjoying the ocean, tried to jump over the shore waves in search of the stick his master patiently tossed over and over again.

I couldn't stop thinking about Dad's book. I thought about how angry he must have been, and I wondered if he'd had any sense of whether or not he was putting his life in jeopardy. The final scenes of *Daughters* haunted me. Pinochet's mistress-daughter had become pregnant, and for the first time, she allowed herself to dwell on what had happened to her mother. She had visions of raising a daughter who would one day supplant her as the mistress. But what if it were a boy? She played one scenario after another in her head. She imagined her teenage son learning the truth about the monster who was his father/grandfather, and she graphically daydreamed about the day her son would exact revenge.

As she slipped deeper and deeper into mental illness, she finally decided there was only one way to save herself and her unborn child. One evening as Pinochet settled into the soft, white leather couch in the apartment he kept for his young mistress, he watched her as she brought him his scotch. She was wearing a sheer silk slip with nothing on underneath. Her belly had only recently begun to show a bulge, which, so far, he found attractive and enticing. She could see he already had an erection.

When Pinochet took the scotch from her, he saw she was holding a large kitchen knife in her other hand. He started to ask her what she was doing, but before the first word came out, she stabbed herself in the belly. Blood spurted onto Pinochet, into his drink, and onto the beautiful leather couch as she plunged the knife over and over until she no longer had the strength to pull it free from her abdomen. She said nothing and did not scream. She whimpered pathetically, and toward the end, she moaned. Her stoicism made the scene all the more horrific.

When she finally fell to her knees in front of her father, she seemed to stare at him for a moment before her eyes rolled back and she fell forward, almost as if she intended to take Pinochet's still-erect penis into her mouth. Pinochet grunted in horror and pushed her away with his right foot. Then he stood, set down his drink, polluted with the blood of his daughter and possibly even his grandchild, and left the apartment.

It was a brutal scene. I wished I could get it out of my head. I closed my eyes and listened to the waves slapping the shore and the dog barking joyfully and a jet flying north, up the California coast. I wondered why Dad had decided to take his hatred for Pinochet to such a personal level. Wasn't there enough to demonize the man based on his record of state-sponsored brutality? Would attacking the very machismo of the man make him more repugnant to his fellow Chileans?

Even as I formed the question, I knew that was the answer. The Chileans would have been weary of the politics, of the endless allegations of torture and murder. Dad must have reasoned there was some disconnect between the populace's perception of political morality and its view of personal morality. While it might have been awful for a politician to torture and kill, it was, after all, what so many had done and were continuing to do all over the world. That was different from being an adulterous pedophile. Dad had drawn a line of morality in the literary sand that had the effect of separating Pinochet from the run-of-the-mill brutal dictators.

I suddenly decided I missed Cheryl and Travis. I needed my friends to keep me sane—or as close to it as I could muster. I pulled out my cell phone and called the office. Cheryl was in court, but Travis said things were mellowing out, at least enough to spend some time together.

It took less than half an hour for me to pack a small bag and book a flight to San Francisco. I grabbed the translated version of *The Daughters of Pinochet* as I was leaving and put it in my bag.

It was a cloudless, blue-sky day when I landed at SFO, but at Divisadero and Sacramento Streets, just a few blocks from my Pacific Heights house, I drove straight into a wall of fog. Two worlds, separated by a couple of yards. I could smell the moisture in the air, and the temperature dropped at least fifteen degrees. I smiled to myself. Back in my bubble. It felt good, calming.

I stood for a moment on my front porch, letting the fog engulf me. I could hear the foghorns in the bay, a melancholy sound I'd grown to cherish. I stood motionless until the chill finally got to my bones.

My cell phone rang just as I walked into the house. I kicked the front door closed and checked the number of the caller: a Vegas area code. I assumed, correctly, that it was Alvin Barker. He sounded different over the phone, younger, less assured, when he said, "Will? It's me, Alvin."

"Hi, Al. What's up?"

"Not much, but I thought I'd let you know I'm heading off to Bakersfield to interview an old UCLA classmate of Evans. We talked briefly by phone, but I got the feeling he had a lot to say, so I'd prefer to interview him in person."

"Good idea," I said. "And just for future reference, you don't need to get my approval for this kind of thing. I want you to do what you think you need to do."

"Thanks," he said. "I'll take that as a vote of confidence." He paused for half a beat before adding, "Oh, by the way, I have Billy watching the townhouse. He hadn't had so much as a glimpse of Evans until early this morning. Apparently, he'd been on a trip.

Billy saw him get out of a taxi with what looked like a carry-on suitcase and go into the house."

"Hmm. I wonder if he was off on a job. It'd be interesting to know what kind of clients they have nowadays, given their implosion among Miscovich's circle of friends."

I heard Barker cough away from the mouthpiece. Then he said, "I'll see if Billy can find out where Evans was."

I asked Barker to call me after he interviewed Chuck's former classmate. I was dying to know what metamorphosis Evans had gone through at UCLA. If his actions spoke for themselves, what made a kid who had grown up with parents willing to uproot themselves in protest of the apartheid regime in South Africa turn into a right-wing racist?

My house smelled a little musty, but it was clear Anna, my longtime housekeeper, was taking good care of the place. My huge ficus tree in the living room was thriving. There wasn't a speck of dust on the hardwood floor surrounding the antique Oriental rug I'd bought on a trip to Turkey some years back. I entered my bedroom and tossed my bag onto the bed. The bedside clock said it was three thirty. I was supposed to meet Travis and Cheryl downtown for a cocktail at 5 o'clock. I wandered back out to the living room and clicked on the television. It was on CNN, so I left it there and plopped down onto my brown leather couch. I kicked my shoes off and stretched out, deciding to let the white noise of the talking heads lull me to a nap. It might seem weird to you that I relaxed to the sound of self-proclaimed experts spouting bullshit about the Middle East or whatever, but left to my own devices, my own brain chatter would keep me awake.

I could feel myself drifting, the words becoming nothing more than a running stream, when something pierced the veil and the words became words again. I opened my eyes and looked at the screen: "Breaking news." *What else is new?* I thought. But I listened to what Don Lemon was saying.

"Miller's body was found this afternoon by his fifteen-year-old son, who had been studying in his room down the hall. According to the Minneapolis police, Miller had been shot through the back of the head. No one else was present in the house at the time of the shooting. Miller's wife and twelve-year-old daughter were out shopping together, according to a family spokesperson.

"Miller's seminal work, *The Failure of American-Style Capitalism*, which was first published almost twenty years ago, had recently been heralded as brilliantly prescient. He eerily predicted almost every economic event, good and bad, of the past two decades, including the growing income and wealth gap among Americans, which, Miller argued, would ultimately lead to the demise of the middle class and the subsequent inevitable collapse of our entire economic and political system."

A photo of Harrison Miller appeared on the screen while Lemon spoke. I knew who Miller was, but I hadn't read any of his work. The photo showed a man who appeared to be in his mid to late '60s. He had collar-length white hair and a large straight nose on a well-worn, wrinkled face. Even a photograph shown on television was able to convey the intense intelligence in his eyes.

"According to the police, there are no suspects at this time," Lemon reported. "Sources close to the investigation tell us that the working hypothesis by the police is a home invasion gone awry. Miller was seventy-one years old."

Don Lemon moved on to other stories, and I sat up straight, staring at the television. You know what I was thinking: *home invasion gone wrong, my ass*. I got up and walked into my bedroom, leaving Lemon behind. My mind was spinning, and I had trouble latching on to any single thought. How long ago had it been that the USC professor—was it Williams?—had been shot from behind? Not long. Was I just overly sensitive to writers being shot in the back of the head while at their homes? There'd been my father, decades ago, and then these two recent murders. Three murders, separated by time and space, did not a conspiracy make. Were there others? Was I turning into a conspiracy theory nutcase?

I took a shower and put on a well-worn pair of jeans, soft leather loafers, and a long-sleeved blue cotton shirt, untucked. I picked up the phone with the intention of calling a taxi to go meet Travis and Cheryl at Perry's, but I changed my mind at the last second and called Travis instead.

"Something's come up," I said. "I need to do a little research. Let's meet at A16 on Chestnut for dinner. I'm buying."

Travis paused before offering a reply. He was probably debating whether he should interrogate me to find out what was more important than cocktails. "Okay," he finally said. "I'll tell Cheryl. Seven thirty okay?"

"That's good. I'll make reservations."

I hung up before he could change his mind and start asking questions. I knew I'd sound like a raving lunatic if I told him what was going through my mind.

Five minutes later I was hunched over my computer, working the search engines. It wasn't going to be as easy as googling *liberal writers who were murdered*. So I took it a step at a time. I did a search for best-known American liberal and progressive writers and made a list of what I found. Then I did a similar search for liberal and progressive activists, then social scientists, then economists, and finally, politicians. *Forbes* had a piece on the twenty-five most influential liberals in America. Then, from each of my lists, I crossed out those whose reputations had been built on environmental and food source issues (such as GMOs). I could always put them back in later, I reasoned, but my hunch was that I was looking for political and social economic liberals.

When I was done, I had a short list of thirty. I'd only heard of seven of them. The rest were all academic types at universities and think tanks, but they were all prolific writers. Both Williams and Miller were on my list of thirty. I didn't include my father, because I'd also set the past twenty years as one of my parameters.

Again, I could always go back later, at which point my father still might not be on the list, since he wasn't that influential as an American liberal.

I googled each name to determine each person's current status. Of the thirty most prominent American liberals in the past twenty years, eleven were dead. Three had died of natural causes, such as heart attack or cancer. But an astounding number of people on my list, eight, to be precise—seven men and one woman—had been murdered. That had to be statistically significant, I thought.

More googling. All but one had died in the course of home burglaries. The one exception had been shot at his university office, late at night. All, including the one murdered in his office, had been shot in the back of the head, execution-style. There was no pattern to their geographic location. They were all over the map, just as Williams had been in Los Angeles and Miller had been in Minneapolis. The shootings were randomly spaced, so there were times when two years had gone by without any murders—at least of the people on my list.

I could certainly see how local police departments had no reason to suspect anything more than what they'd found—burglaries gone bad. Nor was the fact that the victims all happened to be liberal much of an obvious link. Some were journalists, some were academics, and only one was a politician. So it wasn't as if some brilliant cop would jump to the conclusion that someone with murderous intent was stalking liberals.

But there was no way the execution-style murders of eight of the thirty most important contemporary liberals in America could be considered any kind of coincidence. I stared at my handwritten notes, dumbfounded. I had no doubt whatsoever that a politically motivated serial killer was on the loose.

—33—

I was supposed to be at the restaurant in twenty minutes to meet Travis and Cheryl for dinner. I called a cab and stuffed my notes into my pocket. My head was still reeling. It was as if a modern-day Manuel Contreras was operating on American soil. But why? In Contreras and Pinochet's case, they had killed left-wing intellectuals in their geographic region as a way to consolidate right-wing power. What could anyone in the United States hope to accomplish by killing influential liberals? The odds of influencing an American election by silencing outspoken writers just seemed too remote to me. And if Chuck Evans was involved, was he acting on his own out of some ideological motivation, or was he—and possibly Milton Fischer—working for someone else as a paid assassin?

*　　*　　*

A16, a popular Italian restaurant on Chestnut Street, occupies a long, narrow space and boasts an open kitchen. The place was packed and warm, which felt great coming in from the bone-chilling fog. The hostess checked her chart and told me my guests had already arrived, so I followed her past the open kitchen on the right to the rear dining area. Cheryl and Travis were seated at a corner table. I hugged Travis and gave Cheryl a lingering kiss before I sat. I saw they'd already ordered a good bottle of Barolo, and I didn't waste any time pouring myself a glass.

"So," Cheryl said, a half smile playing across her beautiful face, "what was so important that you blew us off for cocktails?"

I enjoyed watching their faces as I took them through my thought process. Their expressions said, "You're a fucking lunatic," then, "Kind of interested," and finally, "Holy shit!" There was dead silence when I was through with my presentation. I removed the list of names from my pocket and put it on the table. Then I drank some wine.

—34—

Cheryl and I ended up at her apartment so she'd be able to dress for work the next morning. We luxuriated in our lovemaking, and I felt more of an emotional intensity than I'd ever experienced during the act of sex. Cheryl must have sensed it—or at least that there was something slightly different—because she didn't make any of her usual wisecracks after we unwound from each other. We just lay there, holding hands, catching our breath, and listening to the foghorns, which sounded more distant from her condo.

Both she and Travis had agreed with me that the killings were clearly not coincidences. What we hadn't agreed upon was what to do with the information. I had argued I should continue my investigation until I had more facts, specifically whether Chuck Evans and/or Milton Fischer were involved. Cheryl had argued in favor of going to the FBI. Travis had listened to each argument before finally siding with me. There wasn't anything more than coincidence and suspicion at this point—certainly nothing to get the FBI excited.

Cheryl had then insisted that Travis take some time off from the firm to work with me. If she needed him, he could work from wherever we happened to be on our quest for truth and justice.

I had intended to spend a few days in San Francisco, and with the unfamiliar level of emotion I was feeling for Cheryl, I was tempted to stick to that plan. But I decided Travis and I needed to return to Los Angeles to see if we could dig up some more information about MKULTRA and Chuck's possible involvement. If Chuck had become a professional assassin, it had all started at UCLA after he had met Milton Fischer.

"I wish you weren't going so soon," Cheryl said the next morning as she rolled onto me and sat over me, her long legs straddling my hips.

I stared up at her magnificent breasts and watched her nipples harden and grow, which, of course, made a certain member of mine harden and grow. "And you think this illegal torture is going to make me stay?" I asked.

"Would you rather be waterboarded?"

Neither of us waited for my answer.

*   *   *

Travis and I were back in the Malibu house by dinnertime. We'd picked up some tacos from a food truck near the airport and washed them down with Pacífico beer as we sat at the dining table and discussed our strategy—or lack thereof.

"We need to figure out a way to get that old professor who was involved in the experimental programs to talk to us," Travis said.

"Maybe we should go and talk to the younger prof"—I riffled through my notes—"Dr. Whiteman. He might be able to tell us how to get through to his colleague."

Travis shrugged and downed his beer. "Or maybe we should go to Vegas and do some investigating there."

I pelted him with a handful of tortilla chips. "Don't worry," I said. "Somehow I think we'll end up back in Vegas before we're done."

*   *   *

It was hazy and cold the next morning as we drove down the coast to the Santa Monica Freeway, which we took to the 405 before getting off at Wilshire Boulevard. UCLA, unlike its archrival USC, is in an upscale part of town, surrounded by Westwood, Beverly Hills, Bel Air, and Brentwood. We turned off Wilshire onto Hilgard Avenue, which runs along the east side of the campus, and parked in a lot close to Franz Hall, which housed the psychology department. It was a boxy building with little character, other than some fancy brickwork at the building's entrance.

Travis knew where he was going, so we skipped the directory and went straight to the behavioral neuroscience department. Dr. Whiteman was in his office. He remembered Travis—who doesn't?—and invited us in.

Dr. Whiteman had to be in his late sixties, but there was a vigor to him that made him seem younger. He was bald, and his whole head had a pinkish glow. Deep creases, most of which looked like laugh lines, etched his face. He had a solid, athletic-looking body. I guessed he played racquetball or squash regularly. His voice was sonorous, and I could envision him keeping the attention of undergrads in a packed lecture hall.

"So you still sniffing around the MKULTRA thing?" he asked in an amused tone.

I had lain awake a good portion of last night, worrying about how best to approach the doctor. In the end, I had decided that, once again, truth would be the best policy—at least most of the truth.

"We're concerned about a person who might have been a participant in the program. That person was my stepfather. He had some serious psychological issues and was so abusive, physically and emotionally, to my mother that she recently committed suicide."

Dr. Whiteman's expression turned from amusement to concern.

"There were some things in my mother's suicide letter to me that led me to believe that he might have hurt other people, as well," I continued. "Travis and I met with a close friend and business associate of my stepfather's, and he basically confirmed that my stepfather was involved in some experiments while here at UCLA."

Travis stepped in. "If this man was psychologically damaged by some experiments that were done on him while a student, we think it's important to find out so he can get some help and not injure anyone else."

The doctor leaned forward as he listened. He had his elbows on the desk and was resting his chin on his linked fingers. As soon as we were finished, he sat back in his chair and, in an almost comical gesture, raised one eyebrow. "Isn't it a little late to be riding in on a white horse to save the world from this guy? He has to be pretty damned close to my age if he went to school here in the late '60s." He looked at me. "I'm truly sorry for the loss of your mother—and for what this man might have done to her—but I hardly think that dredging up old psych experiments will do anything to alleviate your pain and anger. And . . . ." He paused, and his expression hardened just a touch. "No offense, but any statute of limitations for a civil action against the university would have been long passed."

I could hear Travis expel air through his mouth, and from the corner of my eye I saw him sit up straight.

I kept my eyes directed at the doctor and let my expression shift to a cold, hard look I generally reserved for cross-examination. "Doctor," I said, "I have no intention of suing the university or anyone with the university. I'm an attorney, and I'm well aware of the relevant statutes of limitations. But I see it's necessary to expand a little on our reasons for digging into this." I paused and ran a hand through my hair—just a small theatrical pause to make sure the doc was paying attention. "We have reason to believe this man is a killer." I held up a hand to stop the doctor from interrupting. "We have no proof as of yet, but we have strong enough suspicions for me to take time off from my busy practice and for Travis to also take leave to help me. You're right about the man's age, and I doubt very much he'll be marrying again, so we're not worried so much about the way he treats women. We're worried about who he might murder next. If our suspicions are correct, his latest murder was very recent."

Okay, so the bit about me taking time off from my busy practice to investigate Chuck wasn't exactly true, but it was close enough. I was silent while Dr. Whiteman digested what I'd said. I was hoping I wouldn't have to elaborate further.

After a long ten seconds, the doctor leaned forward again, still looking at me. "Okay, so what're you asking of me? I've already told Travis pretty much all I know about the program. I was never involved, and it was terminated not long after I got here."

"We need you to help us get your colleague—what's his name, Dr. Kendrick?—to talk to us," Travis said. "Put him at ease. Assure him we're not looking to sue anyone or point fingers. We just want to find out if the experiments this guy was subjected to might have caused some kind of chemical change in his brain that has affected his personality. We need to stop the killings."

Dr. Whiteman was silent again. He fiddled with a pen, staring down at his desk. The wrinkles in his face had deepened and no longer resembled laugh lines. Seconds passed.

"Okay, I'll talk to him," he finally said. "But I know you're not telling me everything, and I'm guessing he's going to want more details before he agrees to delve into what must have been a very dark period of his career. Can I assure him you will answer all of his questions?"

Travis turned to me, and I nodded.

"Call me tomorrow around ten," Dr. Whiteman said as he stood.

—35—

My cell phone rang just as we hit Pacific Coast Highway. Travis was driving, so I retrieved it from my pocket and recognized Alvin Barker's number on the display.

"I pulled Billy off the stakeout of Fischer and Evans' townhouse," Barker said. "I decided it was a waste of money. So I put Billy on the job of trying to find out where Evans had been. Like you said, if we can get some insight into their current gigs, maybe that'll help. Anyway, a little over a week ago he flew to Chicago, where he spent two nights. I don't know where he stayed or what he did. Then he flew to Minneapolis and spent the rest of the week. He flew directly home from there."

My heart started pounding so hard I could feel it in my temples. Chuck Evans had been in Minneapolis when Harrison Miller had been murdered!

"Will?" Barker said. "You still there?"

"Yeah, I'm here, Al. See what you can find out about the murder of Harrison Miller in Minneapolis last week."

"Who?"

"Harrison Miller, a relatively famous economist. He was shot in the back of the head while at home last week."

I could hear Barker's intake of breath.

"Did you meet with Evans' old classmate yet?" I asked.

"Wait a sec. That was Harrison Miller? I'm writing it down." He paused a moment. "Okay. Yeah, I did. You sound like you're in a car. You driving?"

"Nah, passenger, but why don't I get back to you when I get home so I can hear your account of the interview better—and take notes if necessary."

"Good idea. Call me back."

I looked over at Travis.

"Am I to gather from your conversation that Chuck was in Minneapolis last week," he asked, "during the time frame when that Miller dude was murdered?"

"Yep."

"Holy shit."

"My sentiments exactly," I said.

We said nothing further as we drove along the coast on that dull gray afternoon.

*　　*　　*

It was cold, windy, and generally ugly outside when we got home, but Travis said he needed to go for a run. I probably should have gone with him. I could feel myself slipping into some level of depression, something on the outer edge of my old familiar melancholy. Even the cold, gray day wasn't cheering me up. I put off calling Barker back while I fixed myself a Don Julio on the rocks and then put on a windbreaker and sat on my deck. The beach was deserted except for the occasional runner. I could hear the gulls talking to each other over the breaking waves. I felt the mist from the ocean, brought in by a strong onshore wind. I sipped my drink and let the elements beat me up for a while. When I was sufficiently uncomfortable, I went in and called Barker.

"The guy's name is Steven Arnett," Barker said. "I emailed a transcript of our meeting to you. He's a mid-level manager at the main Bakersfield Bank of America. Seems like a nice enough guy. He remembered Chuck pretty well, considering how long ago it was."

"When did they first meet?" I asked.

"First year. They were in English 101 together. He remembers trying to place Chuck's accent the first time he heard him speak. Arnett had never heard a South African accent before. Anyway, the two became acquainted. They'd sit with each other if they happened to be lunching at the same place. They traded tidbits about their past, where they were from—that sort of thing. Arnett says Chuck was pretty strident about the whole apartheid thing. He said his parents should never have left. They should have stayed and fought."

"So he didn't respect the decision his parents made to move away?" I asked.

"Doesn't sound like it. According to Arnett, he called his father a pussy. 'What good does it do for a cause if you just run away?' That kind of thing. To top it off, Chuck told Arnett his parents pretty much lost everything because of the move. They couldn't get all their assets out of South Africa because of the sanctions, and his father couldn't get a job teaching in the States because he didn't have the proper credentials. So his dad went to work in a hardware store, and his mother took a job as a waitress. She'd never worked before. They'd always had servants in South Africa."

I grunted.

"By the end of their freshman year," Barker said, continuing, "Chuck had begun attending meetings of Students for a Democratic Society as well as marching in antiwar rallies. Arnett would tag along once in a while, although he claims he was pretty nonpolitical. It was at an SDS rally against Dow Chemical that Chuck got arrested, along with about a hundred other protestors."

Barker coughed on the other end of the line. "Hang on a sec," he said.

I heard liquid being poured into a glass, and then he paused, presumably to take a drink. Then he was back.

"According to Arnett, something changed over the summer. Let's see . . . I think it was the summer of 1969. He and Chuck had two classes together, but Chuck seemed different, standoffish. He'd acknowledge Arnett, but he wouldn't go out of his way to be friendly. One of the classes they had together was a psych class, and Chuck would come up with all sorts of weird shit during class discussions."

"What does that mean, 'weird shit'?" I asked.

"Well, one example Arnett gave was when Chuck challenged the professor about some of the human experiments by the Nazis. Chuck's premise was that, although it was of course wrong to experiment on unwilling Jews in concentration camps, weren't a lot of the experiments themselves in the best interests of humanity?" Barker chuckled. "Needless to say, that didn't go over so well in class."

I asked if Arnett had known anything about Chuck participating in experiments.

"Not much," Barker replied. "He knew Chuck was volunteering at the psych department for certain research projects. Apparently he was in dire need of money. He'd come to UCLA on a baseball scholarship but lost that when he stopped showing up for practice and joined the SDS. His parents couldn't afford the full tuition, so he was doing odd jobs for money. I guess volunteering his body for scientific research paid fairly well."

I was sitting at my dining table, feet up on another chair, staring out at the gloomy day, as I listened to Barker. I saw Travis walking up from the beach.

"So Arnett doesn't know anything about whether Chuck was subjected to drug research," I asked, "or anything like that?"

Barker coughed again. I heard him take a sip of whatever he had poured. "Not really. He related a significant personality change from the previous year, but he didn't know what to attribute it to. Next thing he knew, Chuck was hanging around with a quasi-white supremacy group and was going to rallies opposing the creation of ethnic study programs. He got arrested again, only this time when his new hate group got into it with some Black Panthers after an on-campus speech by Stokely Carmichael."

The back door opened, and I heard the surf and the gulls for a moment while Travis entered. I signaled I was on the phone. He nodded.

"Jesus," I said. "That's one hell of a transformation."

"No shit," Barker said. "And that's pretty much all I got from

Arnett. He distanced himself from Chuck pretty quickly that second year."

I didn't say anything. I was wondering what kind of drugs or experiments or whatever could change a person's personality so drastically.

"Oh, Will, one more thing I almost forgot to tell you."

"What's that?"

"Arnett said Chuck got married around the end of his junior year. He heard about it through some mutual friends."

I dropped my feet to the floor and sat forward in my chair. "Married? Really? Any details?"

"Nah, but I can do some digging if you want. He was still Evanovich then."

I heard a thud as a chair was toppled by a sudden gust outside on the deck. The wind was howling.

"No. I'm in Los Angeles, and my legal investigator is down here staying with me. We'll dig around in the records here. We're also hoping to meet with one of the professors who was involved in the CIA research programs here."

Barker gave some kind of grunt, probably wondering if his gravy train had come to a screeching halt.

"What I'd like you to do is check out some travel dates, if you can. I'll send you specific dates and cities, and you see if there's any way you can find out if Chuck was in those cities on those dates."

There was a sigh and then silence on Barker's end. Finally he spoke. "I'll see what I can do. That ain't gonna be easy. Passenger manifest lists are completely confidential. We were lucky with Chuck's trip to Chicago and Minneapolis because it was so recent and I have a special contact with Southwest Airlines." He paused. "But we can give it a try."

We talked a few more minutes, and I promised to get the dates and cities to him by email. Then I sat back in my chair and locked my hands on my head, wondering just what the hell I'd gotten myself into.

—36—

Travis and I left the house at nine the next morning to have breakfast in Santa Monica, where we would kill time before making the ten o'clock call to Dr. Whiteman. Santa Monica was as cold, cloudy, and dreary as Malibu.

The Native Americans who inhabited Santa Monica before the white settlers arrived were the Tongva. They were neighbors of the Chumash. Starting about thirty-five hundred years ago, the Tongva inhabited over four thousand square miles of territory, including the southern Channel Islands. It's said they built sturdy boats that were coated with tar from the La Brea Tar Pits. I've tried to picture the Tongva as they came upon the tar pits, not knowing, of course, that there were the remains of huge prehistoric animals stuck in the depths. "What the fuck is this sticky shit?" one of them might have asked. "I don't know, but why don't we use it to seal our boats?" another might have replied.

Following the Spanish construction of Mission San Gabriel Arcángel, the Tongva were subjected to forced relocation and exposed to diseases that rapidly wiped out huge portions of the population. When Mexico ceded California to the United States, our federal government signed treaties with the Tongva, promising eight and a half million acres of land for reservations. The treaties were never ratified, and by the turn of the century, the Tongva communities were nearly extinct. The remaining Tongva, also known as Gabrieleños (named after the mission), didn't get along all that well. The already shrunken community split in the '90s over the controversy surrounding the building of an Indian casino. Proving themselves to be true Americans, the Tongva groups sued each other.

I felt unsettled as I drove down the Pacific Coast Highway. I wondered how I'd react to an aging professor, a scientist, who'd been willing to experiment with dangerous, mind-altering drugs on unsuspecting students. I lowered the window and let the cold, damp air envelop me, waiting for the calming effect it usually had on me. But it didn't come. Maybe the San Francisco fog had a special chemistry.

"Dude," Travis said, "close the fucking window."

"Sorry, man. Just trying to clear my head. I can't seem to process how a college professor, a doctor, would experiment on students." I closed the window. "I guess I'm a little worried about how I'll react to this guy—assuming we get to see him."

Travis murmured something unintelligible as I turned off the highway onto Ocean Boulevard and then left onto Pico to look for parking. I turned right onto Third Street and then right onto Bay Street. I got lucky and found a spot, and we walked to Main Street and Dogtown Coffee. Despite the chill, Main Street was already crowded, mostly with people sipping coffee and walking their dogs.

"Keep an open mind," Travis said after we'd gotten our coffee and ordered breakfast. "We don't know what this guy knew or didn't know—or even how involved he was." He looked at me with a kind of quizzical expression. "I've never known you to be in such a rush to judgment."

I nodded. "Yeah, I know. I don't know why it bothers me so much. Maybe because it's so reminiscent of the Nazi experiments. I mean, this is the USA . . . ." I let my voice trail off, not knowing what I really wanted to say. Did I not believe our government could do such a thing? Well, it was a fact it had.

As a country, we've committed genocide against our own Native Americans; we've broken promises; we've recognized as law the right to own other human beings; we've turned a blind eye and our backs on the Jews fleeing Hitler, on the genocide in Rwanda, and on the gassing of the Kurds in Iraq; we've killed hundreds of thousands of civilians in Dresden and Hiroshima and Nagasaki; we've supported dictators like Pinochet, who murdered thousands of his own people. There's not a lot of bad shit we haven't done.

The food arrived at our table, and we ate in silence for a while.

"Have you heard from Cheryl?" I finally asked.

Travis shook his head. "I presume that means she's doing fine without me. I'll check in with her later today."

I glanced at my watch and saw it was almost ten o'clock. "I'll step outside to make the call," I said.

Travis nodded and stuffed most of a pancake into his mouth.

"Bob Kendrick will see you today," Whiteman said as soon as I got him on the phone. "Eleven o'clock at his office. Be upfront with him. He's none too happy about this kind of stroll down memory lane."

I agreed and thanked him and then went back inside to finish breakfast.

*　　*　　*

Dr. Kendrick's office was also in Franz Hall, one floor above Whiteman's. It was slightly larger but still cramped. His desk sat perpendicular to the one window. A tired brown couch with exposed stuffing sat against the far wall, while two unmatched chairs faced the desk. Bookcases overflowing with books and treatises lined the wall to the left of the door as well as the wall behind where the professor was sitting. Most of the books looked dusty to me. He hadn't gotten up to greet us.

"Forgive my rudeness," he said in a high-pitched but strong voice, "but my arthritis is acting up something fierce today."

"Not a problem," I said and reached across his desk to shake his bony white hand, which looked brittle, like parchment paper, the veins visible just beneath the skin. His grip was weak, and I gave him my best wet-noodle shake.

Travis followed suit, and Kendrick motioned for us to sit.

I spent a moment studying him as I settled into my chair. Just as the Nazi guards and scientists who had engaged in unspeakable acts had often been ordinary-looking family men, he showed no hint of an evil monster lurking within him. He was rail thin, with wispy white hair and a long, well-etched face. Purple splotches dotted his face. His eyes were dark, maybe brown, but there was a clarity to them that belied the rest of his wasting body. He wore a yellow button-down cotton shirt, frayed around the collar, under a worn brown cardigan. His desk was uncluttered and orderly. His computer monitor and keyboard sat on the right side of his desk, out of the way of his primary workspace.

"So how can I help you, gentlemen?" he asked. "I understand you're interested in some ancient history."

I nodded. "Thanks for agreeing to meet with us. I assume Dr. Whiteman filled you in to some extent?"

Kendrick blinked and picked up a pen, which he absently toyed with.

Must be an occupational mannerism, I thought, remembering Whiteman had done the same.

"Just that you're investigating a man who may be a murderer and who might have been a participant in the experimental drug programs back in the '60s." He blinked again and then shifted in his seat, grimacing slightly as he did so. He continued working the pen like a majorette twirling a tiny baton. "Enough to pique my interest, but not enough to see how I can be of any help to you."

I glanced at Travis, who was smiling pleasantly.

He took the cue. "Well, first we'd appreciate a little background about the program, if you don't mind. We've read the Church report and understand the experiments were funded by the CIA and that various drugs, such as LSD, were used in the experiments—"

Kendrick cut him off, waving his skeletal hand. "Ancient history. It sounds ridiculous now, but you have to remember the times. We were in the height of the Cold War. The government was convinced we had to fight creeping communism around the world. That's why we were in Vietnam." He waved his hand again, dismissively. "The famous domino theory. MKULTRA and its sister programs were misguided attempts to see if human behavior could be modified and controlled. We knew the Soviets were conducting similar experiments."

I couldn't help myself. "So that made it okay to give mind-altering drugs to kids?"

The room fell silent.

I bit my tongue, hoping I hadn't blown it—but knowing I had. "I apologize," I said with as much contrition as I could muster. "I think what we need to know is whether or not any of the drugs that were used in these experiments could cause permanent changes in someone's brain."

Kendrick put the pen down and leaned forward, resting his thin arms on his desk. "You mean like turning someone into a killer?" His tone was intense, mocking.

I shrugged. "Yes, something like that. Wasn't that the goal of the program?"

He sat back, again grimacing at the movement. He looked out the dirty window—at nothing but gray. The seconds passed.

"There are certain types of drugs that affect our nervous system," he finally said, his academic training seemingly taking over. "Whether it's the central nervous system, what we call the CNS, or the peripheral nervous system, the PNS, the brain is the command center and communicates with the body through the nerves and spinal cord. There are four types of drugs that are categorized by their effects on the nervous system." He held up a thin, crooked white finger as he related each one. "Stimulants, depressants, opiates, and hallucinogens. The drugs in these categories can interfere with the way the neurotransmitters send and receive signals. In hallucinogens, for instance, the drug alters the brain's interpretations of sensory input. It can cause hallucinations, affect cognitive ability, and create a state similar to delirium. Mood changes, emotional instability, and aggressive behavior are pretty common effects of hallucinogens."

Kendrick paused, and I followed his gaze out the window, where nothing seemed to have changed outside. He breathed deeply, glanced at Travis and then at me, and then refocused his gaze out the window before resuming his explanation.

"Certain drugs can cause the brain to stop producing its own neurotransmitters or alter the amount of the chemical messengers in the brain, which would, of course, disrupt the normal functioning of the brain. Whether this damage to the brain is transient or more permanent would depend on various factors, such as age, sex, dosage, tolerance, and duration of use."

Travis leaned in toward the doctor. "So the short answer would be that, in certain circumstances, some drugs can actually cause permanent chemical changes in a person's brain?"

Kendrick gave a slight nod. "Sure. If neurons are destroyed, the chemical signals to the nervous system will be altered. But," he said and held up a hand again, "that would be pretty rare. Generally speaking, I think it would be safe to say that the most likely cause of any significant change due to prolonged use of any of these drugs would be the effect on a preexisting personality disorder."

I waded back into the breach. "Did that happen to any of your subjects?"

Kendrick shook his head. He looked briefly at me with what I took to be some measure of disgust. "You don't understand," he said. "Once again, you have to put things in the perspective of the times. My daughter grew up having nuclear bomb drills in elementary school. The children were taught to drop to the floor under their desks and cover their heads." He let go a tinny-sounding chortle. "As if that would protect anyone from what we did to those souls in Hiroshima! The poor thing didn't know about Hiroshima or Nagasaki, but like all the kids, she saw enough on television to understand that an atomic bomb would wipe out all of us. She knew hiding under her desk at school wouldn't protect her. She began to have nightmares." He ran a ghostly hand over his eyes. "Can you imagine what we were doing to these kids? What kind of horrors we'd implanted in their formative minds? My wife and I were at a loss over what to do. We tried to tell her she'd be fine, that we'd all be fine, that no one would dare drop the bomb on us. But then why were our schools instructing the children to hide under their desks?" He shook his head—a statement of some kind.

Travis and I said nothing.

"You're too young to remember how close we came to all-out nuclear war over the Cuban missile crisis. I had to do something," Kendrick said. "I felt powerless . . . ." He stopped and straightened in his chair.

I could see the pain in his face, and I imagined it was more than just physical. If he'd ever actually talked about what he and his colleagues had done, it had been a long time ago. We waited for him to continue.

"It sounds so absurd now," he said "Like the tests the CIA talked us into doing. But back then most of the country had bought into the red menace bullshit. Just like we bought into the weapons of mass destruction bullshit four decades later. We listen to the idiotic pronouncements of the warmongers as if they really do know what they're talking about, and then we blindly follow them until enough of our young people are dead that we finally start asking the hard questions we should've asked before our first soldier died."

Kendrick's face had turned red so that the purple splotches now looked angry, and there were little globs of white forming at the sides of his mouth. I wanted him to take a drink of water, but his mind was elsewhere. I heard a woman's laugh somewhere down the hall.

"So when our department head came to us and asked us to listen to a proposal by a 'government spokesman,' " he said, making air quotes with his fingers, "we listened, and most of us signed up." He paused and finally reached for the bottle of water that had been sitting on his desk.

Travis and I said nothing while he took several long gulps.

He set the bottle down and screwed the cap back into place. He looked at us and this time did not look away. "You must think me an idiot," he said. He didn't wait for a reply. "But think about it. We're scientists. Most of us had already been doing some kind of research into mind-altering drugs. I'd been involved in a project researching the American Indians' use of peyote and how that affected their spirituality and what passed for their science. A close friend of mine at Stanford had been involved in a project to research whether drugs were used in various Aztec and Incan rituals to get subjects to actually volunteer to be human sacrifices." Kendrick sighed heavily. "He's the one who talked me into buying into the CIA program." Then he smiled for the first time, his thin lips breaking into the crepe paper cheeks. "At least he got a world-famous writer out of his batch of subjects."

"Ken Kesey?" Travis asked.

Kendrick nodded. "So of course it was all a load of crap. I don't think any of us really thought we were going to create some kind of *Manchurian Candidate* killing machine that would save the world from communism. But when you think about what the growing array of drugs we had to work with could do to the human mind, the possibilities seemed endless." He spread his arms, palms up, in a strange gesture. "One of my pet projects was to see if we could eliminate, even temporarily, a man's inclination, or even willingness, to commit violence." He coughed without covering his mouth. He looked tired and spent as he fell silent.

I glanced at Travis, who discreetly raised an eyebrow at me. It hadn't escaped our attention that the doctor hadn't answered my question about whether any of the subjects had undergone a personality change.

"Dr. Kendrick," I finally said, "do you remember a man named Milton Fischer? He supposedly worked for the CIA."

Kendrick stayed silent for a moment, and I wondered if he'd heard me. But then he looked me in the eyes and nodded. "Sure, I remember Fischer," he said. "A true believer. A true prick."

"Why do you say that?" Travis asked.

"Fischer wasn't all that interested in turning people into peace-loving citizens. He was interested in turning them into killing machines. He'd seen experiments with some of the hallucinogens and amphetamines where previously docile subjects turned violent and wanted us to develop a protocol from which we could create a real-world on-off killing machine switch."

"Was Fischer in charge of the program?"

Kendrick shook his head. "No, thank God. He was a minion—a sleazy, nasty, scary little ghost soldier."

So, I thought, *Fischer lied about his involvement in the program.*

"Do you know what happened to him after the program was shut down?" I asked.

"No idea," Kendrick said. He took a deep breath and grimaced as he tried to get comfortable. Then he looked from me to Travis and then back to me again. "Time to put your cards on the table, gentlemen. Just who is this *possible* killer who was *possibly* in our little CIA-funded project?" Despite everything he'd revealed only moments earlier, his voiced dripped with sarcasm.

I glanced briefly at Travis before answering. "He goes by Chuck Evans now," I said. "Back then, I think he was called Charles, or Chuck Evanovich."

The blood drained from Kendrick's face. The small smirk faded into a look of shock—and possibly even fear. He sat back in his chair, almost as if he'd been pushed in the chest. But he said nothing.

"What is it?" Travis asked. "Obviously you know him."

Kendrick still said nothing. It was as if he'd gone into shock. His lips moved, but nothing came out. He wiped his mouth with the back of his left hand before putting both hands on his desk, left over the right, perhaps hoping we hadn't seen his right hand shaking.

Travis and I exchanged glances but said nothing. I'd never seen anyone react so severely to hearing another person's name.

I leaned in toward the desk, toward Kendrick. "Doctor," I said softly, gently, "what is it?"

Again Kendrick looked as if he was about to speak, but again, no words came forth. He swallowed heavily.

"Evanovich was one of your subjects," Travis said, as if stating a fact.

Kendrick shook his head. His voice was strained, raspy, as he finally spoke. "No," he said. "But yes, I knew him."

We waited for him to explain, but the frail, pale man was clearly struggling to breathe. He closed his eyes and tried to inhale deeply.

I watched him closely, concerned he might be having some sort of cardiac event. I started to rise, to go to his aid, but at that moment he opened his eyes and looked straight into mine. He raised both his hands, palms out, and I took it as a sign to sit back down. Still more seconds passed before he spoke.

"Charles Evanovich married my daughter," he said softly in a voice laced with anger.

A crushing sense of sadness seemed to envelop Kendrick as he told us the story.

"Chuck was different from the beginning," he said. "He wasn't in my program, but we were all aware of him. He was one of Hinckle's—Dr. Hinckle was head of the department," he added in response to my questioning look. "He had only three students in his experimental program, and Chuck Evanovich was one of them." Kendrick ran a hand over his face and then smoothed back his wispy hair. "When Chuck came to the program as a volunteer," he said, "I interviewed him and gave him our test protocols. The tests were theoretically designed to determine whether a particular student would be a feasible candidate for the program."

"What does that mean?" Travis asked. "You thought you could tell how kids were going to react to acid, or psilocybin, or speed, or whatever?"

There was an edge to Travis's voice that I sympathized with but hoped wouldn't cause the doctor to shut down. It didn't.

He produced a wan, almost dismissive smile. "Yes, actually, that's exactly what it was supposed to tell us—to some degree, of course. But Chuck Evanovich's profile was almost too good. He was, to my way of thinking, too malleable. I recommended that he be rejected." Kendrick sighed heavily. "But each candidate's test results were reviewed by our team of four doctors, and I was ultimately overruled. Dr. Hinckle personally took Chuck on as one of his subjects."

"I'm not sure what you mean when you say you thought he was too malleable," I said, interrupting the story.

Kendrick blinked and scowled—whether from his arthritic pain or from the difficulty involved in accessing his memories, I couldn't tell. He took a sip of water, then looked at each of us in turn before answering.

"Bluntly put, I felt Chuck had a borderline personality disorder that would cause the drug experiments to be skewed and unreliable. Although there hadn't been a lot in the way of scientific studies of the effects of many of those drugs at that point in time, there had been anecdotal accounts of psychotic episodes—and even suicide."

"But isn't that exactly what you folks were looking for?" I asked. "Weren't you hoping to turn some of these kids into psychotic killers? Wasn't that the plan?"

Kendrick looked at me with distaste, but I'd already decided that whatever Travis and I said was not going to stop him from telling the story at this stage of the game. He would still try to rationalize what he and his fellow "scientists" had done in the name of patriotism.

"Maybe for some," he finally acknowledged, "but that was never my goal. As I said, I was hoping that drugs could be used to deter violence."

We let that statement hang in the air. I didn't know if Kendrick had really believed that at the time or if that was where his rationalization had finally taken him. He was an old man who'd played God with unsuspecting students trying to make an extra buck. He'd gotten away with it. Or had he? He still hadn't told us what had happened with his daughter.

"So tell us more about Chuck Evanovich," I said. "How did he end up marrying your daughter?"

Kendrick closed his eyes for a moment and then shifted in his seat, and this time I could tell his grimace was one of pain. "I'll get to that in a minute. We all more or less monitored—or at least discussed—each other's subjects in our weekly meetings. No one before or since had undergone the kind of changes we saw in Chuck. I'm a neuropsychologist, but even I have a hard time describing his transformation."

"You mean personality change?" Travis asked.

Kendrick shook his head. "No, at least not in the classic sense. His basic personality seemed to be intact. He was personable, compliant, and generally polite, which is how he'd been when he first came into the program. And he possessed some level of quantifiable personality disorder, although there was no evidence that it affected his daily activities. But there was some sort of ideological shift in him, which I, for one, can't explain by the effects of the drugs he was given."

"Ideological? You mean like turning from a liberal, or radical, to a racist?"

Kendrick was nodding before I was done. "Yes, that's exactly what I'm saying. When he came to us, he was a pretty normal young man with a strong sense of right and wrong, particularly when it came to racial justice. He was from South Africa." Kendrick paused and looked at us. "I don't know if you knew that."

We nodded.

"So he'd been involved in some demonstrations on campus," Kendrick said, continuing. "I think he even got arrested at one. No biggie. But after about two semesters in our program, two things happened. One, we discovered he'd begun doing drugs outside of the program. That was a violation of our rules and resulted in automatic expulsion from the program. That CIA guy, Fischer, tried to intervene and argued to keep Chuck in the program, but even Dr. Hinckle agreed there was no way we could allow Chuck to stay. But Dr. Hinckle did get us to agree that we should continue to monitor Chuck for a few months to make sure everything was okay and that he hadn't suffered any adverse effects from the experiments."

Travis and I said nothing while Kendrick took a sip from his water bottle.

"The second thing that happened was that we heard Chuck had started showing up at the few right-wing demonstrations there were on campus. He'd even gotten involved with a white supremacy group, most of whom weren't students here. I told Dr. Hinckle we needed to bring Chuck in for further testing. Something had gone wrong with him." Kendrick paused. "How does someone go from being an antiapartheid activist to a virtual Ku Klux Klaner?"

"But you said the experimental drugs wouldn't account for an ideological change," Travis said. "So what was there to test?"

Kendrick sighed heavily. "I said I didn't *think* the drugs could cause such an ideological shift, especially without evidence of other personality changes. But I didn't know then whether there had been other personality changes in Chuck. He wasn't participating in the program anymore and literally had to be bribed with cash to show up for the intermittent screening Dr. Hinckle insisted on doing. So I argued for Chuck to be subjected to a whole new battery of tests."

"And did Dr. Hinckle agree?" I asked.

Kendrick shook his head. "No. I think he'd decided it was time to cut Chuck loose. The sooner we cut all ties with him, the more we distanced ourselves from him, the better off we would be."

"You mean so the program wouldn't be terminated or compromised," Travis said. A statement—not a question.

Kendrick gave Travis a look of irritation before nodding slightly. "I guess that would be true."

"Okay," I said, "so Chuck was kicked out of the program and was turning weird, at least politically weird, but you guys had washed your hands of him. I'm not getting where your daughter comes into the picture."

Kendrick, who had been looking at me as I talked, dropped his gaze to his desk. I couldn't tell what was going on until I saw him wipe away a tear. He was crying. I didn't know what to say or do, and obviously Travis felt the same, so we just sat there, waiting for Kendrick to explain.

"Unbeknownst to me," he said after a long and uncomfortable pause, "Kelly, my daughter, had met Chuck in an American history class. Long story short, he hooked up with her and got her into drugs—the drugs he'd been doing outside of the program." Kendrick wiped his eyes again and finally looked up at us. "I can't conceive of her putting up with Chuck's new politics, but I was in the dark and hadn't even known they knew each other. Next thing I knew, Kelly came to me when the semester was over and told me she and Chuck had gotten married and were going away for a while."

Kendrick looked at Travis and then at me. I'd never seen a man's face so corrupted by sadness and pain. It was hard to return his gaze.

"As you can probably imagine, the scene that ensued was awful. My wife, Kelly's mother, had died a couple years earlier, so we were all each other had. I thought we were good. I mean, I gave her a lot of space, but we talked relatively often, and she would sometimes stop by the office to say hello. I hadn't suspected anything.

"We argued about Chuck and about her getting married without even telling me, and, of course, it ended badly. Kelly stormed out, and she and Chuck disappeared. Neither one of them showed up for their senior year. I didn't hear from her all summer and assumed they were traveling, probably hitchhiking around the country like a lot of kids were doing then. I was worried, of course. I didn't like Chuck from the first time I met him and hated what he'd turned into. Then, to have taken my child from me . . . ." Kendrick's voice trailed off.

The silence hung in the air like a thick, heavy fog.

"So what happened?" Travis asked. "I assume they split up and got divorced. What was she like after?"

It took Kendrick a few moments to register the question and respond. His answer took my breath away. "I never saw Kelly again."

—38—

It took me a while to find my voice. "What do you mean, you never saw her again? She won't see you?"

I don't see how it was possible for someone who looked like Kendrick to age before my eyes, but he did. His pasty skin seemed to whither on his bones. His already sad eyes became dull and unfocused. His chest looked as if it was collapsing in on itself.

When he spoke again, his voice was flat. "The police say she is presumed dead. They were in Alaska, about two months into the marriage, staying in some hostel near Denali, when Chuck claims she went for a hike—alone. No one ever saw her again."

"Went for a hike alone?" Travis asked. "That seems a little hard to believe. That's bear country."

Kendrick waved a hand dismissively. "It's utter bullshit, and we all knew it. But the police say they conducted a thorough investigation and found no evidence of foul play . . . against Chuck or anyone else." His weak voice cracked when he added, "Her body was never found. Chuck had her declared dead seven years later."

"Did you ever see Chuck again?" I asked.

He shook his head. "No. I never saw him nor heard from him again. I got the court notices about her being declared dead, but he never contacted me—never even to give his condolences."

* * *

"Holy crap, was that about the weirdest conversation you've ever had?" Travis asked once we were back in our car.

I nodded. "Yeah," I said softly. My thoughts were all over the place. Had the very program Kendrick participated in cost him his daughter? Had Chuck killed Kendrick's daughter, or had she really just walked off as he had claimed? Was Chuck's ideological metamorphosis real or feigned?

We drove to Malibu in silence.

"I wonder how many other wives Chuck had," I said once we were seated at the dining table with sandwiches and beer.

It was still cold and windy outside. I couldn't help thinking it would be a perfect day to build a fire, make love to Cheryl, watch a movie, and then make love again.

Travis grunted. "And how many are still alive."

"Jesus," I said. I paused to let the thought sink in and then repeated the word.

We ate our sandwiches, sipped our beers, and listened to the wind howl. The sliding glass doors were wet with sea spray.

"I think I'll run into downtown L.A. this afternoon and see what I can dig up from the county registrar," Travis said. "I'll do a search for both Evans and Evanovich. Do you want to come? Or do you need the car for anything?"

I shook my head. "Nah. I'll stay here and ponder things."

Travis snorted. "Yeah, well, don't hurt yourself."

*   *   *

The wind picked up forcefully after Travis left. Sliding glass doors rattled. Patio chairs tipped over. Sea spray drenched the ocean side of the house, coating the windows with salt residue. I wandered from room to room, remembering what the house had been like when Mother was still alive and Josephine was bossing me around. I found myself wishing I'd gone with Travis. I felt so lonely it was actually physically painful.

I wanted to bury my face in Cheryl's neck and smell her. I wanted to talk to her about what I was doing, to ask her if she thought it was time to turn over whatever we had to the cops and then let it go. She'd always had the most sense among the three of us.

I sat down at the computer, unsure what I was planning to do. I was adrift. I thought about Dr. Kendrick. Before meeting him, I had assumed he was some kind of monster. Maybe he was. Maybe the program he had willingly participated in had created a monster of its own—one that ended up taking the one thing that was most precious in his life. Whatever he'd been, whatever price he should have paid for playing God with young people's minds, he did not deserve the punishment he ultimately suffered.

I flinched as a huge blast of thunder jolted the house.

Forget Dr. Kendrick, I told myself. *Think about Chuck. What did he do? What did he become?*

Of course, I had no answer to those questions—not yet. There was only my—*our*—conjecture that he'd become a cold-blooded killer. I thought again about going to the authorities. But what did we have besides our conjecture? We knew Chuck had participated in the drug experiments. We knew his first wife, Dr. Kendrick's daughter, had disappeared without a trace. We knew the police investigation had absolved Chuck of any involvement in her disappearance—or at least had been unable to prove any involvement. We knew my mother had suspected him of killing my father. We knew he had been abusive toward women, at least toward my mother. And we knew he'd recently been to Minneapolis during the same time frame when yet another liberal academic had been murdered.

I'd been making a list on the computer of the things we knew, but now I stopped and read what I'd written. It was laughable in terms of legal proof, much less logical assumptions. I leaned back in the chair, clasped my hands on top of my head, and closed my eyes, letting the sounds of the storm outside clear my mind.

Then a thought came to me: *Augusto Pinochet.* For my family, this had all presumably started with Pinochet and the novel my father had written. Mother's theory had been that Pinochet, through Manuel Contreras, had ordered my father assassinated. For all the other theories about Chuck to pan out, absent some bizarre and cruel coincidence, we somehow needed to determine if there was any connection between Chuck and Pinochet and, ultimately, my father.

—39—

Augusto Pinochet was indicted for human rights violations in Chile in October of 1998. He'd already fled to Great Britain, where he was the darling of the conservative set. Even after he was arrested, six days after his indictment in Chile, he was only confined to house arrest. Margaret Thatcher, former prime minister of the U.K., occasionally stopped by to have tea with him.

How awfully civilized compared to how Pinochet had treated my father and the thousands of others he'd had arrested.

The British ultimately released Pinochet, and he returned to Chile on March 3, 2000. Below is a passage from a news report at the time:

> *Former Chilean dictator General Augusto Pinochet will not be extradited on torture charges and is free to leave the U.K., Home Secretary Jack Straw has decided.*
>
> *Mr. Straw believes the general is medically unable to stand trial in England.*
>
> *General Pinochet slipped out of the Wentworth estate, Surrey—where he has been under house arrest— in a convoy under police escort just before 10:00 GMT, avoiding angry protesters and media.*
>
> *His motorcade has arrived at RAF Waddington, Lincolnshire, where a Chilean Air Force Boeing 707 is waiting on the runway to take him and his entourage home.*

The following 2004 BBC account shows the reaction of Pinochet's oldest daughter to the Chilean government's report on his tortures and detentions:

The eldest daughter of Chile's former military ruler has said the use of torture during his 1973–90 regime was "barbaric and without justification."

Lucía Pinochet Hiriart spoke after a report on torture and detention during the rule of Gen Augusto Pinochet was submitted to the president.

The report has not yet been published, but it is said to detail horrific and degrading treatment of detainees.

"I knew there were detentions . . . but nothing like this," said Ms. Pinochet.

Last year, Ms. Pinochet complained that history had been distorted and her father was demonized while the man he overthrew, Salvador Allende, was depicted as a saint.

Despite being determined too ill to stand trial in Britain, Augusto Pinochet lived until December 10, 2006. Below are excerpts from a *New York Times* article, published on December 11, 2006:

Santiago, Chile, Dec. 10—Thousands of demonstrators took to the streets in celebration here on Sunday almost immediately after news circulated of the death of the former dictator Gen. Augusto Pinochet. But within hours the revelry was marred by violence, with confrontations breaking out and the police using tear gas and water cannons against a large group marching toward the presidential palace . . . .

The government called for calm on Sunday night. "We call on the detractors and supporters, if they're going to demonstrate to do it peacefully. And for this, we've deployed a major security force," said Felipe Harboe, the Undersecretary of the Interior.

*After General Pinochet's death, at 2:15 p.m.,
President Michelle Bachelet met briefly with cabinet
ministers and then released a terse announcement
through her spokesman, Ricardo Lagos Weber, covering
only funeral and memorial considerations with no
other comment. Mr. Lagos said that General Pinochet
would not receive a state funeral, but would receive
military honors. The president authorized flags to fly at
half-mast at military installations, but did not decree a
period of national mourning . . . .*

*A few hundred mourners gathered in front of the
hospital Sunday afternoon, with some weeping or
chanting, "Viva Pinochet!"*

*"Pinochet rescued and transformed Chile into the
country we all feel proud of," Hernán Guillof, president
of the Pinochet Foundation, said to a group outside the
hospital. "Once passions subside, he will be given his
place in history as architect of our nation."*

*But many more focused instead on the brutality and
terror of General Pinochet's 17-year rule, in which
more than 3,200 people disappeared or were killed and
tens of thousands were detained, tortured or exiled.*

*Some rights advocates said they had mixed feelings
about General Pinochet's death. Hiram Villagra, the
prosecuting attorney in dozens of human rights cases
against the general, said he would have preferred that
he lived long enough to be sentenced in the trials he
was facing.*

*"The air will feel lighter tomorrow, we will feel a
sense of liberation," Mr. Villagra said. "But I lament
that Pinochet has died without having been sentenced.
However, in all serious charges against him, he has had
his immunity lifted and has been indicted. Pinochet
does not die an innocent man."*

The following passage, taken from the same article, really stuck in my throat:

> *A spokesman for the White House, Tony Fratto, said:*
> *"Augusto Pinochet's dictatorship in Chile represented*
> *one of the most difficult periods in that nation's history.*
> *Our thoughts today are with the victims of his reign*
> *and their families."*

How hard would it have been to say that the United States regretted the role it played in bringing Pinochet to power and in providing covert support in the form of monetary aid and CIA expertise to his brutal regime? But then I guess we'd end up having to apologize for the roles our country played in Panama, Nicaragua, Iran, Iraq, Saudi Arabia, Vietnam, and everywhere else in the world where we've supported totalitarian states and crazy dictators.

I got up from my computer and stretched. I had an idea and went upstairs to find the box in which much of my father's personal effects were kept. I found his address book near the top and flipped to the letter *M*. There it was: a Chilean phone number for Nikolai Muñoz. Nicky, as my dad had called him, was a distant cousin. He had been an up-and-coming prosecutor before being arrested and jailed for refusing to prosecute several anti-Pinochet demonstrators, who had not broken the law other than to speak out against the dictator.

Nicky spent over a year in jail. When he was released, he was allowed to practice law in private practice so long as he did not engage in any political activity. He had come to Santa Fe on a couple of occasions to visit with Dad. I remembered him as a soft, corpulent man with a formal Van Dyke beard and piercing green eyes.

Nicky had gotten his revenge after Pinochet was arrested and Nicky was appointed to the prosecuting team. He'd been instrumental in compiling the long list of abuses, outrages, and crimes attributed to Pinochet's reign. I was certain that if anyone in Chile could help me—or at least steer me in the right direction—it would be him.

When I got the housekeeper to hand the phone over to Señora Muñoz, I explained who I was.

She screamed with excitement. "*El hijo del gran Señor Muñoz!*" She explained that her husband was now a judge and was at his office at the courthouse. She gave me his number. "*Venir al Santiago para visitar,*" she said before saying good-bye.

I assured her I would come visit one day. Then I called Judge Muñoz. Thankfully, he spoke English much better than I spoke Spanish.

"Ah, yes, Will. I remember you." His voice was deep and authoritative, which made sense, I guess, considering he spent his days issuing rulings from on high. "Of course, you were so young then." He sighed audibly. "Those were such happy times for your father and mother."

We worked our way through the formalities while slowly approaching the reason for my call. When I realized we'd reached that point, I explained how my mother had always believed Dad had been assassinated on orders of Pinochet. I mentioned *The Daughters of Pinochet.*

Nicky snorted a laugh. "Ah, yes, I heard all about that book. It was the worst-kept secret in Santiago. I heard Pinochet was apoplectic over it."

I told Nicky that I hadn't planned on doing anything further about Dad's death but that certain things had begun to make me suspicious—and make Mother seem not so crazy.

"I understand this may sound farfetched, and maybe even a little mental to you," I said in an apologetic tone, "but please try to bear with me."

Nicky grunted his approval to continue.

So I talked about Chuck Evans and how he'd beaten my mother. I talked about the two threatening notes my mother had received. I talked about how Chuck had repeatedly alluded to being her protector, even as he had continued to beat her. I explained that he was some sort of security consultant and in partnership with Milton Fischer, who'd been with the CIA in the '60s and into the '70s. And finally, I explained that Chuck had been involved in a CIA-sponsored drug experimentation program in Los Angeles.

"Ah, yes, I remember hearing something about those programs. The CIA later tried to cover them up, correct?"

"Yes," I said. "But they missed a bunch of paperwork that confirmed the programs and the funding by the CIA. There was a whole congressional report, the Church report, which chronicled the illegal program."

Nicky exhaled heavily. "The CIA," he said derisively. "Didn't I hear that one of the goals of the experiments was to see if they could turn ordinary people into killing machines?"

"Maybe," I said. "Although I talked to one of the doctors involved in the program, and he claims he was searching for the exact opposite."

Nicky snorted again. "Right."

"So," I said, trying to get back on track, "we—that is, my investigator and I—are trying to find out if there was any connection between Fischer and Pinochet's government." I paused, assuming I would be interrupted with a dismissal, but when Nicky said nothing, I continued. "If Pinochet was as upset about my dad's book as you and everyone says, and if he thought nothing about using violence to solve problems, and if he was already in bed with the CIA, wouldn't it make sense that, if he wanted to kill someone in the States, he'd use the CIA or an ex-CIA operative?"

There was silence on the line when I finished, but I could hear Nicky breathing, so I knew he was still there. I let him think.

"And so," Nicky said slowly, "you think this CIA fellow might have been in contact with Pinochet's people and was your stepfather's controller?"

As I listened to Nicky, I realized how absurd the whole scenario sounded. "Does it seem absolutely crazy?" I asked.

Nicky laughed. "My young friend, if you had lived through what I've lived through here in Chile, you would not ask that question. Our Chilean people will suffer the scars of your CIA atrocities for many years to come." The anger in his voice was palpable. "I don't know if there would ever have been a *Presidente* Pinochet if it hadn't been for the CIA. And so long as Pinochet and Contreras, who we know was on the CIA's payroll, continued to make communist and left-wing activists disappear, the American government continued to be grateful and cooperative."

Nicky paused to take a couple of deep breaths. When he spoke again, the calm judicial demeanor had returned. "I know for a fact your father was on Pinochet's enemy list. I have seen such a list with my own eyes."

I could tell Nicky was thinking out loud, playing through the process. Since I was no help whatsoever, I said nothing, even when he'd stopped talking. The silence lasted almost a full minute.

"I think that your father might have been on Pinochet's hit list well before Pinochet heard about *The Daughters of Pinochet*."

His remark took me by surprise. I'd been operating under the assumption that whatever link there was between Pinochet and Dad's murder stemmed from the novel.

"Why?" I asked. "I thought Dad's relocation to the U.S. would have appeased Pinochet."

I thought I heard Nicky sigh. "Have you ever heard of Orlando Letelier?"

"No. Who is he?"

"He *was* a high-ranking member of Allende's cabinet. He served as ambassador to the United States, foreign minister, minister of interior, and minister of defense. After the coup on September 11, 1973, Letelier was the first of Allende's cabinet to be arrested. Long story short, after being imprisoned and tortured and eventually released and ordered to leave Chile, he ended up in Washington, D.C., where he was a strong activist against the Pinochet regime."

Nicky paused, and it sounded like he covered the mouthpiece while talking to someone close by, presumably one of his staff. Then he was back.

"In the spring of 1976, I heard Letelier had visited your father in Santa Fe. I don't know any details, but you can rest assured that Pinochet heard about it. According to a statement made in court by Manuel Contreras in . . . let's see, it would have been 2005 . . . a former CIA deputy director by the name of Vernon Walters told Pinochet that Letelier was preparing a Chilean government while in exile. According to Contreras, Pinochet himself gave the order to have Letelier assassinated. When we hang up, do an internet search for Michael Vernon Townley. He was the American assassin of Letelier."

"How does that relate to my father?" I asked.

"If Pinochet thought your father was working with Letelier and his people to overthrow the regime, it would make sense your father would end up on a hit list, as well."

I thought about what Nicky had said. "But didn't you say that this Letelier guy was killed in 1976? That was twelve years before my father was murdered."

"True, but your father continued to write articles in opposition to Pinochet. I think it's also possible that Pinochet might have been so angered by your father's book that it was the proverbial last straw. Everything else aside, he certainly would have wanted to stop the publication of *Daughters*."

"Which he did," I interjected.

"Yes, but not forever. Your mother could have published it. Now you could . . . if you wanted to."

"Thus the scary letters to Mom," I said.

Nicky agreed to see what he could come up with. He had a law clerk named Ernesto, whom he trusted and who was a veritable bulldog when it came to research. He said he'd put Ernesto to work digging through some files. In the meantime, Nicky himself would ask around.

I asked for the name and spelling of the assassin I was supposed to google and wrote it down.

Nicky said he'd try to get back to me by next week.

—40—

After talking to Nicky, I googled the assassin he had mentioned. I learned the following:

Michael Vernon Townley was born in Iowa in 1942. His father moved the family to Santiago de Chile when he was appointed to head up Ford Motor Company in Chile. The elder Townley had already established a relationship with the CIA when he'd been in the Philippines and soon became involved in Chilean politics. Michael, meanwhile, married a Chilean woman named Mariana Callejas, who was an informer against the Marxists for the Chilean military intelligence. Michael himself had contact with the CIA, but I was unable to determine if he was in the actual employ of the "The Company."

In 1967, Michael Townley moved to Miami, where he hooked up with several former CIA operatives with links to the Cuban Nationalist Movement known as CNM. He subsequently became an electronics expert and planted bombs under cars of targets in the Miami area. He became, in other words, an assassin.

In 1969, the CIA sent Townley back to Chile under the alias Kenneth W. Enyart, where he allegedly became an operative of one David Atlee Phillips, a career CIA man. Their mission was to prevent the election of Salvador Allende. They failed, and Allende, a Marxist, became the president of Chile (the first democratically elected Marxist anywhere).

But the CIA, being the CIA, didn't take defeat lightly. Phillips, Townley, and others worked toward the overthrow of Allende's government. Chile's chief of staff, General René Schneider, refused to assist the CIA in a coup against Allende, and in October of 1970, his car was ambushed and he was shot and killed.

Chilean courts later found that he was assassinated by groups that were allegedly receiving support from the CIA.

Meanwhile, our boy Townley was said to be instrumental in causing the resignation of General Carlos Prats, the head of the Chilean army. You can probably guess which general replaced him. Yes, it was Augusto Pinochet. That happened on August 21, 1973. Just a few weeks later, on September 11, a military coup resulted in the death of Salvador Allende and the takeover of his government. Pinochet became the not-so-democratically-elected president of Chile.

Michael Townley went to work for General Juan Manuel Contreras, the head of DINA, the new secret police. One of Townley's early victims appears to have been General Prats, who was then living in Argentina and writing his memoirs. On September 30, 1974, Townley and a team of assassins allegedly murdered Prats and his wife by way of a car bomb, Townley's specialty.

In September of 1975, former Chilean Vice President Bernardo Leighton and his wife were gunned down in Rome. A month later, my father left Chile and obtained asylum in the United States. A month after that, leaders of the military intelligence services of Chile, Argentina, Bolivia, Paraguay, and Uruguay met with Manuel Contreras in Santiago de Chile. The objective of the meeting was to coordinate the actions of the security services to eliminate Marxist revolution in the area. Operation Condor was born and was given tacit approval and support from the United States, ever fearful of a region-wide Marxist revolution. Operation Condor targeted and assassinated lefties. Michael Townley was said to be involved with the organization.

On September 18, 1976, Orlando Letelier and a twenty-five-year-old woman named Ronni Moffit were killed in a car bomb in Washington, D.C. Moffit and her husband were campaigning for a democratic Chile. The husband survived the bomb.

At that time, the director of the CIA was George H. W. Bush. According to what I'd read, he was immediately told that DINA and its agents were Letelier's assassins. However, the CIA leaked to their people in the press, including William F. Buckley, that the CIA had concluded the Chilean secret police had nothing to do with Letelier's death.

*   *   *

My head spun as I read through everything I could find about Pinochet, Contreras, Townley, Operation Condor, and the CIA's role in everything. I assumed these people, like Dr. Kendrick, didn't think of themselves as evil. They had probably rationalized every insane and awful decision as being necessary to protect the integrity of . . . not Marxism. I needed some of Dr. Kendrick's good LSD just to wrap my head around this shit.

Oh, and by the way, just in case you think it was conjecture that Townley—and thus DINA—had a hand in Letelier's assassination, Townley later confessed that he'd hired five anti-Castro Cuban exiles to help booby-trap Letelier's car. He later entered into a plea bargain with the U.S. government, wherein he pleaded guilty to conspiracy to commit murder and was given a ten-year sentence. His wife testified in exchange for not being prosecuted. Michael Townley was freed after serving sixty-two months in prison and lives under the Witness Protection Program.

Your tax dollars at work.

41

By the time Travis got home, I had a serious headache. This Michael Townley character was living proof that a U.S.-born assassin had killed people inside and outside of the U.S. for Augusto Pinochet and the right-wing cause. If not in the actual employ of the CIA, he'd had CIA support at various times. This wasn't the movies; this was real-life shit. Was it much of a leap to think that Milton Fischer and Chuck Evans had played in the same muddy playground?

The day had cleared, and the ocean was once again pacific. There was a chill in the air, but we nonetheless took our newly opened beers and, appropriately bundled up, situated ourselves in the chaise lounges on the deck. It took me fifteen minutes and a bottle of beer to fill Travis in on my conversation with Nicky and what I'd found in my internet search of Michael Townley. Travis didn't have much to report. He'd found the marriage documentation for Chuck Evanovich and Kelly Kendrick and for Chuck Evans and my mother as well as the court-decreed death certificate of Kelly Evanovich and the divorce decree for my mother. There weren't any other marriages recorded for Evanovich/Evans in the state of California.

Neither one of us said anything for several minutes after we finished debriefing. I listened to the gulls and to the gentle lapping of the waves on the beach. A mongrel-looking dog without an owner in sight ran along the edge of the surf, occasionally barking at a gull. The gentle scene before us was far removed from the filth of the political intrigue I'd been immersed in all afternoon. Travis looked as tired as I felt. Rummaging around in public records could be mind-numbing work.

"So now we have another motive for the assassination of your father," Travis said. "If he was still involved with anti-Pinochet activists, particularly guys like this Letelier dude, then it wouldn't take a nasty novel for Pinochet to want to kill your pop."

I said nothing. A good-looking couple, both wearing tight skins to ward off the cold, jogged by. The dog barked at them and began to chase them but then got distracted by another gull. I thought about Cheryl.

"Let's head up to San Francisco tonight," I said, turning to look at Travis. "There's not much we can do until I hear back from Nicky, and we can give whatever direction to Al from anywhere."

Travis gave me a sideways look and then smiled. "Yeah, let's go see Cheryl."

*　　*　　*

We were in the city by dinner time and went straight from the airport to meet Cheryl at Capannina on Union Street. It was a chilly, breezy night, and she was wearing a red leather skirt, black tights, black boots, and a black cashmere turtleneck sweater. Cheryl looked magnificent, and after sharing a short kiss that sent shivers down my spine, we held each other for several long seconds before sitting. I knew for certain that the increased intensity of emotion I'd been feeling toward her had not been imagined. The cynical, perpetually melancholy side of me still wasn't willing to acknowledge that it was anything more than a transient surge in passion brought on by the heightened awareness of life and death. But there was no denying its existence.

We ordered a bottle of Barbera d'Alba and opened it to let it breathe while we sipped our respective martinis. Cheryl brought Travis and me up to speed on the office issues. She'd settled a couple more of my troublesome cases and was happy to see those clients out the door. Her big drug case was taking a lot of time—

so much time that she was thinking of bringing in co-counsel. We kicked around some names of the best litigators in town. There were a lot to choose from, but I suspected few were willing to play second fiddle.

"So," she said after we'd finished with the legal stuff and had ordered food, "what have you boys been up to?"

We spent most of the ensuing dinner bringing Cheryl up-to-date on what we'd learned.

She said little during the briefing, although her facial expressions implied a panoply of responses, including but not limited to "OMG," "WTF?" and the ever-popular "You're out of your fucking mind!"

When Travis and I were done with our storytelling, we ordered a tiramisu for the table and sipped the last of our second bottle of wine.

"The key is Fischer," Cheryl said after she'd swallowed her first bite of the dessert. "If you can connect him to any of those CIA and DINA people who worked in Chile, then I think it's pretty safe to conclude Fischer and Evans were involved in your dad's death."

I glanced at Travis, and we both nodded our agreement. As usual, Cheryl had cut to the chase. The odds of Nicky or his people finding direct evidence that Pinochet had ordered the assassination of my father were slim. But if they were to find any reference to a CIA man—or ex-CIA man—by the name of Milton Fischer having been in Chile during the time period in question, that would be a huge step toward connecting the dots.

"I'll call Nicky back tomorrow and ask him to have his people do a search for any reference to Milton Fischer," I said.

"Might as well include Chuck Evans while you're at it," Travis said.

We kicked around some other ideas for a while, but I was eager to be alone with Cheryl, and we called it a night as soon as the wine ran out. Since I hadn't been home yet and had my carry-on bag, Cheryl and I agreed to spend the night at her place. Travis headed off on his own. I doubted he was headed straight home.

*　　*　　*

Cheryl snuggled against me. She'd thrown one long, perfectly shaped leg across my legs. I had my left arm wrapped around her, so I could feel the softness of her breasts pressing against the side of my chest. I buried my face in her short dark hair and caught the familiar scent of her shampoo, which contained a trace of honey. Our lovemaking had been slow, gentle, and passionate.

"What's up with you, pards?" Her voice was muffled against my skin, and I could feel the warmth of her breath.

"What do you mean?" I asked, although I knew exactly what she meant.

"I don't know. You just seem so much more . . . *something*." She pulled her head away from my body so she could look at me. She smiled a sly, almost catlike smile. "You know perfectly well what I'm asking, because you know what you're feeling. So tell me, and don't make me find words that I'm not sure apply or, worse, that might come out wrong."

I moved to sit up a little, but in doing so, I threw the whole snuggle thing out of whack. She pulled her leg off me, and I withdrew my arm, which was starting to go to sleep anyway. We sat up side by side, and I took her right hand in my left. My mind raced as I tried to decide what to say.

"You know I love you," I began.

"Uh-oh," she said, interrupting me. "Sentences that begin like that usually come with a big 'but' attached to them."

I laughed, not letting go of her hand. "This one doesn't. What I want to say is that I've loved you ever since we got together. But I've always felt compelled to hold back, to not fully commit." I was struggling to find the right words.

"I know," Cheryl said tenderly. "You forget how well I know you. We've loved each other in the best way we knew how. I wouldn't have wanted to take more out of what you wanted from our love any more than I would have let you take more from me than I wanted—if that makes any sense."

"It does, and you're kind of letting me off the hook here, which I appreciate. But what I really want to say is that something's changed in me. I don't know, exactly. Maybe it's Mother's death. Maybe it's the separation from you. Maybe it's the horrible shit I've been digging up. But I've been missing you so much I actually ache. I've been feeling like I need and want you more than ever before." I let go of her hand and ran my hand through my hair. "I'm not saying it right. I don't know if I ever can." I paused to look at her, stroking her cheek with my fingers as I did. "Maybe I'm still scared—too scared to say how strongly I feel." I took my hand away. "I'm fucking this up, aren't I? I'm trying to explain how I don't understand how I could possibly love you more than I have, but I do."

Cheryl let loose a deep, throaty laugh that always made me smile. Then she climbed on top of me and looked me in the eyes. "Just shut up. I love you, and you love me. Plus, as an added bonus, ladies and gentlemen, we actually like and respect each other. So let's do what we want."

She was sitting on top of me now, and I was starting to get distracted by her breasts.

"Quit staring at my tits, and let's finish this conversation," she said in a mock-stern voice that wasn't quite as scary as the one she reserved for imitating a judge.

"You really want to keep listening to me blather?" I asked. I could see her nipples had grown hard.

"Oh, forget it," she said as she put me inside her.

42

Almost a month passed without anything significant happening on the investigative front. I wasn't doing much other than reading up on the Pinochet regime and on the MKULTRA project. Mostly I was waiting for Nicky to call or for Al Barker to come up with something.

Travis was deep into investigating a water diversion case in central California that had left one town completely out of water and two more towns on the verge of running out. The case was essentially a case of water piracy by a huge agribusiness. We—I mean *they*—represented the little guys, who were literally getting their water sucked out from under them. The aquifers were being depleted at an alarming rate. Cheryl explained to me that unconfined aquifers took years to replenish—that is, if they didn't collapse when the water was sucked dry, while confined aquifers, the deeper ones, could take hundreds to thousands of years to replenish. Central Valley farmers, who'd been using two-hundred-foot wells to irrigate their crops, were now drilling a thousand feet and more.

Once again I thought about the kind of world we'd created—and worse, the kind of world we'd chosen not to fix. Then I thought about how, in my not-too-distant-past, I might have been representing the big agribusiness.

Cheryl and I were living together. Although I preferred my house in Pacific Heights, we were staying in her luxury condo in the Millennium Tower and enjoying majestic views of the city, the bay, and AT&T Stadium. It was closer to her work, and I had to admit, it was nice to be able to walk to some of the city's best restaurants, one of which, Prospect, was in the building.

Since I pretty much wore blue jeans, loafers, and long-sleeved cotton shirts every day, I also had less to move in with than she would have had.

It was an amazingly smooth transition for me, considering I'd been living alone since college. Cheryl and I had spent so much time together already that we knew and respected each other's moods. She could discern when I needed cheering up and when I needed to be left alone. I quickly realized it had been my personal demons—and resulting melancholia—that had been one of the driving forces in my fear of personal commitment. I'd been afraid that my psychological issues would make me a high-maintenance partner—needy and weak—so I'd shied away from putting myself in that position. But in doing so I had grossly underestimated Cheryl. She already knew I was all fucked up and exactly how to handle me.

For her part, I was still looking for flaws. She was unperturbed if I needed time alone. She didn't get angry if I left the toilet seat up. If she wanted to do something I didn't want to do, she'd simply go and do it by herself or with a friend. When she got angry, it was usually about some antic her opposing counsel had pulled or some ridiculous ruling by a judge. I'd get her a glass of chardonnay and let her rant.

My routine was to get up and eat a light breakfast with Cheryl before she left for work. Then I'd mess around on the computer for a few hours, acting as if I was investigating Chuck Evans. But invariably I'd get sidetracked by something.

I was reading up on the Operation Condor assassination squads one morning when I ran across a tidbit about how Henry Kissinger's underlings at the State Department had drafted a démarche, a diplomatic policy statement. I figured the continued use of a word of French origin was a tip of the hat to the days when French had been the language of diplomacy.

Now fully diverted, I had to find out if there was evidence that Kissinger had known what was going on with our "friends" to the south. The démarche had basically instructed the U.S. ambassadors in the realm of Operation Condor to meet with their counterparts and express "our deep concern" about the "rumors" of assassinations. Although initially approved by Kissinger, that démarche was never sent, and the assassinations continued. In fact, the Letelier assassination occurred five days after Kissinger's decision not to send the démarche.

Argentina, of course, was not only a participant in Operation Condor, the numbers of dead and missing Argentinians during the reign of terror is said to run in the tens of thousands. Here is a record of a conversation Kissinger had on October 5, 1976 with Argentina's foreign minister:

> *Look, our basic attitude is that we would like you to succeed. I have an old-fashioned view that friends ought to be supported. What is not understood in the United States is that you have a civil war. We read about human rights problems but not the context. The quicker you succeed the better . . . . The human rights problem is a growing one. Your Ambassador can apprise you. We want a stable situation. We won't cause you unnecessary difficulties. If you can finish before Congress gets back, the better. Whatever freedoms you could restore would help.*

Here's how I read that quote: "We want you to win, so kill as many left-wing subversives as fast as you can. It'd be best if you got it done before Congress gets back so we don't have to deal with all those pesky human rights issues. Oh, and it would be great if you can make it look as if you're restoring some appearance of freedom."

What more is there to say?

*   *   *

When I wasn't "researching," I would go for long walks, usually along the Embarcadero. The Indian summer days were a thing of the past, and the weather had turned dreary and cold. I bundled up and walked for miles, enjoying the city in a way I hadn't done since we were college kids at Berkeley. When Cheryl and/or Travis had the time, I'd meet them for lunch, usually in a South of Market restaurant close to their office. They'd talk about cases, and I'd often give my two cents, but I didn't miss work at all.

Sometimes it scared me how happy I felt. In fact, I'd been thinking that very thought when my cell phone rang. It was Nicky.

—43—

"Sorry I took so long getting back to you, Will," Nicky said. "But after you gave me the names to check on, I figured I'd wait until I had as much as possible to report."

"No problem," I said. "It's been kind of nice not thinking too much about it for a while." I felt a tightening in my gut. I had no idea what to expect. "So what did you find?"

"One sec."

I heard Nicky speak rapid-fire Spanish in what I took to be a harsh tone.

"Sorry," he said to me. "One of my clerks has been a little too interested in why I put Ernesto to work on this project. Just now I noticed her lurking outside the door to my chambers." I heard him sigh. "Even now there are many in Chile who think fondly of Pinochet, or at least think we should let sleeping dogs lie. Anyway," he continued, "I have confirmed as best I can that your dad was targeted for assassination by Pinochet."

I gasped—and realized I hadn't been breathing. I didn't trust myself to speak, so I just waited for Nicky to continue.

"I spoke directly with one of Contreras's confidants," he said. "There aren't many still alive. Anyway, your father had been on Pinochet's enemy list for many years, which your father knew and which is why he left Chile. But this fellow didn't know of any direct order to assassinate your father until after Pinochet somehow got and read your father's book. According to my source, Pinochet ranted and raved to Contreras and then gave a direct order to have Ricardo Muñoz killed." Nicky breathed heavily. "In fact, in 2005, when Contreras was on trial for the murder of Letelier—I assume you read up on him?"

"Yeah."

"Well, during that trial Contreras sang like a bird and gave up all sorts of names of people he'd known to have been on assassination lists. There were hundreds. After talking to my contact, I dug around and found that your father's name was among those Contreras named."

I felt a chill go up my spine. How strange it was to hear, quite matter-of-factly, that a president of a country had specifically ordered my father to be killed.

"Did your contact know who killed my father?" I asked in a voice I barely recognized as my own.

"No," Nicky said, "but I had Ernesto go back through records, starting from 1980 and up to '88—"

"The year my father was murdered," I whispered.

"Precisely," Nicky answered. "Anyway, he looked through archives documenting visits to Contreras's office and to Pinochet. He even found some DINA notes detailing the comings and goings at the American embassy." Nicky snickered. "Paranoia knows no boundaries. Long story short, Milton Fischer showed up in Chile in 1987, supposedly as an American businessman. Oil, I think it was. He'd been noted by DINA's people in immigration as entering the country under the name Oscar Gillespie, and on that same day, he visited your embassy. We don't know who he met with that day, but someone in DINA identified him as Milton Fischer, formerly of the CIA. The next day he supposedly had a meeting with our minister of energy but met instead with Contreras himself. The meeting lasted less than half an hour. There are no minutes of the meeting, and my contact was not present."

I was silent for a good ten seconds after Nicky stopped talking. I didn't know what to say. He'd just essentially proven—to me at least—that Chuck Evans, through Milton Fischer, had carried out a hit on my father at the order of Augusto Pinochet. My poor, scared, and supposedly deranged mother had been right all along.

Finally, the lawyer in me kicked in. "Do we have any kind of documentation I can use?"

Nicky sighed audibly. "I don't know yet. I had to pull some strings with my old friends at the Department of Justice to get Ernesto access to those documents. They aren't public record. I'm going through channels now to see what I can get copies of." He chuckled again. "I tend to doubt that the DINA records of spying on the American embassy will be declassified."

I realized just how far Nicky had stuck his neck out for me, how he must have loved my father.

"I can't thank you enough," I said. "Regardless of what I'll ever be able to prove, it means a lot to me to know how right my mother was. I'm going to have to figure out how to process the fact that we lived with the man who probably murdered my father. It's one thing to be a paid assassin but quite another to marry the widow of your victim."

"I understand, my friend. It's hard to fathom. Unfortunately, I've seen enough sociopathic human behavior that it sometimes seems like all elements of shock and surprise have been eradicated from my psyche." He paused for a moment. "Look, Will, I've got to get to court now. I'll keep trying to get documentary proof, and I'll tell Ernesto to keep digging when he has the time. He had a great time working on this. I think it was a good history lesson for him. I'm glad I was of some help. Keep in touch."

With that, Nicky was gone.

I hung up the phone and sat dumbly at the desk in Cheryl's posh condo.

"My God," I said out loud.

—44—

I sat in the stillness of Cheryl's condo for a long time. Just thinking. The abstraction of my mother's suspicions and even my so-called investigation had been just that: an abstraction. Suddenly it was real. Chuck Evans' mentor, controller, and partner had been to Chile the year before my father was murdered and had met with Manuel Contreras. The question now, of course, was what to do with this information.

I have many flaws—too many to enumerate—although you, dear reader, have been made privy to some. As I've said, I have some anger issues, but I've learned to control them quite well. That's probably because most of my anger stems from the death of my father at the hands of someone whose identity I thought I would never know—someone who took my father away from me at the most vulnerable time in a young man's life. So my anger has always been diffused and thus diluted. Yes, I'd disliked Chuck—maybe even hated him—but that had always been tempered by the fact that my mother had chosen to be with him. I had tried to like him but had simply been unable. Okay, maybe I had never really tried very hard, but that was irrelevant. When my mother had finally thrown him out of the house, I'd been pleased, but after that I hadn't given Chuck a second thought. He was gone from our lives, and that was good enough.

Now, however, I felt a kind of hatred that was completely new to me. It was a scary, burning kind of hate. I looked down at my hands and saw that they were clenched tightly into fists, as if I were ready to do battle. I could feel the blood pulse in my skull. It shocked me to realize that if Chuck and Milton were here with me now, I could kill them.

I forced myself to breathe deeply. Gradually, slowly, I felt my-self begin to relax. I wondered if everyone had such a capacity for hatred lurking inside them. We tend to write off murderers and evildoers as psychological aberrations, yet over and over again the world has seen regular people commit genocide, murder po-litical and religious opposition, and even kill their own spouses and children. Is anyone capable of murder? Was I?

I finally decided to go for a walk. I needed to try to clear my head, calm myself. I needed to know what I wanted to do with the information I now had. It was predictably cold and windy outside, and the Embarcadero was almost deserted as I strolled, head bent into the wind.

In terms of evidence, I had nothing new. I tried to picture a conversation with the authorities. Perhaps the method of execu-tion of my father and the liberals on my list would be enough to generate interest and investigation. Perhaps not. The liberal con-nection was tenuous at best. There was no other commonality among them; not even their professions were the same. Home invasions or burglaries gone bad were commonplace; people were shot from behind all the time.

In my windblown mind I could hear Cheryl telling me to turn my information over to the FBI and be done with it. I'd done the best I could do with my limited resources. And maybe she'd be right. Hell, probably she'd be right. Travis was, to my mind, less predictable. He had agreed with me the last time the three of us had entertained the turn-it-over-to-the-cops discussion, but would he still be in favor of our quasi-vigilantism? I thought his position might hinge on whether he'd be intimately involved with any continued investigation or whether he'd be stuck in the of-fice—on the inside looking out, as it were.

The cold was finally getting to me, and I ducked into the Ferry Building and into the Waterbar. The pre-lunch quiet was pleas-ant, and the bartender, a beautiful thirty-something Asian woman, was obsequiously attentive. I ordered a Don Julio Silver on the rocks in a voice I hoped was dismissive without being rude. The smooth, earthy, familiar tequila tasted good, and I resisted the temptation to shoot it all at once.

Sitting alone at the bar, I realized the problem I was having was one of closure, which, frankly, was surprising to me. I'd never been a big fan of the concept when there was nothing one could do to change past events. A victim's family praying that the murderer would be executed so they could have closure seemed so pointless and illusory to me. A family of a plane-crash victim hoping the body of their loved one would be recovered so they could have closure seemed sadly impotent to me. So here I was, thinking about what it would mean to me to have closure when it came to the death of my father. Was I playing the role of the victim's sad, pathetic family? Did I want something that would change nothing?

No, I told myself, there was a huge difference between the concepts of closure and justice. Despite my wayward, hypocritical lawyering and heretofore lack of political agenda, I believed in justice. And I especially believed in justice where injustice would otherwise continue. If Chuck Evans and Milton Fischer were not brought to justice for their crimes, whether against my family or others, they would continue to kill. That, I concluded, would be neither closure nor justice.

*   *   *

I made my arguments for continued investigation to Cheryl and Travis that evening over cocktails after I'd filled them in on my conversation with Nicky. We were in the bar at Prospect, downstairs from Cheryl's condo.

Cheryl's rebuttal was predictable and cogent. We were dealing with murderers who would think nothing of killing anyone who got in their way. Either they were still killing on their own, or they were working for someone on a contract basis. Either way, it was too dangerous for me to go it on my own.

I took a sip of the Malbec I'd ordered and smiled at her. "You'd be one hundred percent correct if what I could turn over to the cops was enough to cause them to open an investigation. But I don't think it is. We've got hearsay out of Chile that Fischer was there and that my father was on Pinochet's hit list. We've got some semblance of connectivity in a handful of murders occurring over a couple of decades."

"But that's the point," Cheryl said. "Give it to the cops and let them connect the dots. They're the ones with the power to do that. You're too limited in what you can do. How the hell do you think you can prove Fischer went to Chile to get a contract to murder your father? He wasn't even with the CIA anymore at that point."

She exhaled, clearly frustrated. "How do you connect Chuck or Fischer to those liberals you think they murdered? There won't be any personal connection to them if you're right and they were assassinations. Maybe you can find enough circumstantial evidence that Chuck was in the cities where the murders took place on the dates that they took place, but that ain't gonna be easy."

"What if," Travis said, "we could prove Chuck was in all those cities on those dates? Would that be enough to get the feds interested?"

Cheryl and I both looked at him.

"How you gonna do that?" I asked. "I already talked to Al about that. Passenger manifests are confidential. Hotel registrations are confidential. Credit card charges are confidential." I shook my head. "I've been racking my brain trying to think of a legal way to get that information."

Travis smiled and sipped his Tito's rocks.

Cheryl aborted the sip of wine she'd been about to take. "Oh, no. No, no, no." Her voice was firm and edgy. "We're lawyers, Will." She pointed a finger at Travis. "You *work* for lawyers. We are obligated to follow the law. I will not stand by while you risk destroying everything we've built so you can pursue some personal vendetta." Her eyes were huge, and her face was flushed with anger. She looked beautiful.

I held up both hands. "First of all," I said in as calming a voice as I could muster, "this isn't just some personal vendetta. If we're correct, these men are serial killers."

Cheryl started to say something, but I held up my hands again. "Wait. Second of all, no one said anything about doing anything illegal. We just acknowledged that so far, we can't think of how to get the information we need legally."

Travis had been watching our exchange with one of his patented shit-eating grins. Cheryl and I turned in unison toward him, and when he saw our expressions, he stopped grinning and assumed a serious countenance. He looked like a child trying to appear contrite, and Cheryl and I cracked up at the same time. The tension was alleviated.

"Well, okay then," she said. "I just don't want to have to worry about you children."

After Cheryl left for work the next morning, I called Alvin Barker in Las Vegas and filled him in on what I'd learned from Nicky.

"Wow," he said when I was finished. "This is some serious shit."

"So what have you been up to? Anything new on your end?"

"Not much," he said. "I put Billy on surveillance of the town-house every once in a while, but it's too random to do much good. I was just hoping to stumble onto something unusual. Mostly the guys hang around the house during the day and then go out to dinner. Maybe some gambling at night. No more trips that I've been able to tell." He paused and said, "Hand me that notebook," to someone, probably Billy. "I'm on the track of another fellow who went to school with Evans," he said to me. "It's a guy who was involved in the white supremacist group with him. He would know what Evans was like during his junior year, before he got married and took off. But I'm having a hard time getting to him. He's apparently still into that racist stuff, only now he's one of those survivalist types, as well. He's living somewhere in Idaho. I've been trying to get a message to him to contact me."

"That could be interesting," I said.

Barker coughed right into his mouthpiece, and I involuntarily cringed. "Yeah, well, I don't know if it'll happen," he said, "but I'll keep trying. In the meantime, anymore ideas?"

"Not unless you can figure out how to legally determine if Evans was in those cities on those dates I gave you," I said.

He was quiet, and I could hear Cheryl's voice in my head.

"Al," I said, "don't do anything illegal. I mean it. I don't want to get disbarred."

He grunted what I took to be his acknowledgment, and we hung up.

I sat still a moment, looking out at the bay on a clear, chilly day, and wondered if I should have left the legal niceties more ambiguous.

*   *   *

Three days later, after nothing new, I was lounging around in the living room of Cheryl's condo in jeans, a long-sleeved T-shirt, and moccasins. The television was on and tuned to PBS, but mostly I was swiping through *Huffington Post* stories on my iPad—until something being said on television pierced my brain. I turned toward the TV and saw a talk-show interview setup with desk and chair. The guest was a middle-aged man with a full head of gray hair. The show host behind the desk, also male, had slicked-back black hair and a fake-looking tan. I turned up the volume.

". . . have to admit your book is going to be seen as inflammatory from pretty much every side of the political and social spectrum," the interviewer said.

His guest, who was wearing pressed khaki pants, a blue work shirt, and a professorial corduroy jacket, complete with leather patches at the elbows, wrinkled his brow and shrugged. His body language suggested disagreement, but his eyes and his mouth were smiling. "Maybe," he said, "but frankly, I don't care."

He sat forward, leaning in toward his interviewer in an obvious display of intensity.

"Look, we tiptoe around the subject of race in this country like we're too immature to have an adult conversation. As a white man, there's no way I can pretend to know how it feels to be black or Latino, but I am able to look at socioeconomic factors and work toward developing some level of understanding and empathy. But that's exactly what we as a society seem to shy away from doing.

"Whenever Barack Obama comments on any issue dealing with race, the right cries, 'Race card!' "

The author shook his head in a gesture of wonderment and sat back in his chair.

"Yet who's more competent to comment on issues of race than our first black president?

"A city could be burning to the ground because of race riots, and if Obama uttered so much as one word that could be construed as being conciliatory to the demonstrators or their cause, he would be vilified. The new racism in America is the right's pretend game that there is no racism except for whenever Obama or Eric Holder speak out against racism, which the right then claims fans the flames of racial divide. Meanwhile, Republican legislatures around the country are passing some of the most restrictive voter registration laws this country has seen since the Jim Crow days."

The camera zoomed in for a close-up of the guest, and I could see the intensity in his blue eyes. From the confident, authoritative way he was speaking, I assumed he was an academic of some sort. A caption at the bottom of the screen identified him as Mark Greenberg, author of *The Rise and Fall of America*. But it also read: 1956–2017. The guest was dead. This was obviously an old interview being shown in some sort of tribute to his passing.

"We've got some black celebrities," Greenberg continued, "who come out and condemn the blacks in the ghettos for acting like hoodlums, gangsters. When that happens, the statements of the black celebrities are sent around the right-wing internet at the speed of lightening. 'See,' the conservatives say, 'even the black men who work hard and make it are saying their brothers in the projects are bums. They do drugs, and they kill, and they live off welfare. They're forced to act as mean as possible. Otherwise, they face being condemned by their fellow gangsters as not being black enough. Just look at all the looting that goes on when a demonstration turns into a riot,' these people say. 'They're making their own race look bad by the way they act.' "

The interviewer looked as if he was about to interject something, but Greenberg held up a hand to indicate he wasn't finished.

"The point I'm making is that these guys who aren't acting the way we want them to, these guys we see looting on camera, these guys who get into gang fights and kill each other—they aren't thinking about whether they're embarrassing their race, their fellow black men, or their fellow Latinos anymore than the white idiots who riot and burn cars and loot stores because they won a football game are thinking about whether they are embarrassing the white race.

"These guys don't give a damn what you or I—or even some famous black athlete—think of them. They know perfectly well we don't give a damn about them, so why in the world should they worry about what we think? It's not like anything would change if they didn't loot or do drugs or fight. Our society has created their world for them. We have put them into communities where hopelessness and unemployment go hand in hand. We send them to schools that don't educate, that can't educate under those circumstances."

Greenberg looked as if he knew he was rapidly running out of time.

"The point is we've created these segregated compounds in our inner cities and even in some rural areas, where blacks and Latinos are nothing more than third-class citizens who know they're not respected and are not cared about and who, in turn, simply don't give a crap about what the rest of us think. Yet they're the ones who are supposed to pull themselves out of their situation. If only they would work hard and not rely on welfare or food stamps or give in to the only temptations offered them that would afford some relief from their abject poverty, then they could become anything they want to become, because, after all, this is America and we elected a black president."

"So," the interviewer said, "you're basically an apologist for all the bad actors in the inner cities. You're—"

"Jesus Christ, no!" Greenberg leaned forward again, and this time there was an edge to his voice. "You're missing the point entirely. It's not a question of being an apologist. It's a question of understanding so that we can effect change. It's wonderful when some lone wolf—maybe with a unique talent, with a strong family support group—is able to break out and achieve some semblance of the so-called American dream. But the odds are so stacked against that happening it's downright criminal. We—you and I and our forefathers—created this scenario. We did it. But we blame the blacks or the Latinos who can't fight their way out. It's not apologizing, although we damn well should apologize. It's *acknowledging*. It's *understanding*.

The liberals in this country have become so cowed by the label 'liberal' that they've abandoned their basic ideals. Government really is capable of helping people. Government can begin to undo these segregated outposts of poverty and hopelessness. We need—"

"Dr. Greenberg, I'm so sorry to interrupt, but we're almost out of time. Before we go, however, I want to ask you about a chapter in your book that you dedicated to essentially demonizing Larry and Joseph Carson, the billionaires who invest so much money in conservative causes. Why them, when there are a number of other billionaires who are doing the same thing on both sides?"

The camera zoomed in, revealing another close-up of Greenberg, whose eyes seemed to sparkle with humor.

"The Carson brothers have distinguished themselves from their fellow oligarch wannabes. They're a couple of hateful, greedy, manipulative racists whose conservative agenda is far, far to the right of the mainstream Republican Party. Their father, Peter Carson, was a full-fledged member of the KKK back in his home state of Alabama. He was among the founding members of the John Birch Society. When his sons inherited their immense wealth from their father, it was soon clear they had also inherited his politics."

Greenberg stopped and gave the camera a wry smile.

"That chapter in my book lays out example after example of what they stand for: from the politicians they have sponsored to the causes they have supported to the business decisions they have made, which in one way or another were racist or antigay or anti-immigration or just plain anti-poor."

The television screen faded to black, and then the same interviewer, wearing different clothes and alone behind his desk, appeared on the screen, a sad look on his face.

"That was my 2014 interview with Dr. Mark Greenberg, the noted sociologist from the University of Chicago and author of the controversial book, *The Rise and Fall of America*. It's a fascinating look at how race plays such a pervasive role in American politics, economics, and social issues yet is largely ignored or, more accurately, *avoided* because it's too volatile an issue for people to address.

To recap, Dr. Greenberg was found murdered in his Chicago Columbus Circle apartment Tuesday. The police believe the doctor must have interrupted a burglary in progress and might have been trying to flee, since he was shot from the rear. Dr. Greenberg, a widower, is survived by his son, Matthew, who is thirty-four, and his daughter, Martha, who is thirty-one. Dr. Greenberg was fifty-eight years old."

I turned off the television. Another murder of a liberal academic. I picked up my iPad and typed Greenberg's name into my search engine. There were multiple hits. I clicked on the *Chicago Tribune* story about his death, which had occurred two days ago. There wasn't much more information other than an enumeration of his many academic accomplishments. *The Rise and Fall of America* had been his third book. As best I could tell, the overarching theme throughout his work was the ignorance of Americans, and in particular American politicians, when it came to the sociology of American culture. Greenberg had argued that as a general rule we don't make an effort to educate ourselves about other people. Without education and understanding, there can be no empathy. Instead, we listen to our preferred media of information and incorporate the messages we receive from that media into our personal belief system without ever having taken the time to investigate the facts or formulate opinions on our own. Hence the widespread belief that helping poor people buy food or pay their rent makes them so dependent that they have no desire to go to work and better their lives—a belief that multiple studies over the years have proven false.

I scanned the rest of the article, hoping to find more information on the murder itself, but concluded the police were withholding most of the details. I dropped the iPad to the couch and sat back. You know what I was thinking.

I called Alvin Barker and asked him if, by any chance, he'd had Billy watching the Evans/Fischer townhouse over the course of the past week. He hadn't. Then I asked him if his friend at Southwest could check to see if Chuck had traveled to Chicago again. Al said he couldn't do that. He'd already called in his one favor, and his buddy had made it clear he wouldn't risk his job any further.

—46—

All I had accomplished three days later was three more incredible lovemaking sessions with Cheryl; a visit to the de Young Museum, coupled with a long, cold walk through Golden Gate Park; a lengthy email to a friend of mine who I hoped, thanks to his father's ex-CIA status, might be able to advise me how to go about finding certain things; and a quick read of Donald Freed's *Death in Washington: The Murder of Orlando Letelier*.

I was just about to contact Captain Morrisey of the Santa Fe Sheriff's Office to ask if he thought there was enough to turn the investigation over to the FBI when Alvin Barker called.

"I'm meeting a man named Samuel P. Jones in Boise tomorrow," Barker said. "He's the guy I told you about who was in school with Evans—or Evanovich, I guess it was—and was involved with the white supremacists. It's been something of an ordeal getting him to meet. Apparently he's one of the leaders of a white supremacist, survivalist, antigovernment group that lives commune-style in northern Idaho. He wouldn't let me come to him, so we finally agreed to meet in Boise." Barker cleared his throat. "And, uh, I agreed to pay him a thousand bucks and cover his hotel room."

I chuckled. "I guess even antigovernment survivalists don't mind getting their mitts on some greenback now and then." I thought for a moment. "I want to come with you. I'll charter a plane and pick you up in Vegas, and then we can fly to Boise. I'll bring the grand in cash."

Barker was silent for a few seconds, no doubt debating whether he wanted me there. "Okay, but, Will?"

"What?"

"We need to come up with a different last name for you when I introduce you to Samuel P. Jones. He hates everyone who's not white, so I don't think introducing you as Will Muñoz would be a good start."

This time I snorted. "How about my mother's last name—Montrose? Nice and English-sounding."

"Good. And while you're at it, make yourself look as white as possible." Barker laughed and hung up.

*   *   *

We checked in at the Boise downtown Hampton Inn at two o'clock the next afternoon. Snow dusted the mountains visible to the north, but the sky was clear and crisp. I hadn't been to Boise since I'd argued some motions there on a case eight or so years before. The downtown had come a long way. There was a hip vibe that I hadn't noticed before. For a city with a high Mormon population, its downtown boasted a lot of bars and cool new restaurants. It always helps to have a university nearby.

Samuel P. Jones refused to tell us where he'd be staying, just that he wanted an extra $100 for a room. We finally agreed to meet in a popular watering hole and steak house called Chandlers, home of the fairly famous Ten-Minute Martini. Both sides wanted other people around—but with enough confusion that no one would be eavesdropping—so once Barker assured Jones we'd be picking up the tab, he reluctantly agreed to meet at the high-end establishment. Barker had warned Samuel P. Jones that he'd be bringing his client and again assured him that we would have no recording devices. Everything would be off the record, whatever "everything" was.

Barker and I had gotten there early and had just been served our martinis, which had sat in a ten-minute ice bath prior to serving, when we saw a scruffy-looking man enter the bar and start sizing up the place. He had to be our man. He was big—about six feet, three inches, which made him a few inches taller than me—and solid. He would have been around Chuck's age, which would be in the early sixties, but his face was so weathered that, had it not been for his hard body, I would have guessed his age to be closer to seventy. He had narrow, squinty eyes; a broad nose; and thin, snarling lips. His long white hair, worn in a ponytail, was turning yellow.

Barker signaled to him, and Samuel P. Jones nodded and came our way. He smelled like cigarettes and musky body odor. I noticed a couple of hipster couples at the next bistro table wrinkle their noses and whisper to each other. His odor stayed close to his body, fortunately, and the hipsters soon appeared to forget about him and moved on to more important topics. Jones sat without shaking any hands, which was fine with me. He looked at Barker and nodded, and then I watched him study me.

"You look like you could be a Mexican," he said with a smoker's rasp in a tone that was easy, not menacing.

I smiled my best courtroom smile and shrugged. "Pretty much all Englishmen in my genealogy," I said, "although some of them were missionaries—and you know what they're like."

I suspected he didn't have the slightest idea what I'd meant by that statement.

After a brief pause, he turned back to Barker. "So what's all this about? I told you I haven't seen Chuck Evanovich since we were juniors at UCLA. He never came back to school after that summer, and I left after one more semester."

Barker nodded. "Yeah, I understand that. But we're looking into that part of his life because it might have been an important turning point for him. He'd gone from being a left-wing radical to a far-right conservative in a span of a year. Then, decades later, he married a black woman, his third wife, and had three children by her, so he seemingly turned again. We're working for the children of his second wife, a white woman, who believes they were wrongly cut out of his will."

Barker and I had worked out this cover story during the plane ride. We figured the best way to get our potentially uncooperative witness to spill the dirt on Evans would be to get Jones angry with him. What better way to do that than to say Chuck was screwing over his white kids in favor of his black kids?

The risk, of course, was that Samuel P. Jones had been lying to Barker and had been in contact with Chuck all along—which is why I found myself holding my breath as Barker laid out our little fairy tale.

I was relieved when Jones spoke as soon as Barker was done. "He did *what?*" he said, his voice rising in anger. "You mean to tell me that fucker went and married a nigger?"

I looked around to see if anyone was paying us any attention. Thankfully, no one appeared to notice the slur.

Barker nodded sympathetically. "Imagine how his rightful family felt," he said. "By the way, you knew his first wife, didn't you? The one he married just at the end of his junior year?"

Jones nodded. He didn't acknowledge the waitress, who'd just put a beer in front of him. "Sure. Kelly something," he said. "Her pop was one of the crazy scientists giving Chuck all sorts of drugs. Chuck was fucked up almost every time I saw him." Jones smiled for the first time, exposing a set of crooked yellow teeth.

"Yeah, we know about the drug experiments," Barker said. "But let's go back a little. When did you first meet Chuck, and what were his political leanings at that time?"

Jones took a swig of his beer and didn't bother to wipe the foam from his upper lip. He just talked until it dissolved. "We met at a meeting of a group called Students for a Better America. It was more or less a Republican-sponsored group. Pretty mild shit. Chuck showed up one day and sat through a meeting, not saying a word. I'd seen him around but didn't know who he was. He always had a kind of stoner look about him." Jones gave another yellow-toothed grin. "Course, I later learned he was on mescaline or acid or some such shit most of the time. He started coming to more and more meetings, and eventually he opened up. He told us he'd been involved in left-wing politics, but lately it didn't make sense to him.

Some of what Jones told us, we already knew. Chuck was originally from South Africa and had been strongly opposed to apartheid, but he'd left as a kid and hadn't really known any blacks other than family servants. Once he started being exposed to blacks in America, he realized how different they were, said Jones.

"He said the LSD really opened his eyes. He could see that they were really a different species." Jones stopped talking and looked at me. His eyes narrowed. "You probably don't agree that the blacks and Latinos are ruining America. They're all living off the backs of the law-abiding, taxpaying white people who've made this country what it is. Now these people are turning our cities into centers of crime and corruption and little welfare states. The Muslims over in Iran and Iraq are recruiting Mexicans to cross into the United States and release viruses like Ebola in our cities."

Jones stopped his rant as suddenly as it had begun. He turned back to Barker, and I ordered two more martinis and a beer.

"Anyway," he said, "a few of us in the group found we were like-minded about the whole racial, anti-welfare thing and eventually founded our own group. We had to be circumspect about things, since college campuses at that time were pretty much full of lefties. We called ourselves Americans for America." He paused and looked almost embarrassed. "I know, pretty hokey, but as I said, we had to be subtle."

"So you and Chuck Evanovich were founding members of this group?" I asked.

Jones nodded. "Pretty much. There were a couple other guys that were in the first group of members. Chuck wasn't really much help getting things organized since he was fucked up most of the time. But every once in a while he'd come up with some great idea."

"So this transition from left-winger to right-winger was a real, politically based change?" Barker asked.

"What d'you mean?"

"I mean, you felt his change in ideology was for real? He was working with the CIA in the drug experiment program, after all. He could have been a spy."

Jones laughed out loud. It sounded more like a dog barking, but it was a laugh. "Let me tell you a little story," he said. "A few months after we'd started this new group, Chuck and I dropped some acid and went for a drive. He was driving. Next thing I knew we were passing the Coliseum and the USC campus, and we were suddenly in the heart of darkness." He paused, presumably for dramatic effect. "We were smack dab in the middle of Watts. I asked him what the fuck he was doing; we were going to get ourselves killed. Them niggers don't like whiteys coming onto their turf. But Chuck just smiled and kept driving. It was early evening, before daylight saving time, so it was dusk. We turned onto a street that was pretty industrial, and deserted . . . until we saw this teen-ager throwing a basketball against the side of a building. There wasn't a hoop or anything, but the stupid fuck would pretend like he was going in for a layup and throw the ball up against the wall."

Jones halted his story when the waitress arrived, although again, he didn't acknowledge her when she put his second beer in front of him. I made a mental note to double her tip. Jones took a swig of beer and resumed his story.

"So Chuck pulls the car into the lot where the kid is, and the kid turns to face us, holding his free hand over his eyes to block the glare of our headlights. He had this funny, puzzled look on his face. Chuck says, 'Watch this,' and reaches under his seat and pulls out a gun. Before I can say shit, he gets out of the car and walks toward the kid. I could see the little nigger's eyes go big, just like in them old-time movies where everybody overacted. There was a big-ass white guy coolly walking toward him with a gun in his hand. The kid dropped his basketball, and it rolled away. He raised both hands in the air. I guess he thought we were robbing him. But without saying a word, Chuck shot the fucker in the face. I don't know what kind of gun it was. It was too dark for me to tell, but whatever it was totally blew the kid's face apart. He went down like a sack of cement."

Jones smiled again and then shook his head, apparently enjoying the memory.

"The gunshot seemed like the loudest thing I'd ever heard. It reverberated off the cement buildings, and I heard it echo. I gotta admit: I was pretty scared. I was also stoned on acid, so I was getting pretty fucking paranoid at this point. But Chuck walked back to the car, slow as could be, and got in. He calmly put the gun back under his seat. Then he turned to me. There was a wild look in his eyes, but he was grinning ear to ear. 'Well, that was fun,' he said. Then we drove away."

We were silent after Jones finished telling his story. I sipped my new martini, and Barker did the same. I was maintaining my best poker face, as was Barker. But I felt like vomiting—not just because of the horrific story but because of the way Jones had told it, as if it was one of the coolest, funniest incidents he'd ever experienced.

"Well," Barker finally said, "I guess that answers that question."

Jones snorted his dog laugh, and for a brief moment I thought he was going to blow beer out his nose. "You think?" he quipped.

The noise level in the small bar had intensified as the dinner hour neared. People were standing three deep at the bar.

"So do you know how Chuck and Kelly met?" I asked over the din.

"Not really," Jones said. "She just started showing up with him. I guess I assumed they'd met in a class together."

"Was she into the whole white supremacy thing too?" Barker asked.

"Nah. I don't think so. But she put up with it. I think she was into the drugs Chuck had. I think she'd have put up with pretty much anything so long as he kept her on a steady diet of dope."

"Did they seem happy together?" I asked.

Jones seemed to do a lot of shrugging, and he did so again. "Who knows? Mescaline and acid and pot and some of the other shit they took can make you laugh a lot, so if you went by that, they were happy as clams."

"Did you hear anything about her death?" Barker asked.

"Only that she'd disappeared, never to be seen or heard from again."

"Do you think Chuck could have had anything to do with her death?" I asked. It was a silly question, but I asked it anyway.

"Man, after what I saw Chuck do that night in Watts, nothing about that fucker would surprise me."

We were silent again for a while.

I wasn't sure what else to ask, but then I remembered Milton Fischer and asked if Jones had known him.

"You mean the CIA guy? Sure. Chuck called him Uncle Miltie, his benefactor. Even after Chuck got kicked out of the CIA program, Uncle Miltie kept furnishing him with drugs."

"Did you ever meet him?" Barker asked.

"Who? Uncle Miltie? Nah, just saw him once from a distance. I was walking with Chuck toward his off-campus housing, and we saw this guy—skinny fuck—leaving the building. Looked like a Jew to me. He was too far away to hear Chuck call to him, so Chuck just let him go. He must've had a key to Chuck's place, since there was a package sitting on Chuck's desk when we got inside. Drugs, according to Chuck."

We'd all finished our drinks, and I'd run out of questions. I looked at Barker, and he nodded to me, which I took to mean he didn't have anything more, either. I slid an envelope containing eleven hundred dollars across the table.

"So," Jones said as he grabbed the envelope and stuffed it into his pocket in a flash, "what're you gonna do about Chuck and his little nigger family?"

I glanced at Barker, who smirked at me.

"Not a fucking thing," I said as I smiled and signed the tab.

—47—

I didn't feel like staying in Boise that night, and since it was such a short hop to Vegas, we checked out of the hotel and went straight to the airport. The pilot had been instructed to be on call, so he was there and ready to go by the time we got to the plane.

"Good to see Samuel P. Jones put his college education to such good use," Barker said once we were strapped in. He shook his head. "What a piece of work."

I nodded but said nothing as the engines revved and we began the taxi to the runway. I was thinking about Chuck shooting that kid in cold blood. I'd done my share of drugs while at Berkeley, but I'd never been tempted to kill someone. There had to be some underlying sociopathic or psychopathic disorder that had been released by whatever drugs he'd been taking. Was that possible? Probably, I thought. After all, just in the past few years I'd heard of many cases of guys on meth engaging in unprovoked homicidal and suicidal attacks.

I felt a shiver go up my spine as I thought about Chuck having lived with us—having slept with my mother. He had killed that black kid in Watts. He had probably killed his first wife. He had probably killed my father. It was possible he was the serial killer of left-leaning academics. I wondered how close he'd come to killing my mother.

*   *   *

Barker dropped me off at the Palazzo, where I checked in and went right to my room to call Cheryl and Travis on a conference call. I filled them in on Samuel P. Jones, who, according to Barker, always referred to himself by his full name.

"Sounds like a seriously weird dude," Travis said.

"No shit," I said. "But nothing compared to our boy Chuck Evans."

Cheryl hadn't uttered anything other than a few exclamations as I recounted Chuck's murder of the black kid, but now she was ready to weigh in on the matter. "Will, darling, you've got to call this off. Now. Turn over what you have to the authorities and let them handle it. You're playing with more than fire here. Your ex-stepfather is seriously mentally ill. He's obviously capable of anything." I could hear pain and fear in her usually strong voice. "I don't want anything to happen to you," she said.

The line was quiet. I knew the ball was in my court to say something, but I wasn't sure what to say. Platitudes about being careful? I didn't even know how to be careful. If Chuck wanted to kill me, he could do so pretty much whenever he wanted. After all, that was apparently his profession.

I let out a big sigh. "The problem is, even if the feds or who-ever start investigating Chuck and Milton, it's not like they won't find out about it at some point. And when that happens, who do you think they'll suspect set the ball in motion? Remember, I've already confronted Fischer about Chuck. They know I suspect Chuck of killing Dad, and maybe others."

Cheryl started to say something, but I cut her off.

"Cheryl, you know I'm right. Barker agrees with me that it'd be almost impossible to convince the FBI to open an investigation based on what we have. And individual cops, already over-worked, aren't going to start investigating across jurisdictional lines on the basis of my suspicions."

"So you're going to keep pushing?" Cheryl asked. Her voice had calmed, but there was still an edge to it.

I knew our newly intensified love was the underlying current throughout these conversations now. I'd finally worked through my fears enough to admit she was all I wanted, that I was finally ready to commit to our love, yet now I was putting everything at risk by putting myself at risk.

"I'm not going to let a probable serial killer keep killing if I can help it," I said. "I need to figure out a way to prove at least one of these cases. Then I can go to the cops, and from there they should be willing to look beyond that one case."

After another brief silence, Travis finally jumped in, probably hoping to defuse the tension. "So what's the plan?" he asked.

I exhaled through my nose, which must have sounded loud through the phone. "That's what I need to figure out. I'm going to stay here tonight and meet with Al again tomorrow. Hopefully we can devise some sort of plan."

Cheryl huffed her disapproval, while Travis simply said, "Okay."

I was about to say good-bye and hang up when Cheryl spoke up. "If anything happens to you, pards, I'll kill you."

"Love you too," I said and hung up.

*   *   *

I'd brought a travel bag, thinking I'd be staying overnight in Boise. So I showered and put on my jeans, cowboy boots, and a clean blue dress shirt. Then I went downstairs to the casino level, took a seat at the round bar in the middle of the casino, and ordered a Tito's vodka on the rocks. I let the sounds of the casino wash over me. Maybe I was thinking that the noise would erase the visions of the hateful depravity with which I'd become infected. Bells and whistles and groans and cheers and laughter were doing nothing to elevate my mood. Neither was the booze.

I downed the drink and moved on. It was getting late, and although I hadn't eaten anything more than the light snacks on the chartered jet, I didn't feel hungry. I just felt anxious. So I wandered the hotel. Over to the Venetian side and around the canals.

Back upstairs on the Palazzo side, and through the halls of high-end shops, many closing down for the night. I didn't feel like going back to the room to get my coat, so I stayed in the two adjoined hotels and walked until I could feel myself getting tired—and then I walked another big loop. When I finally went to the room and climbed into bed, I felt mentally and physically exhausted—almost the way I felt after a day in trial. I didn't even need the white noise of the television to fall asleep.

—48—

Although some of my previous opposing counsel might laugh out loud at this statement, it is nonetheless true that I firmly believe in the rule of law. I've done my share of manipulating the law to zealously represent my clients, but I've never crossed the line and broken the law (if you don't count smoking dope and experimenting with a few other recreational drugs when I was in college). Our American system of jurisprudence is probably the best in the world, but it isn't without flaws, and we might be rapidly approaching a point where changes will need to be made.

One opinion I share with libertarians and conservatives is that we have too many laws on the books—too many absurd and unevenly enforced laws. As new legislators at both the state and federal levels get elected, they often seem to think that they need to make their mark by authoring or sponsoring new laws. So the laws grow exponentially and unnecessarily.

Laws against murder—and especially murder-for-hire—are not laws I think are unnecessary. There was no way I was going to let Chuck Evans and Milton Fischer get away with murder. The only question in my mind as I went to meet Alvin Barker was this: How far was I willing to go in order to bring them to justice? And at what risk?

If this were a movie or television script, our vigilante hero wouldn't hesitate to break the law in the name of justice, and the audience would think nothing of it. They'd applaud it, in fact. I had no intention of illegally beating the shit out of someone for information, but somewhere along the line last night, I'd made two decisions. The first was to see what Barker thought he could accomplish if left to his own devices. The second was to turn a blind eye to his tactics.

Which is why I didn't call Cheryl or Travis to report on my two-hour meeting with Al.

49

By the time my chartered jet landed in San Francisco, I had four voicemail messages. Two were from Cheryl and Travis, respectively. One was from Nicky in Chile, and the other was from my friend whose father was ex-CIA.

I called Cheryl and Travis, in that order, and asked if they wanted to meet for cocktails and an early dinner. We agreed on a time and place.

I waited until I was home at my Pacific Heights house before returning the other two calls. It was just after noon in San Francisco, which meant it would be just after 5 p.m. in Santiago de Chile. I wasn't sure what the work hours were in Chile. Did they take afternoon siestas as they do in Spain?

Nicky answered the private number he'd given me on the first ring. "Will! Thanks for calling back. I've got two bits of news for you." He sounded excited.

I sat down at the desk in my small study and made sure I had pen and paper handy in case I needed to make notes. "Go ahead," I said.

"The first and most important thing, I think, is that Pinochet put a one-million-dollar reward out for anyone who could bring him the original and all existing copies of *The Daughters of Pinochet*."

I heard myself involuntarily gasp. "Really? A million bucks?" I paused for just a second and then asked, "How would he know if he really got all existing copies?"

Nicky chuckled before answering. "He couldn't know, of course, but then again, who would be so bold as to demand a million-dollar reward from Augusto Pinochet and double-cross him?"

My mind raced. "So that would explain why Chuck Evans was caught snooping around our attic."

"Yes, I remember you telling me your maid caught him," Nicky said. "He was looking for the manuscript. I suppose an argument can even be made that he married your mother so he could get access to your father's treasures, find the book, and claim the reward, but frankly, I find that a little extreme. He could have just broken into the house."

"Yeah," I said, "assuming he didn't think Mother was keeping the manuscript in a safe deposit box or with a third party."

Nicky grunted.

"So I assume that expired when Pinochet died?"

"Ah, that's one of the interesting things about this reward. He put the million dollars in an account controlled by one of his attorneys here, but there were no instructions about what to do if someone came forward to claim the reward after Pinochet was dead."

"So are you telling me the offer of reward still stands?" I asked.

"No." Nicky chuckled again. "I don't know if this would be considered irony or not, but one of Pinochet's daughters learned about the reward and about five years ago withdrew the offer—and the million bucks."

I'd been doodling on the yellow legal pad sitting on my desk and noticed that I'd written the number one and six zeros. I wondered if anyone had ever been paid a million bucks *not* to publish a book.

"How in the world did you find this out, Judge?" I asked.

"Nicky. Call me Nicky, just like your father did. I happen to know one of the partners in the law firm Pinochet used. He was just an associate back then, but he'd been assigned to that particular senior partner and was privy to most of the old guy's cases."

"Wow," was all I could think to say. I remembered Nicky had said he had two things to tell me. "So what's the second thing? I don't think it could be quite as mind-blowing as the first."

Nicky laughed. "No, it won't cause your head to explode, if that's what you mean, but it's damned interesting, nonetheless.

Ernesto pieced this together from various notes and papers in the DINA archives, much of which had since been catalogued for various trials, including that of Manuel Contreras. In the winter of 1975, Michael Townley, who had CIA ties but by then was actually on DINA's payroll, introduced a man going by the name of Oscar Gillespie—whom we know was Milton Fischer—to General Contreras. Now remember that Operation Condor had just begun in September of 1975. That's important. From what we can piece together, Fischer told Contreras that he used to be with the CIA but now ran a security consulting company that could provide various services within the United States and throughout Central and South America. For some reason, he told Contreras he didn't want to work inside Mexico."

Nicky coughed and cleared his throat. I used the pause to scribble a few notes.

"Anyway," he said, continuing, "Fischer seemed to know all about Operation Condor, even though the participating intelligence services had just met in Santiago de Chile on November 25. So this was just a couple of weeks later. Fischer said he had a man available to do freelance assassinations. Prices were to be determined on a case-by-case basis."

I'd used the phrase "mind-blowing" without thinking, forgetting that Nicky might not have been as familiar with the idiom as an American might, but now, after hearing Nicky's information about Milton Fischer, I did in fact feel as if my head was going to explode.

"Will? You still there?"

"Yes, sorry. Uh, Nicky, I'm just so shocked I don't really know what to say. So when Fischer posed as Oscar Gillespie and met with Contreras in the '80s, they were already acquainted with each other. They had maybe even worked together."

I paused, trying to piece it all together. Fischer, as Gillespie, had gone to Contreras in 1975 to offer his services as an assassin.

We didn't know if he had gotten any work from Contreras, but just over a decade later, still using the name Gillespie, Fischer had again met with Contreras. Within a year, my father had been murdered.

"How in the world did Ernesto find all this?" I asked.

Nicky chortled softly. "I told you the kid's good. He loved it. And, not to take anything away from him, a lot of people have been working many years to assemble these archives, referencing and cross-referencing for the various trials. We think your man Fischer must have met Townley at some point when Fischer was still with the CIA. In the late '60s, Townley was living in Miami, working with Frank Sturgis and anti-Castro groups, which we think included several former CIA agents. We don't know if Fischer was involved with Townley and those groups then, but it's most likely the two met either in Washington, D.C., or Miami during that time period."

"Hmm," I mused, "that would have been just before he got involved in the MKULTRA program in Los Angeles."

"A tangled web indeed," Nicky said. "That's all I have. Probably all we'll ever have on this end."

"I'm grateful to you, Nicky. You can't know how much you've helped me." I felt myself choking up. "If nothing else, you've helped me understand Mother more."

"And," Nicky said, "I hope you understand what a great man your father was." Again, that deep-throated chuckle I was just learning to appreciate. "Not many men scared the hell out of Augusto Pinochet, but your father did."

"Thank Ernesto for me, and love to your wife. Hopefully I'll get down to visit one of these days."

I hung up the phone and sat quietly for a few minutes, just thinking. Then I remembered the other call from my friend Freddy Welch.

*   *   *

"Will! Goddammit, it's been a long time!"

I moved the phone a couple inches away from my ear. Freddy always sounded as if he'd just won the lottery.

"Yeah, Freddy, it has. Sorry I haven't been better at keeping in touch."

"Not to worry," he boomed. "Old friends are friends forever. So your email was pretty darn mysterious, I must say. Have you had some kind of run-in with this Milton Fischer guy?"

I had only told Freddy that I was looking into an ex-CIA man by the name of Milton Fischer. I implied it was related to a case I was working on, and I'd asked how much information I might expect to get out of the CIA.

"Just looking into something," I said. "Had your father heard of him?"

"Never met the man," Freddy said. "Although he asked a couple of his old cronies if they'd heard of him. One had. Dad got the impression his friend didn't much like Fischer. Said he was too gung ho. He got into some kind of trouble working with some anti-Castro groups down in Florida, so they moved him out to Los Angeles to work on that crazy drug experimentation program. The personnel files are confidential, so this is all hearsay, but my father's friend said he'd heard Fischer was asked to resign from the agency when he got caught with his hand in the pot o' drugs . . . pun intended."

Freddy's laugh was infectious, and I had to laugh along, even though I wasn't exactly sure what we were laughing at besides a bad pun.

"You mean he was stealing drugs from the drug experiment program?" I asked.

"Just hearsay, but yeah, that's the word on the CIA street."

"Yikes," I said. We'd learned from Samuel P. Jones that Fischer had been supplying Chuck with drugs after Chuck got kicked out of the program. Maybe he'd been giving Chuck extra doses even while Chuck was still in the program. In either case, it sounded as if Fischer had been stealing the drugs from the CIA.

"Thanks for the info, Freddy. Should I assume any attempt to FOIA the CIA on his personnel file would be blocked?"

"Ha! Good assumption, my man. Dad says the CIA is mostly exempt from the Freedom of Information Act. You wouldn't get jack, except maybe some increased frustration. Those guys are so danged tight-lipped I'm surprised Dad was able to get anything at all."

We talked a little longer, catching up on our lives and promising to stay in touch.

I got up and stretched and then retrieved some fresh clothes to take to Cheryl's. As I closed the dresser drawer, I mulled over the conversations of the day, first with Alvin Barker this morning and then with Nicky and then Freddy just now. I was going to dinner with Cheryl and Travis. I wouldn't be mentioning my meeting with Barker, but after my calls with Nicky and Freddy, now at least I had something to talk about.

50

It was after midnight by the time we'd had cocktails and dinner, and Cheryl and I had gone home to her place to make love. We were still entwined in each other's arms and legs, and I felt totally spent. I reveled in the softness of her skin, her familiar scents, and the heat of her body. I could feel myself drifting off to sleep.

"What aren't you telling me?" she asked.

I opened my eyes to see her face just a few inches above mine. She was wide-eyed and staring at me.

"This is a hell of a cross-examination technique," I said glibly.

"C'mon, Will. I'm not letting you go to sleep until you tell me the rest of what's going on." She gave me a wicked smile. "You don't think I know you? For an attorney, you're the worst liar I've ever met."

"Am not."

"Are so." She rose above me so that I was staring into her breasts. Her brown nipples were still hard and erect. She had her hands on my chest.

I sighed. I'd thought I'd gotten away with the omission at dinner, but obviously I hadn't.

"I haven't lied to you guys," I said, but I could hear the feebleness in my voice.

"Lying by omission is still lying," Cheryl countered. She hadn't moved from her position, which was lovely if I could ignore the dialogue. "What plan did you and Barker hatch that you're afraid to tell me?"

Jeez, she was good. I sighed again and resigned to come clean.

"He's going to see if his son Billy can do a little computer hacking to trace Chuck and Milton's travels, particularly on the days of the murders. That's all. No biggie."

Cheryl rolled off me and climbed out of bed without saying anything. I watched her shapely figure and her perfectly round butt as she walked to the bathroom and closed the door.

I woke up when I felt her climbing back into bed. I must have only been asleep for a couple minutes. We lay there in silence as I struggled to stay awake. God, I was tired.

Finally she said, "Okay. You're a big boy, and you're going to do what you think is best. Just don't be more stupid than you need to be. And don't screw up a legal case by tainting the evidence. We won't talk about this anymore, and I don't think we should say anything to Travis. I don't want his license in jeopardy."

She was on her side, looking at me as she spoke, and when I knew she had finished, I nodded, kissed her, and then fell fast asleep.

* * *

When I awoke the next morning, Cheryl had already left for work. I rolled over and looked at the clock on the bedside table. It was nine thirty. It was rare for me to sleep in so late. I sat up and rubbed my eyes. I still felt tired and groggy. My whole body felt limp and fatigued when I forced myself out of bed and into a shower. It didn't help. I didn't feel like shaving, so I did a half-assed job of brushing my teeth, put on a robe, and went to make some coffee. Cheryl had one of those individual-cup coffee makers, so I was sitting in her breakfast nook and staring out at the bay with coffee in hand in a matter of minutes. The day was clear and glorious. The bay was calm. I wished my mood matched the day.

I was in a dark place, well beyond any semblance of "gentle sadness." I could feel the depression as if it were a real and tangible thing living inside me, pressing against my organs and vessels and muscles so that I felt as if I would explode. I sipped my coffee, hoping the caffeine would open my blood vessels and ease the pain, but it didn't. I felt as if I was going to cry, but I didn't know why. I sighed repeatedly, thinking that something terrible was about to happen. I had no idea what that terrible thing might be, but the notion planted a hollow feeling in the pit of my stomach.

Maybe more sleep would pull me out of whatever dark place I was inhabiting. I thought about going back to bed. Instead, I opted for getting out. Maybe some exercise on a perfect day would snap me out of my dismal mood. Although it looked inviting out there, I knew it would be cold, so I bundled up and put on my walking shoes and hit the pavement.

It was chilly, but it felt good to be moving. I walked briskly past the Ferry Building and the piers, and by the time I was at Fisherman's Wharf, I could feel the endorphins kicking in and some sense of clarity seeping back into my brain.

Why had I gone into such a funk? Was it that I had violated my principles by giving tacit approval to Al Barker to do some illegal snooping? Was it because I had tried to hide that fact from my best friends? Or was it because, despite whatever progress I thought I'd been making, the reality was that I was on a fool's errand? Despite what I knew, there was no way I was ever going to be able to prove that Chuck had murdered my father and that he and Milton Fischer were serial killers.

Who knew? Maybe it was a combination of everything. Maybe the stress of thinking I was the only one trying to stop more murders was just too much for me.

When I got to Maritime Park, I slowed down, climbed into the concrete bleachers, and sat. There were a few people—Polar Bear Club members, I presumed—swimming laps in the lee of the breakwater. I looked out at the bay. Alcatraz looked close from this angle. The wind had kicked up a little so there were gentle whitecaps surrounding the former prison island. I involuntarily shivered.

I thought about calling off Barker, but how else, I wondered, could we get the information we needed? I couldn't think of any other way. I thought about what Cheryl had said about tainting the evidence. If I could prove murder in just one case, I felt I'd then have the capability of convincing the authorities to look into the other killings.

I was too cold sitting there, so I got up and started walking again. I walked through Fort Mason and onto Marina Green. It was almost noon, and the green had its usual share of dog walkers and Frisbee players, plus a few hardy souls lying on blankets, reading or doing nothing but enjoying the sun. I'd just turned to start the long trek back when my cell phone rang. I saw it was Cheryl.

"Hey," I said.

"How are you?" Her voice was gentle and kind.

"Fine," I lied. "Out for a long walk to clear the cobwebs. Why?"

"Why what?"

"Why are you asking how I am?"

I heard her exhale. "Because I love you, and sometimes I worry about you. You had a really shitty night, so I thought I'd make sure you're okay. If that's all right."

I stopped walking. "Of course it's all right, darling. It's kind of nice to have someone worry about me. I'm just not used to it, I guess."

"I've cared and worried about you since we met," she said.

"Yeah, I know, and me too. But it's different now. We're an actual couple, you know? Not that thing you always called us."

She laughed, and it was good to hear. "Fuck buddies. God, you can be such a prude sometimes."

I smiled. "I know. I'm all fucked up, but you already knew that, so tough shit."

"Okay. I give. Glad to hear you're fine. Where are you, anyway?"

"Standing just outside the Palace of Fine Arts, about to head home."

"You walked all the way there?"

"Sure," I said. "I'm trying to build up my stamina so I can keep up with you in bed."

We hung up, and the remnants of depression seemed to rush out of me like a demon during some exorcism.

51

By the time I got back to the condo—after a short stop to scarf down some fish tacos at Fisherman's Wharf—my mental state had retreated to my usual cloud of melancholia. In other words, I felt good.

Did you know that in the United States about 15 million people a year suffer from some form of major depression? It's a serious and debilitating disease, and true to my state of melancholy, I felt guilty to have pulled out of my depressive state in such short order.

On the walk back, I'd decided that my sense of helplessness over my so-called quest was probably contributing to my angst. I felt as if I was sitting around, waiting for other people to figure out stuff. What I needed was some kind of personal action.

I spent the next week and a half familiarizing myself with the published works of the nine liberals who'd been murdered over the years. I was searching for connections. Did any one issue, university, publication, city, or state serve as a common element? When certain technical phrases were used, I'd hunt around to see if the particular phrase popped up in the others.

I'd taken to going back to my house to do my research after Cheryl left for work each day. That was because, after a couple of days of me doing the research at her place, Cheryl's condo had begun to resemble a student dorm in the days leading up to final exams. Papers and books were strewn everywhere. I'd purchased two more laptops, so there were three computers running at any given time. On day three, Cheryl got home from work and I saw the look on her face as she eyed her perfectly decorated living room, now a disaster zone. I knew I had to take it on the road. It was better that way, anyway. It would make it seem as if I was actually going to a job, and it would create some semblance of separation between my "quest" and my new life with Cheryl.

When I made the discovery, it was the old-fashioned way. I'd started to notice references to the right-wing Carson brothers in one or more writings of the various victims. I went back through the articles I'd read before, this time noting the mentions. Now my job was much easier. I was specifically looking for Carson brother references in the writings or speeches of the rest of the group. It was one hundred percent. Every single one of the dead liberals had, at some point or other, ranted and railed against the actions of Larry and Joseph Carson and their many ventures.

The Carson brothers called themselves entrepreneurs, which I suppose was technically correct, although some American journalists referred to them as "vulture capitalists." Their business stories were eerily reminiscent of the most egregious examples of Mitt Romney's Bain Capital buyouts and sell-offs.

I went back through my notes and began to list the brothers' real or perceived offenses, as noted by each murder victim:

> *1. Randolph Horton: referred to himself as a "social economist." Was a professor of economics at Harvard. In one of his books, The American Dream Revisited, Horton referred to the Carsons' closure of three manufacturing plants in Georgia back in the early '90s, with the resulting relocation of the plants to Thailand. Larry Carson was quoted as saying that they'd become disgusted with the work ethic of the mostly black workforce in Georgia. They couldn't effect the changes they wanted, he claimed, because they weren't allowed to hire only whites, most of whom wouldn't work for those wages, anyway. "At least the slant-eyes work cheap without complaining," he said.*

2. Calvin Bright: professor of political science at Princeton University. Well-known lecturer on social issues that affect the political arena. In 2003 Bright gave a series of lectures at universities across the country wherein he repeatedly lambasted the Carson brothers' modus operandi of buying moderately successful companies, mostly in poor economic areas, and then stripping out the assets, including intellectual property assets, such as patents, and selling them off piecemeal. All of the employees were summarily fired, thus making the poor economic areas even poorer. In the meantime, of course, the Carsons poured millions of dollars into the campaigns of right-wing candidates that abhorred any kind of welfare benefits, including food stamps, as being motivationally disastrous.

3. Harrison Miller: author of The Failure of American-Style Capitalism. Detailed the financial dealings of the Carson brothers, showing how they'd avoided paying taxes in the United States on the vast majority of their income, which Miller estimated to be in the range of $300 to $500 million annually.

My list of dead liberals only went back twenty years, and Randolph Horton was the first death I noted. He had been murdered in 1995. The most recent, Mark Greenberg, had been murdered just a matter of a few weeks ago. Every single one on my list had singled out Larry and Joseph Carson as modern-day villains who, though acting within the law and in the best traditions of Ayn Rand capitalism, were someday going to be seen as major architects of the destruction of America's economy and, by extension, its political system.

Greenberg's premise brought to mind George Santayana's 1905 quote in *The Life of Reason*: "Those who cannot remember the past are condemned to repeat it."

Did you know that as of 2014, the top 5 percent of Americans control 60 percent of the wealth? Thomas Piketty's best-selling treatise, *Capital in the Twenty-First Century*, predicts that inequality will continue to grow and that wealth will be inherited and concentrated even more in the decades ahead.

I felt a twinge of guilt as I thought about how I'd acquired most of my wealth—through inheritance. I wondered how many more empires would fall because of economic inequality before the oligarchs realized they needed to heed the lessons of history.

In any event, I'd found my connection. But what did it mean? Were the Carson brothers having their detractors murdered? Were they a two-man Operation Condor, intent on killing liberal dissent? Did that even make sense?

I sat in my study, staring down at my notes. I knew the other murder victims had no relation to my father's assassination. Augusto Pinochet had had my father killed either because of his dissent or because of his book. My working theory was that Milton Fischer had gone to Chile to solicit work, which included assassinations. Whether he and Chuck had killed anyone else for Pinochet or Contreras was basically irrelevant to me. It seemed pretty clear that Fischer had been hired to assassinate my father and that Chuck Evans had carried out the actual murder.

Was it now reasonable to theorize that Fischer and Evans, along with maintaining their regular security consulting business, had gone into the business of murder-for-hire? Were the Carson brothers, who appeared bent on killing off liberals who spoke ill of them, Fischer's and Evans' major—or possibly *sole*—client?

I glanced at the clock and saw the afternoon was drawing to a close. Time to wrap it up for the day. I gathered my notes, put them in my old, worn leather briefcase, and drove back to Cheryl's condo. I'd been circumspect about my work over the past week and a half, but tonight I would lay out my findings for Cheryl and Travis.

52

I told my story well—slowly and dramatically. I knew I was telling it well because Cheryl's and Travis's expressions transitioned from skeptical to dubious to interested to excited. If they'd been jurors, I'd have known I had them hooked.

We were at Mamacita's, on Chestnut Street. I'd forgotten that the chef/owner's last name was Contreras, which made me laugh out loud when I read it on the menu. I'd gone through several margaritas as well as my grass-fed beef enchiladas rancheras with a perfect Oaxacan mole by the time I was finished. As I expected, no one said anything for a while.

Finally, the ever-practical Cheryl was the first to speak. "So where does that leave you now? With some damned interesting theories but still no proof."

I glanced at Travis, who was still eating, and then back at Cheryl. We'd agreed not to say anything to Travis about my implicit approval for Barker to engage in a bit of illegal hacking.

"Still trying to figure that part out, I guess," I said. "But I'm pretty damn sure I'm onto something. Everything fits."

Travis was chewing on the remnants of his goat cheese–stuffed chile relleno, but he spoke up anyway. "Mostly," he said, "but I'm having a hard time with the logic of these two racist, reactionary, billionaire motherfuckers offing a bunch of no-name academics because their feelings were hurt."

I nodded. "Yeah, me too. But it's the only link among the nine victims. That can't be coincidental."

Cheryl raised her margarita in a toast. "Well, whatever it all means, I think you're getting closer, and the closer you get to turning all this shit over to the cops, the happier I'll be."

It didn't sound like much of a toast, but we all toasted anyway.

*   *   *

Cheryl and I were lying on our backs in bed, holding hands, the covers askew from our lovemaking. The muskiness of our sex mixed with Cheryl's slightly citrus fragrance. I was still breathing hard, and I could feel the pleasant, solid thump of my heart.

We hadn't talked about my "quest" since leaving the restaurant, but I knew Cheryl, and I knew she'd been thinking about it. Christ, it was hard not to. If I was correct, I'd stumbled upon one of the most bizarre political murder-for-hire scenarios ever. It was so strange that it was easier to disbelieve than believe.

"*Sooo*," she said, "find your link to one murder and then stop there. You don't want to screw up everything by letting Barker and his kid go hog-wild. Make the connection and then present your case to the cops, the FBI, or whoever."

I grunted my agreement.

She pulled her hand from mine and turned onto her side, staring at me. "Promise me."

I smiled at her. "I promise."

And I really meant it.

—53—

I wonder if the Muwekma Ohlone people got depressed after they were officially declared extinct. They were the native peoples that populated the San Francisco Bay Area and were ultimately "missionized" by the Spanish, which, predictably, didn't go well for the Indians. Like most tribes in California and elsewhere, once they made contact with the Europeans, they began dying off.

Disease was the No. 1 killer, but the changes in diet and living conditions imposed on them were another. Once geographic authority had been ceded to the United States, treaties were drafted that would have granted the California natives millions of acres of land on which to peacefully live. But the abundance of riches the region had to offer—as well as the land that could be sold to the white settlers moving west—was just too much to give up for the handful of rich barons who controlled the wealth of California. The treaties were never ratified, and the Indians continued to die off.

At one point, after noting the dilution in pure Ohlone blood vis-à-vis intermarriage, anthropologists determined the tribe was officially extinct. This probably came as a surprise to the Ohlone people who were still living in the Bay Area. Although that anthropological finding has since been reversed, the Muwekma Ohlone Tribe has been fighting for decades within the federal regulatory and judicial processes to obtain federal recognition.

The good news for the oligarchs who prevented those treaties from being ratified is that there weren't enough Muwekma Ohlone people left to rise up in revolution. Do you think modern-day oligarchs like the Carson brothers think they can just make all the minority and poor people extinct so they won't rise up in revolution?

*   *   *

Over the next few days, I took long walks between my research sessions on Larry and Joseph Carson. I had to take long walks just to clear my head of the anger I felt building inside. I was searching for motive, since I tended to agree that being skewered by a bunch of ineffectual liberals didn't justify murder. But the more I read about the brothers, the more I began to believe that could be all there was to it. The Carsons were so hateful, so willfully ignorant, and so arrogant that it was becoming believable to me that their egos simply wouldn't tolerate the kind of intellectual vivisection these academics had performed on them. They were old. They were billionaires. They controlled hundreds of right-wing politicians. They'd successfully financed gerrymandering in scores of districts, which would now elect Attila the Hun if ordered to do so. And they'd set the tone and much of the dialogue in the right-wing propaganda media. In short, they were probably the most politically powerful men in America today. So why should they tolerate dissent any more than Pinochet and Contreras?

When Alvin Barker called, I'd just been rubbing my eyes, ready to pack it in for another day.

"Can you come to Vegas to meet?" he asked without preamble.

"When?"

"Tomorrow. Hell, *now* if you can."

I trusted Al to know when something was important enough to discuss in person, so I made no attempt to question him. I told him I'd be there first thing in the morning. Then I called Travis to see if he wanted to come with me.

—54—

We took a chartered jet out of Oakland early the next morning. It was a gorgeous winter day in the Bay Area. There wasn't a cloud in the sky, and the bay sparkled joyously. I was in a good mood. I figured Barker wouldn't have summoned me if he didn't have something good and important. Travis and I had brought overnight bags, just in case.

The weather was clear all the way to Vegas. We speculated on what Barker might have but soon succumbed to the view out the windows as the Sierra Nevada, lightly dusted with snow, transitioned to desert. As I stared out at the seemingly endless stretch of the Mojave Desert, I allowed my mind to wander. What would I do if we finally had enough to turn the investigation over to the authorities? Before all this had started, one of my plans had been to volunteer at the Innocence Project. That still seemed like a pretty good idea, but I kept going back to the involvement of the Carson brothers. I certainly wasn't going to become a politician, but in the course of my research, I'd become convinced that something needed to be done to curb the dangerous power of the mega-wealthy if we were going to avoid becoming an oligarchy, which, I was convinced, would mean the ultimate destruction of the America I believed in. I had nothing against mega-wealth. Hell, I was sitting in a chartered jet only a tiny percentage of Americans could afford. I was only against those who believed their extreme wealth entitled them to impose their personal ideologies and insatiable thirst for more power on the rest of the country. I was, I realized, becoming political for the first time in my life. I was becoming my father's son.

When the jet landed at McCarran Field, the temperature was just hitting a comfortable 68 degrees Fahrenheit. I'd ordered a car and driver to meet us at the Signature Flight Support Terminal. I made sure the car company didn't send a limousine, which, knowing Vegas, would probably have been expected. A well-dressed Filipino man met us with his white Lincoln Town Car.

Barker's office was on Meade Avenue in a shabby one-story building that also housed a radiator shop. The area was zoned for small industry and lower-income housing, mostly two-story apartments. The plate-glass window on the left side of the building had peeling, faux gold-leaf lettering on the window that read *Barker Detective Agency, Discreet Inquiries and Investigations*. Bars covered the window.

The front door was unlocked, and a buzzer sounded when we entered the reception area, a medium-sized rectangular room with fake wood-paneled walls. A faded dark green sofa sat to one side, and a metal desk with a computer on it occupied the space next to a closed door, which I presumed to be the door to Barker's private office. The door had an old-fashioned photo calendar hanging on it. The photo for this month was of a vintage red Camaro. I figured the calendar came from the radiator shop next door.

At first I didn't see anyone. "Hello?" I called out as I walked toward the receptionist's desk.

I stopped so fast that Travis ran into me. Then he saw what I was looking at: a woman was lying behind the desk next to a basic secretarial chair that was tipped over on its side. It had probably fallen over when she had. I grasped she was a woman because of the dress. Whatever face there had been was now a mass of blood, cartilage, and brain matter.

"What the—"

Travis pushed me aside and produced a handgun. "Get back, Will."

But I stood there stupidly, staring down at the corpse. I could smell the metallic warmth of the blood.

"Now!" he barked at me.

I stepped back, toward the front door. I felt nauseated. My heart was pounding.

Travis moved slowly toward the door to the inner office. I didn't know where he had acquired his skills. I thought I'd known everything about him, but he was good. He opened the door and entered the room, gun held outstretched in a shooter's stance, in one motion. I didn't even know he'd brought a gun.

Nothing happened. There were no shots, no cries for help, and I knew then that Alvin Barker was dead, too.

I walked to the inner door and stood behind Travis. I could see Barker slumped motionless in his high-backed chair.

Travis motioned for me to stay where I was while he went to the one other door in the room and opened it. It was a closet—empty except for a couple of men's dress shirts and three sport coats. Travis lowered his gun and went to Barker. When Travis felt for a pulse in the left side of Barker's neck, the body shifted toward Travis, so that even he let out a gasp and jumped back. It was then that we could see that the entire right side of Barker's face had been blown off. Travis didn't need to go back to checking for a pulse.

"Call 9-1-1," he said. His voice was low and husky—solemn and scared.

*   *   *

We waited out front for the police to come. I tried to get Billy Barker on the phone but kept getting voicemail. At least we hadn't found his body in the office, as well.

It took the better part of the afternoon for us to give our statements, first to a detective at the scene and later in much greater detail to two more detectives at the station. I suggested they call the FBI, which, for now, they declined to do. I told them the whole story, from my father's death to my theory about murders-for-hire. I explained that Barker had been investigating Chuck Evans and Milton Fischer on my behalf. I didn't tell them that Billy Barker had been planning to try to hack into their accounts. I told them I didn't know what other cases Barker had been working on. No, I didn't know if Barker kept any valuables in his office—I'd never been there before.

I didn't know what the detectives believed. They had good poker faces.

By the time we checked into the Palazzo Hotel, I was an exhausted wreck. I kept hearing Cheryl's voice in my head, telling me to be careful, stressing that if we were correct, we were dealing with treacherous men. I'd known it was all true, of course, but until today it had just been an abstraction, a puzzle that needed to be solved. Now I'd caused the death of two people.

Travis knew what was going on in my head, and he kept trying to assuage my guilt, telling me it wasn't my fault, that Barker must have slipped up somewhere to alert Evans and Fischer. That was assuming the deaths had even been related to my investigation, which was still only an assumption.

I begged off getting a drink and went straight to my room. It was not yet five in the afternoon, but I tore the covers off the bed, took my clothes off, and climbed in. I curled up in a fetal position, holding a pillow against my chest. I couldn't picture the secretary—I'd never met her—but I kept seeing Al Barker in my mind. I couldn't wrap my head around the fact that I was responsible for the death of these people. I closed my eyes and willed myself to cry, but there were no tears. No tears, but a profound sense of failure, mixed with equal amounts of anger and guilt.

* * *

I awoke to the musical melody of my cell phone. I sat up in bed and grabbed the phone from the bedside table. It was a Las Vegas number.

"Hello?" My voice sounded small and childlike to me.

"Mr. Muñoz? This is Billy Barker." His grief was palpable.

"Billy. You heard? You okay? I've been trying to call you . . . ." I was rambling, and I was glad he interrupted me.

"I'm okay," he said. "It's all my fault, though. I hacked into their business account at Bank of the West, and I must've gotten sloppy." His voice cracked. "They must have traced my IP address. I don't know. I'm not exactly sure. I underestimated them."

I heard him blow his nose away from the phone. I waited, staring out the floor-to-ceiling window at the glistening lights of the city. The Treasure Island Hotel and Casino sat across the street. My heart felt as if it was going to break in two.

"Where are you?" I asked. "Are you safe? You can come over here. I'll get you a room."

He was silent for a moment. "I'm okay, I think. I'm at my mother's. She and Dad are divorced. She doesn't even use the same last name."

My mind raced. "Look, Billy. Fischer is ex-CIA. Obviously we're not fucking around with amateurs here. Why don't we get both you and your mother to a safe place? One of the other hotels on the Strip. Just for a few days until we know what's up."

More silence. "Maybe you're right," he finally said. "Tell me where."

"I'll go over and set you up in a suite next door at the Wynn. They'll want to see a driver's license when you check in. Do you have any fake IDs?"

"Yeah, uh, hold on a minute." I heard him fumble with something. "Put the room under the name Walter Fleming. I think they'll only need the one ID. I'll get rid of this cell and get a prepaid one on the way over. Then I'll call you on your cell. You might want to get a new cell phone, also. If they know you're the client, it'd be easy to find you with their obvious resources. When I call, you can give me your new number. Then turn off your old cell."

He was right. I hadn't thought about being traced. I'd been too busy wallowing in my guilt. I needed to get my act together if I was going to protect Billy—and not get killed myself. We hung up, and I took a quick shower to wash off the smell of sweat and fear. I put on my jeans, boots, and the one fresh shirt I'd brought.

Then I walked to the Wynn and prepaid three nights for a two-bedroom suite under the name of Walter Fleming. I explained he was a business associate and would be arriving soon.

I found a Verizon store in the big shopping mall across the street and purchased two prepaid cell phones. Then I found a RadioShack.

When I got back to the Palazzo, I used a house phone to call Travis. He met me in the lobby a couple of minutes later. I gave him one of the new cell phones and explained my plan.

—56—

Our meeting with the hotel manager on duty didn't take long. I'd already called Sam Olson, the lead detective in Barker's murder case, and he had agreed to call the manager before we met. I arranged for Travis and me to each get another room under assumed names. We would keep the two rooms under our names. When I told the manager I'd bought some motion sensor cameras at RadioShack, he laughed and summoned the Palazzo's head of security, a big, ruddy-faced man named Paulie O'Conner.

"Put that shit away," O'Conner said when he saw what I'd purchased. "Leave it to us. We'll have it all set up within the hour."

Billy called moments after we left the manager's office. I gave him my new cell number, and he hung up and called me back. We arranged to meet at Grimaldi's Pizzeria, upstairs in the Palazzo.

He came alone, for which I was thankful. I didn't think I could bear to face his mother, even if she was Al's ex-wife. I'd never met Billy. He called me from the front of the restaurant, and I told him where we were, which was as far back in a dark corner as possible.

Billy looked to be in his early twenties. He was big, like his father, but better looking, which was obvious despite his reddened eyes. He had short dark brown hair, dark eyes, a prominent nose, and a mean five o'clock shadow. He wore a long-sleeved light blue cotton dress shirt and gray pants.

"I'm so sorry, Billy," I said after we'd all introduced ourselves. "We both are. Your father was a good man." The words sounded awful and hollow to me, and I remembered the litany of impotent condolences following the death of my mother. "I feel responsible," I said, feeling as if I needed to get that on the table.

Billy met my gaze. "Don't. It was a job with risks. We knew we were investigating possible murderers. If anything, it's probably my fault. I must have led them to us."

We were all silent, letting the guilt and the loss hang in the air.

"We might be making assumptions that aren't necessarily accurate," Travis said. "I mean, we don't know yet if Evans and Fischer had anything to do with your dad's death. It does seem pretty likely, considering, but we're kind of jumping to conclusions." He looked at Billy. "Have you talked to the cops yet?"

Billy shook his head. "I assume they've called the house and left messages for me, but I wanted to talk to you guys first." He looked to me. "I was breaking the law by hacking into their accounts. You were our client. I don't want to get you in trouble. So I was wondering what to say."

Shit. I leaned back in my chair and ran a hand through my hair. I looked at Travis, whom I'd earlier briefed on the Barkers' high-tech snooping plan, and then back at Billy.

"You've got to tell the truth," I said at last. "They need to know why we think it was Evans and Fischer, and they need to know how they found your office. I'll be surprised if anyone presses charges against either of us, but if they do, I'll cover the costs of an attorney, and we'll do everything we can to protect you."

Another long silence followed.

Finally Travis asked what I'd been too chickenshit to ask. "Did you find anything from hacking into their accounts?"

Billy smiled sadly and nodded. "Too much, apparently."

Before he could elaborate, however, I asked another pressing question. "How come you weren't there at the office, Billy? I would've thought you'd be the one presenting your findings." I saw him start to answer, but I held up a hand. "And," I continued, "how'd you hear about it if you haven't talked to the cops yet?"

Billy was nodding before I'd finished. "Yeah, I should've been there. But I was running late. My mother fell on the stairs at her house and hurt her ankle. She called me, and I rushed over. We thought it might be broken, so I took her to the E.R. It wasn't broken—just a bad sprain. So after I got her home, I was in the process of arranging for one of her friends to come over and help her out when she got a call from the cops. She's the one who had to break it to me."

No one spoke for a while. Our pizza came, and we each took a piece, but no one ate. We'd wanted a busy place, but the noise level of the crowded room was starting to bug me. Maybe it was because there was too much laughter.

"So," Travis said after a time, "what was it you found out?"

Billy inhaled deeply and then sighed. He swiped at his right eye with his right hand and then gave us a slight nod. "We can put Evans in the same towns and on the same days as the two most recent murders. For the second murder, we can put both Evans *and* Fischer there. Credit card charges," he added, as if that explained everything. "Dad told me not to chase down anymore than one or two for now. He said you wanted just enough to convince the cops to investigate further. But," Billy said, handing me a thumb drive, "there's a year's worth of activity on that. I don't recall if there were more than the two murders in the past year, but if so, that data should be on there, as well."

I watched Travis take a bite of pizza. I waited, not sure if Billy was done. He wasn't.

"They used Southwest out of Vegas. The charges didn't have the actual travel dates, but I found Marriott Courtyard charges in the two cities on the subject dates. I was working on accessing their Southwest Rapid Rewards accounts to confirm the flights but hadn't gotten there yet."

I'd taken my own bite of pizza while Billy was talking, and now I sat and chewed, digesting both the pizza and the information.

Travis was looking at me. "What do you want to do now? Time to let Billy turn this over to the cops and let them do their thing?"

I nodded. I couldn't think of what else to do. The three of us ate the rest of the pizza in silence. I had a feeling Billy would be spending a good portion of the night at the police station. I told him to take a pizza up to his room for his mother before he arranged to meet the police.

*   *   *

Travis and I stopped by the front desk after dinner and asked if there'd been any messages for us in our original rooms. The clerk checked with the operator and then told me there'd been eleven messages for me. I asked her to transfer them to my new room. Travis had five messages, and he transferred his, as well.

During the elevator ride up to our floor, Travis and I pulled out our permanent cell phones and turned them on. I had seven messages. Travis had five. All of them were from Cheryl, and each had gotten progressively more frantic.

I waited until I got to my room before calling her on the landline.

Travis had the adjoining room and opened the door and went straight for my minibar as Cheryl's voice exploded into my ear.

"Jesus Christ, Will! What the hell's going on? I'm frantic here. Some maniac who I think is your ex-stepfather has called twice. He sounded completely out of his mind—royally fucked up. He demanded to talk to you, then demanded to know where you were. He said he was going to rip your arms off and stuff them up your asshole."

"God, I'm so sorry, Cheryl. Things are all screwed up here too. Al Barker and his secretary were murdered today—just before we were supposed to meet with him, in fact. Travis and I were the ones who found the bodies, so we spent most of the day with the cops. Then we had to make sure Al's son, Billy, was safe."

Cheryl gasped. "Oh, my God, Will. Was it Evans?"

"You mean who killed them? We don't know for sure, but it makes sense. Billy hacked into Evans' and Fischer's credit card accounts. Something must have alerted them." I paused to rub my face with my hand. I felt so tired.

I glanced at Travis, who'd retrieved two bottles of Smirnoff vodka from the minibar and was pouring both of them into a glass. He gestured to me to see if I wanted anything, but I shook my head.

"Are you home now?" I asked.

"Yeah. I've been here, worried out of my mind and trying to call you guys."

"We're fine," I said and then told her what we'd devised with the fake room registrations and gave her our prepaid cell numbers. "Why don't you close the office tomorrow. These guys are crazy, and I don't want anyone getting caught in the line of fire." I regretted my choice of words as soon as they'd slipped out of my mouth.

"You think we could be in danger?" Cheryl asked.

"Only if Evans comes to the office looking for me and gets pissed because he thinks he's getting the runaround," I said. "But I tend to doubt that will happen."

Cheryl sighed heavily. "I'll close down. I don't want anyone getting hurt. When are you guys coming home?"

"Hopefully tomorrow," I said. "I don't know if the cops will want to talk to us some more or not. I suspect they will, once they've heard what Billy has to say." It was my turn to sigh. "Oh, by the way, line up someone to represent us if the cops decide to play rough with the fact that Billy was hacking."

"God," Cheryl said, "what a mess."

*　　*　　*

After we'd hung up, I fell back on the bed. Travis was sitting at the table by the window, sipping his cocktail. He looked fresh. It wouldn't have surprised me if he had announced he was going downstairs for a little blackjack. I presumed Chuck and Milton didn't know anything about Travis, including what he looked like, so I didn't think it would do any harm if he went and had some fun. But he didn't say he was going downstairs to gamble.

"We'll keep the connecting door open tonight," he announced. "Chuck is obviously out of control if he's calling the office and threatening you after having just killed two people. It sounds like he may be unraveling. God knows how Fischer fits into all this weirdness. I'd always assumed it was just business with him."

I nodded and closed my eyes, too tired to engage in any dialogue. I didn't hear Travis retreat to his room.

I awoke to the landline ringing. I looked around, momentarily disoriented. The neon Treasure Island sign glowed brightly from across the street. I looked at the clock. It was 2:17 a.m. I picked up the phone.

"Mr. Muñoz, this is Paulie O'Conner from hotel security."

I sat up, fully awake now. "Yeah. What's up, Paulie?"

"Can you come on down to my office? We've got something to show you."

"Sure," I said, already slipping on my jeans. "I'm going to get Travis, my investigator, to join us, if that's okay."

O'Conner gave the okay for Travis to come along, and as I stood up to go wake him, Travis appeared in the adjoining doorway. He was buttoning his shirt and looking as fresh as ever. I put on my cowboy boots and untucked dress shirt, and we left to meet Paulie O'Conner.

*   *   *

O'Conner's office was not decorated to impress. It was spacious and functional. A wall of television monitors and several desktop computers sat on his large desk. He motioned to us to pull up chairs beside his desk and then swung one of the computers around to face us. He still hadn't told us what this was all about. In fact, he hadn't said anything, really, beyond thanking us for meeting him.

He pressed a key on the computer, and a clear picture of an interior hotel door appeared on the screen. I recognized it immediately as the entry door and hall of a Palazzo room—presumably my old room. The door flew open suddenly and struck the side wall with a loud bang. Chuck Evans appeared in the hall. O'Conner touched the keypad, and the camera zoomed in on Chuck's face. His expression was wild—wilder than I'd ever seen it, even when he'd been fighting with Mom.

The picture was in color, but the lighting was such that I couldn't tell if Chuck's eyes were as fiery red as they appeared. The unshaven face was the face of an absolutely crazy person. I wouldn't have been surprised to see white foam coming from his mouth.

"Will! Will Muñoz, you motherfucker, where are you?" His voice was higher than I remembered, almost shrill.

O'Conner panned out as Chuck advanced into the room, and it was only then I saw he'd been holding a gun. I didn't know enough about guns to know what kind or caliber it was.

It took a matter of seconds for Chuck to conclude I wasn't in the room. He turned and left as fast as he'd come.

I turned to O'Conner.

He shook his head, already anticipating my question. "My guys didn't get there in time to catch him. He's long gone. Was that your man?"

I nodded. "That was him—in all his lunatic glory."

"He looked totally fucked up," Travis said. "Stoned on something."

O'Conner, who had probably seen his share of drug-addled crazies, nodded. "I agree." He turned away from us and picked up a phone. "I'm calling Olson."

*   *   *

"Sounds like our boy Chuck is about to self-destruct," Travis said once we were back in my room.

"Unless Fischer can get him back under control," I said.

"Hmm. You're assuming Fischer controls Evans."

I shrugged. "I don't see how they've gotten this far without some kind of control on Chuck. That's what that whole MKUL-TRA program was all about."

We said nothing for a couple of minutes. Then Travis asked if I was going to go back to bed.

"I don't know. I feel too wired to sleep now."

Travis gave me a grin. "Want to go down and play some blackjack?"

Despite everything, I had to laugh. "Talk about crazy. You go ahead. If Chuck is still wandering around, I don't want to be responsible for him spotting me and going nuts in the middle of a casino. I think I'll lie around and try to figure out how we can convince the authorities to include the Carson brothers in their investigation."

*　　*　　*

I must have drifted off to sleep, because I awoke lying on the bed, fully clothed. I heard a sound like the door to the room closing and then locking shut. I sat up and swung my feet to the floor.

"Hello?" I asked in a timid voice. "Is someone there?"

From where I was sitting on the bed, I couldn't see down the hall to the front door, so I stood up. The hall closets were mirrored, but there were no lights on. I thought I could make out a large shadowy figure. My heart was pounding. I heard a slight noise, but no one had answered me. I felt a coldness inside of me—pure fear. I hadn't moved since I'd stood up. I was afraid I couldn't move.

Then there was sound and movement, and before I could react, he was standing in front of me, gun in hand. The colorful lights from Treasure Island across the street cast intermittent shadows in the room and now on his face.

As I stared at the man who had been my stepfather, I felt the cold fear turning to ice, as if I was going to explode. I'd never known such all-consuming, debilitating fear. My mouth was so dry I couldn't even cry out to Travis, assuming he was even in his room next door.

Chuck looked like he had in the surveillance video taken by hotel security. As the neon lights from outside crossed his face, his wild eyes flashed red. His face hardly looked human. I inanely wondered how he'd been able to walk around the hotel in such a state without someone reporting him. I noticed that the gun was shaking in his right hand—his whole body was shaking. He was barely in control.

"You motherfucking piece of shit. Why couldn't you just leave it alone?" The words tumbled fast and furious from Chuck's mouth, but I understood his slurred words just fine.

"My father . . . ." It was all I could choke out. I could feel the fear loosen its grip on me just a bit as my mind raced.

"Fuck your commie spic father." Chuck spat the words at me through clenched teeth, his rage raw as he stepped toward me. His gun hand was still shaky, but not enough for him to miss from such close range.

I glanced around for something to defend myself with, but other than a clock radio several feet away, I saw nothing that wasn't bolted down.

For a split second, Chuck's enraged expression softened, giving way to a look of deep sadness. "I loved your mother, you know. But I was never good enough for her."

His voice had fallen to a despondent whisper, but it still harbored a menacing edge, and when the unhinged snarl returned to his face, I knew those were the last words he intended to speak. This wasn't the movies. I wasn't going to get him to confess, all while waiting for the cavalry to come to my rescue.

I did the only thing that came to mind: I stepped toward him and kicked him in the groin as hard as I could with my right foot. He was wearing lightweight khaki pants, and I could feel the point of my cowboy boot make contact with the softness of his nut sack. The gun in his right hand went off so close to my left side that I could see the flash in my peripheral vision and instantly smell the acrid odor of gunpowder. It was loud, but not like an explosion. More like a loud pop. I felt a stabbing pain in my left shoulder and knew I'd been hit. I also knew both from the sound and from the fact that I still had most of my shoulder that it wasn't the same gun he'd used on Al Barker.

Chuck had doubled over in pain, but he wasn't down—and he still held the gun. Although he was close to twenty-five years older than me, he still had several inches and a good thirty pounds on me.

There was no way I'd beat him in a straight-up fight, even if I was able to knock the gun out of his hand. So I took advantage of the fact that his head was bent down almost to my waist level and kicked him again, this time aiming for his left temple. I heard the thud of my boot against his head as I fell backward, off-balance.

He fell to the side, toward a dresser, and I saw him reach out with his right arm to protect himself. The gun in his outflung hand hit the side of the dresser, and Chuck dropped the weapon as he groped for a handhold. His face was so grotesque I couldn't tell if it was from pain or drugs or both. He was hanging onto the dresser and breathing hard through his mouth. Blood seeped through his pants at crotch level. I had hurt him badly with that first kick, but he wasn't out of it yet.

I knew I wouldn't have time to bend down and pick up the gun. He would be on top of me before I could straighten. I fought to regain my balance, took two quick steps forward and kicked the gun away as hard as I'd kicked Chuck. My shoulder was starting to burn, and I could feel blood dripping down my arm. My foot hurt, and I didn't think I'd have the strength to get in another good kick.

I frantically looked around for something to hit him with.

Chuck unloosed a loud, animalistic cry and lunged at me.

I reached out to my left and grabbed some kind of ornamental glass ball that was sitting on a wrought-iron stand on the dresser, and just as Chuck tried to wrap his arms around me, I hit him on the right side of his head with the ball. I got lucky and struck him close to his eye. The ball was solid glass with bubbles inside, but part of it broke against his upper jawbone and cut him badly.

He howled like a banshee again, and we went down to the floor, with Chuck on top. He muttered something unintelligible as blood dripped from the cut on his face onto mine. Then he raised his upper body and reared back with his left fist to deliver a furious blow. He had me pinned, and there was nothing I could do. I closed my eyes and turned my head to the side.

The blow never came. Instead, I heard another shot.

I opened my eyes to see Chuck still hovering over me, but the rage was melting from his face. He fell over on top of me, and I closed my eyes again and tried to push him off. I lacked the strength. Our faces were inches apart, and I could smell gin on his breath.

I cried out for Travis, assuming he had shot Chuck. The pain in my shoulder was intensifying, probably because the adrenaline was wearing off. I opened my mouth to call out to Travis again just as someone pulled Chuck off of me.

A second later, I was looking up into the faces of Travis and Paulie. Both men were holding guns.

—58—

I didn't get to ask any questions before an EMT unit pushed into the room and started working on me. I'm assuming morphine was part of their protocol, because the next thing I knew I was pleasantly drifting, only half aware that I was the center of attention. At some point I fell asleep.

I awoke in a hospital room with an IV in my right arm and a clear plastic tube with two prongs stuck in my nose—oxygen. My left shoulder was bandaged, and the whole arm was immobilized. Cheryl was sitting on the side of the bed, holding my right hand. She was staring off toward the one window in the room and hadn't noticed I was awake. It was light outside. I moved my head slightly and saw Travis slouched in the room's single chair.

Cheryl must have detected my movement. "Is it too early to say I told you so?"

"I'll concede the point," I said, slurring my words. I closed my eyes as she caressed my face with her cool hand. "How's my shoulder?" I asked after a few moments.

She took her hand away, and I opened my eyes. She wore no makeup and was wearing blue jeans and a tailored blue office shirt. God, she looked beautiful.

"It'll be okay," she said. "There was some muscle and ligament damage and only a minor chip out of the humerus."

"You trying to be funny?"

"You're still stoned," she said.

"Duh," I said. Then I turned to where Travis was still sitting. "So, T, did you shoot Chuck?" I could tell I was still speaking with a slur, but it was getting better.

Travis stood and came to the side of the bed opposite Cheryl. "Nah, I was just about to, but then Paulie barged in and didn't hesitate." He smiled. "Good thing too, since I'm not licensed to carry in Nevada." He paused for a beat. "Besides, the caliber gun I had would have probably gone through Chuck's body and into you."

"So you're not my white knight?" I asked.

Cheryl laughed.

"Dude, I ain't your white anything."

I'm sure we would have continued our witty repartee, but Detective Sam Olson entered the room. Cheryl let go of my hand and moved away from the bed, making way for Olson. He was tall and thin except for a paunch in his midsection. I placed him in his mid-fifties. He had sad eyes and a big crooked nose set between two ruddy cheeks. He stared down at me for several seconds.

"You okay?" he finally asked.

"Fine," I said. "Is Chuck dead?"

He nodded.

"How did Chuck find me?" I asked. "And get into my room?"

Olson sighed and then frowned. "You used your mother's last name to register in your new room—Montrose."

"Oh, shit," I said. "How stupid am I?"

Olson gave me a half smile. "Easy mistake to make. Once he had your name, it wasn't hard to find out which room you were in. He could have bribed someone or gotten access to any one of the hundreds of computers around the hotel. Then he stole a master code key from housekeeping." He paused for a moment. "It wasn't rocket science."

Nonetheless, I felt pretty stupid.

"Did you find Fischer?" Travis asked.

He shook his head, turning slightly to address Travis. "No. By the time we got to their house, he was long gone." He rubbed the back of his neck with his right hand. "In fact, I got the impression he took off some time ago, probably when Evans started going nuts. There wasn't a trace of Fischer in the house."

It made sense. If Chuck had learned Billy had hacked into his accounts and that the shit was about to hit the fan, he had probably begun ingesting whatever combination of drugs he liked in order to get into killing mode. He had probably been scared and had taken more than usual. Fischer, meanwhile, would have realized that he could no longer control Chuck and that it was time to get the hell out of Dodge.

"Do you have any leads on him?" I asked.

"Not so far. Being ex-CIA and all, he was probably ready to run at any time." Olson shrugged. "Could be anywhere by now."

"Fuck," I mumbled.

"I don't think you have anything to worry about," Olson said. "Fischer's a pro. He knows he's toast if we catch him. Coming after you wouldn't do a damn thing except add another victim to his list. I doubt he's the vengeful type." He eyed my bandaged arm. "But we'll keep someone on you for a while. You'll be safe."

I pulled the oxygen tube from my nose. It was tickling me when I talked. "I wasn't worried about me. I'm just pissed because this was really all about him. He's the one who got Chuck into drugs. He's the one who turned Chuck into an assassin. He's the one who solicited murder contracts from Pinochet and then from the Carson brothers." I stopped talking and stuck the tubes back into my nose and closed my eyes.

I heard Olson's voice. "Is there anything more you can tell me about Fischer that might help find him? Anything at all?"

I was drifting on morphine. What more could I know about Milton Fischer besides what I'd already told the cops? Had I told them he was an asshole? I smiled to myself. The dope almost made me tell Olson exactly that, but I stopped when another thought came to me through the haze.

I pulled the oxygen tube from my nose again. "Oscar Gillespie," I mumbled.

Olson leaned closer. "Who?"

I took a deep breath, trying to clear my head. "Fischer traveled to Chile twice on a passport under the name Oscar Gillespie," I said. "Maybe he'll use it again."

I stuck the oxygen tube back into my nose and closed my eyes again. I was tired—very tired. I listened to Cheryl, Travis, and Olson talk some more, but I had no interest in participating.

"Did you find anything of interest in Chuck's house?" Cheryl asked. "Besides the disappearance of Fischer?"

"Yeah, we found the notebook you referred to." He must have nodded toward me but then saw I was out of it and turned back to Cheryl. "It was hidden on an upper shelf in Chuck's closet. We also found enough drugs to hold a reenactment of Woodstock. Mostly psychedelics but also a lot of speed and downers."

"You gonna call in the FBI?" Travis asked. "That notebook and the information we gave you should be enough to convince someone to start investigating this as a serial killer case."

"We're talking it over, but yeah, my bet is the FBI will be in charge of the case by the end of the day."

Olson's tone had turned brusque, causing me to open my eyes. He turned back to look me squarely in the face.

"Mr. Muñoz," he said, "I assume you realize that hacking stunt probably got Mr. Barker and his secretary killed." He paused. "And almost got you killed."

I didn't say anything, and after a few moments Olson grunted and turned to leave.

More than a year had passed since my ex-stepfather had been killed trying to kill me. The scrapbook he had kept contained newspaper accounts of the death of my father, plus all eight of the liberal writers I had identified as possible targets. But there was more. It included Mark Greenberg, who hadn't been on my list and had been the last one to die. It included two Chilean journalists, both of whom had led strident opposition to Augusto Pinochet and both of whom had been assassinated before my father's death. I presumed those murders had been carried out pursuant to Milton Fischer's business solicitation to Manuel Contreras in Chile in 1975.

Following my father's assassination, there were five murders documented in the scrapbook between 1987 and 1995, the first year on my list. Of those murders, only one, the last one, had any connection to the Carson brothers. I had concluded that whatever possible relationship Fischer and Evans had cultivated with the Carsons had begun just before that murder in 1994. The circumstances had been almost identical to all the subsequent murders. The victim had been a well-known left-leaning economist who had lambasted the Carsons in a series of articles for *Rolling Stone* pertaining to their purchase and closure of three manufacturing plants, all within a five-square-mile neighborhood in Detroit. That neighborhood had been one of a handful of predominantly black neighborhoods still thriving as solidly middle class. Following the last closure, the neighborhood had predictably died a slow and, at times, violent death. The Carsons had made a fortune on the sale of the assets from the three plants while consigning about a thousand previously proud workers to poverty and welfare.

* * *

Special Agent Emilio Rodrigues had been assigned to the case once Olson and his superiors had made the inevitable decision to turn the investigation over to the FBI. Rodrigues had come to San Francisco to interview Travis and me on a couple occasions, and we had hit it off. I hadn't asked, but as far as I had been able to tell, Billy hadn't told the authorities that he'd done the hacking at my behest. But it hadn't seemed as if it had mattered much, anyway—no one had been making any noises about filing charges over computer hacking. The feds had been subpoenaing the very kind of records Billy had hacked into and had confirmed that Evans— and sometimes Fischer too—had been in all of the cities on all of the dates the murders had occurred. Their hotel of choice? Marriott. Ballistic tests had tied four of the murders to a Beretta 92A1 9mm pistol found in Chuck's room with only his prints on it. Rodrigues had told me it was a fairly new model, which explained why it hadn't matched the evidence from earlier crime scenes.

The gun used to kill Barker and his secretary had been a .357 Magnum loaded with hollow-point bullets. Rodrigues theorized that Chuck had probably wanted more firepower than he had needed for the assassinations of academics. That gun had yet to be found.

The gun Chuck had shot me with had been a small .22, a Beretta Model 21 Bobcat. I was lucky it hadn't packed more firepower. My shoulder had healed with only minimal residuals.

Fischer and Evans had taken a lot of trips to Chicago, which was where the Carson brothers were based, but so far any further link had been elusive. Large sums of money had been deposited in the Fischer-Evans accounts in the days or weeks just before and after each murder, but there was nothing to tie the payments to the Carsons.

Meanwhile, Fischer had effectively disappeared. He was, after all, a pro—as Olson had said. He would've had a fake passport and

ID at the ready. He would've had a great deal of cash and, presumably, even more money stashed away in some offshore accounts. According to Rodrigues, it would take blind luck to find Milton Fischer. Nevertheless, he had been indicted on seven of the murders, with the few remaining ones, such as my father's, still pending. He had been added to the FBI's Ten Most Wanted list.

*   *   *

Travis and Cheryl and I had enjoyed many a long conversation, usually over cocktails, about whether the MKULTRA program had had any effect on turning Chuck into a cold-blooded murderer. Our conclusion was that it had had an ancillary effect. It had introduced Chuck to drugs he had obviously enjoyed, drugs that had enabled him to abandon any sense of morality. The toxicology report on Chuck had revealed LSD, methamphetamine, psilocybin, and a couple other, more innocuous substances present in his brain at the time of death. Certainly the drugs had helped fuel his rampage the night he had come gunning for me at the Palazzo.

Maybe the drugs administered through the MKULTRA program had caused chemical changes in Chuck's brain. Maybe not. In any event, we decided that Milton Fischer's killing machine had been a sociopath who, when high on certain drugs, had killed without remorse.

We couldn't decide if Milton had authorized the killing of Alvin Barker, but I tended to doubt it. It had been too blatant and too easy to link to Evans and Fischer. The cops would have merely had to find Barker's client list and figure it out from there. I was sticking with my original premise: that Chuck had probably started taking his hallucinogenic cocktail of drugs after he'd found out they'd been hacked, after which he had taken it upon himself to kill Barker. When Fischer discovered what was going on, he had probably gone ballistic, which had probably caused

Chuck to take even more drugs. Chuck's resulting craziness had probably helped Milton come to the conclusion that Chuck was finally out of control and that it was time to cut and run.

*   *   *

As for closure—and the little discourse I'd had with myself on the subject during the heat of my quest—I thought it would be nice if the authorities could find Milton Fischer. I thought it would be even nicer if they could figure out a way to bring down the Carson brothers. But I wasn't obsessing over any of that. As far as I was concerned, we had proved that Chuck Evans had murdered my father at the behest of Augusto Pinochet and had been a paid assassin. He had also tried to get the million-dollar reward from Pinochet by finding my father's manuscript. Whether that had been why he had married my mother I couldn't say.

I couldn't get Chuck's words about having loved my mother out of my head. I hated that he had said that. Could that really have been true? It seemed so impossible. Yet I had caught a glimpse of real emotion, of pained honesty. Or maybe I had just imagined it, hoping in that moment to see some sign that he wasn't about to kill me.

To me, it was equally possible that he had just been a sick motherfucker who had decided he wanted to have the wife of one of his early victims. Bottom line, Chuck Evans was dead, and the odds were that Fischer was through with the assassination game. I told myself that that was closure enough for me.

—60—

Cheryl and I married in June. I rented out my Pacific Heights house and fully moved into her condo, where we'd pretty much been living for the past couple of years, anyway. I'd been scared out of my mind to marry and then give up my house. It seemed so . . . permanent. Sometimes I still feel scared and vulnerable—as if something bad is going to happen to make all this happiness go away. I guess the scars of our youth are hard to erase.

Anyway, as time passed, I became ever more comfortable in our love and our life. Cheryl had turned the law office into the kind of firm we'd originally dreamed of. She and Travis reveled in the ability to help the powerless, to take on the arrogant people who thought their money and power imbued them with special privileges and indemnities.

Eventually, after we'd jumped on the opportunity to take over the office space next door, I moved back into the firm. I'd volunteered with the Innocence Project for a while, but after seeing the kinds of cases Cheryl was taking on, I decided I could do more good going back to work at our firm.

For the first time since my father's murder, I felt a connection to him. I felt as if I'd finally discovered the great man everyone admired, and I couldn't help but think that, for the first time since his death, he would have been proud of me. It hadn't escaped my attention that Mother's suicide, which had sent me on my quest, had coincided with the first day I'd planned on acting upon my epiphany by walking away from the law. I couldn't help but wonder whether it had been fated, like something in one of Dad's complicated novels.

I was still a good litigator, and we settled into a routine. Cheryl chose which cases to take, and I handled most of the litigation. I guess she didn't want me turning back into a complete dick and taking any high-paying case that came through the door, although I liked to think that wouldn't happen. I was thoroughly enjoying the role of representing the underdog. I liked being . . . not a dick.

Sometimes I liked to imagine that the all-powerful defendants I was suing were surrogates for the Carsons.

*   *   *

In July, a little over a month after we'd married and things had slowed down at the office, Cheryl and I took two weeks off and drove down Highway 1 to Los Angeles, where we stayed at the newly renovated and decorated Malibu house. I didn't have the heart to sell it. Sometimes, when I'd lie on the chaise on the deck listening to the surf and the gulls, I'd let my mind wander and would pretend that Mother and Josephine were sitting at the kitchen table, sharing some tidbit of gossip.

On our third day in Malibu, my cell phone rang. The office had been given strict instructions not to bother us, absent an emergency, which Travis had to verify.

It was Special Agent Emilio Rodrigues. "Hey, Will. Congratulations on your marriage."

"Thanks, Emilio, I appreciate that." I waited, knowing that wasn't why he had called.

"So they arrested Milton Fischer in Mumbai. He was about to board a flight for Malé, in the Maldives."

"Wow. That's a surprise. Was he using his own name?"

Rodrigues laughed. "He's not that stupid. He was trying to travel on a passport issued to Oscar Gillespie. Your tip that he had used that passport to get into Chile in 1975 and then again in 1986 paid off. He'd been renewing the passport ever since, but we put a red flag on it, and when he entered India using that passport, we were contacted."

"So," I said, "not stupid, but not as smart as he thought. Do we have extradition with India?"

"Yeah, we do. But not with Maldives, which I assume is why he was going there."

"When did this happen?" I asked.

"A few days ago. We got a team there as quickly as possible. Fischer's already made a deal. He'll accept extradition to the U.S. and will testify against Larry and Joseph Carson, against whom he claims to have a great deal of evidence, including recordings. He has probably gathered all sorts of evidence over the years as insurance against this very occurrence."

"And what does he get out of the deal?" I asked.

Rodrigues snorted. "Don't worry. He's not going to walk. He'll plead to conspiracy to commit murder and will probably serve ten years or so. It hasn't all been worked out." He paused for a beat. "The main thing is we got him, and it sounds like we'll get the Carsons, as well."

I thought about Michael Townley, the assassin who had worked for DINA. He had done a deal and had pleaded guilty to a single count of conspiracy to commit murder for the car bomb assassination of Orlando Letelier. He had killed two people in that act, injured another, and had assassinated God-knows-how-many other people. He'd been sentenced to ten years in prison but had served much less than that and was now living free, protected by the Witness Protection Program.

"Good news," I said, not bothering to hide the disappointment in my voice.

"You don't sound very excited," Rodrigues said.

"I guess I'm past all that. You guys have done a great job. But I would ask one thing from you."

"What's that?"

"If you get anything from Fischer about my father's assassination, I'd like to hear about it."

"You got it. Thanks for all your help, Will. And again, congratulations."

EPILOGUE

Cheryl and I sit on the deck in Malibu, glasses of chardonnay in hand. The sky has erupted in an explosion of oranges, reds, purples, and pinks. No gradient. No dissolution. Just pure color. The beauty and perfection of it hits me hard, like a blow to the chest. Like a nonlethal myocardial infarction. I can barely breathe, yet I am so enthralled, so entranced, that I couldn't care less.

I don't consider myself to be an absolutist. In fact, I consider such people to be ridiculous, arrogant, and, in the end, intellectually vapid. But this spectacle before me now is, without question, absolute. Its perfection of beauty is not subject to any form of debate or qualification. I have never seen anything like it. I have never *felt* anything like it. This feeling is so . . . not me. There is no gentle sadness. It's foreign to me, and I'm unsure what to do.

I finally tear my eyes from the sky and look at Cheryl, only to experience such a profound sense of completeness that I feel I could cry.

I force myself to take a deep breath, and I feel some semblance of reality seep back into me. My being? My soul? I don't know. Whatever it is that takes the blow and feels the enormity of the moment. And then, too soon, I see the edges of the colors begin to dilute and fade, and soon it's just another beautiful sunset.

I smile.